CHILD OF THE MOON

RIFT MAGIC: BOOK 2

MIRANDA HARVEY

CHAPTER 1

Luca strode back and forth, his boots clicking on the stone floor, pausing every third rotation to put his ear to Skylar's door. He could just make out the sound of the centaur's voice inside, talking to the Ruling Council about allowing their petition for Zara to return to Wundor. Though muffled by the oak door, Skylar's voice sounded tense, dropping to a deeper octave occasionally, which signalled he was attempting to control his temper. From the few words that Luca could make out, it didn't sound as if it was going very well. He had begged Skylar to let him be in the room when he made the petition, but he had been denied. His emotional involvement, as Skylar called his love for Zara, would cause him to overreact. Over two months had passed since he had seen Zara. Another Guardian, a werewolf named Marx, had been assigned to the farmhouse, and Luca worried that she would think that he had deserted her.

Hearing Skylar bid farewell to the Council members,

followed by the chime which indicated that the projection spell had been disabled, Luca knocked sharply on the door. "Come in," Skylar ordered, and Luca pushed the door open eagerly. But one look at the Commander's face and his hopes fled. "When I told you to wait, I didn't mean outside my door," the centaur said, brow creased in a scowl.

"I'm sorry, Skylar, but I couldn't wait. I need to know if the Council has made a decision. Have they?"

Skylar sighed."They have not. They refuse to hear my petition until the culprits in the kidnapping are brought to trial."

"Have they set a date at least?" Luca asked.

"No. The Council said they are still gathering evidence. Without the ringleaders, they believe that they do not have enough evidence to convict."

"What about Zara's testimony?" Luca demanded indignantly.

"First of all, Zara was here without their permission. They, therefore, deem her witness statement inadmissible. Secondly, in their opinion, a human cannot be trusted, and they believe that there is a good chance she may have misinterpreted what she saw."

"How the hell does one misinterpret torture?" Luca was fuming. "What about Alick's testimony? He isn't human, so surely that should count for something." Luca despised Alick for betraying the Guardians, but his testifying might start to change Luca's feelings towards him. Might.

"Alick has recanted his version and is no longer willing to testify. It would seem that he has been badly beaten by other prisoners and is now in no state to take the stand. For his own safety, he is being held in isolation until he recovers, which may take a considerable amount of time. At the moment, he is too injured to even shift form to aid with the healing. And, before you ask, I requested access for Celeste to help heal him, but it was denied."

Luca swore under his breath. "What about all the Silver dealers that we tracked down? Surely they must have some evidence?"

"While the Council is appreciative of the hard work that you, Helo, and Symon have put into decimating the Silver trade here in Lightfall, they can find no direct link between the dealers and those who kidnapped Wysh."

"So it was all for nothing then?" Luca asked bitterly.

"Nothing?" Skylar stamped one hoof in agitation. "No. You have made the town that this Guild is sworn to protect a safer place. You have taken a nasty element off the streets. I know it is not the result you wanted, but it was a noble act."

"What about my reassignment back to Rosa Brook?" Luca asked. If he could at least see Zara in her world, then her inability to return to his would be made bearable.

"I'm afraid my answer is still no." Luca was about to complain when Skylar held up one hand, silencing him. "Do not try and dissuade me, Luca. I know how much you care for her, and I know how much she sacrificed to save the unicorn. But we are being watched. After Alick's betrayal, I did some investigating. I believe that there may be spies here within the Guild's walls. Spies for the Council and also, perhaps, for a darker element I cannot yet name."

Skylar's words silenced Luca. Taking a closer look at his Commander, he noticed for the first time the strain on his face, the dark circles forming around his eyes and the disappointment that he was trying desperately to hide.

Instead of berating him for his decision, Luca asked, "What can I do?"

Skylar sighed. "For the moment, nothing. Keep what I have said a secret, even from your friends."

"Surely you don't suspect Helo or Symon of betraying us?"

"No," the centaur shook his dreadlocked head, "but I also don't want to give those that are false any warning that we are aware of them. It may take some time to sift them out. Until then, I need you here. I know that I can trust you, and for that, I am grateful." Luca's heart swelled at Skylar's words. He was not one to give easy compliments, so this demonstration of his high opinion touched Luca deeply. "If you can keep an ear to the ground, report anything unusual. Also, I hope I don't need to remind you to keep your nose clean and stay out of trouble. The fact this has happened at our Guild means my leadership and our whole existence is being questioned. We cannot give the Council any reason to doubt our loyalty."

"But we don't answer to the Council?" Luca asked, confused.

Skylar lowered his voice as he continued, "No, but they created the first Guardians, a decision I believe they may have come to regret. Some sit on the Council who believe that we have been given too much power and would gladly see us fall."

Luca was stunned to hear Skylar talk this way about

the Council, especially so openly. He must indeed be worried to voice concerns such as these out loud."What will you do?"

"I am going to call a meeting of the Guardian Commanders. But first I need to find the spies," Skylar answered as he rubbed his forehead.

"Then I will leave you to it. But know that if you need anything, I am here."

"I know," Skylar replied, smiling for the first time since Luca had entered the room.

Leaving Skylar's office, Luca went in search of Helo and Symon. He found the elf and bear shifter in the hall, playing a game of cards. Nero lay stretched out at their feet, snoring. Two half-empty tankards of ale sat on the table. Next to them, a crust of bread was all that remained on an otherwise empty plate. The sight made Luca's stomach rumble, reminding him that he had missed the evening meal while waiting for Skylar. Helo, looking up from his hand of cards, greeted Luca, "Judging by the dejected look on your face I'm guessing your petition was declined again?"

Luca nodded.

"They are refusing to make a decision until after the trial." He gently nudged Nero out of the way with his boot and slumped into one of the chairs. He thought about mentioning Alick's injuries, but knew the bird shifter would find no pity at this table. The others despised Alick as much as Luca did.

"Shame, this place could really do with something beautiful to look at besides me," Symon said teasingly, trying to lighten Luca's mood. "Want to play a round?" He invited. "Helo is wiping the table with me; at this rate, I'll be doing his chores for a month."

"No, thanks. You should know better than to play against an elf, a lesson you should have learnt by now," Luca declined. "But I am going to go and help myself to whatever supper is left. I haven't eaten since breakfast. Are you two busy tomorrow morning?"

"My morning is completely free," Helo answered, with a smirk at Symon.

"I have to muck out the stables," Symon moaned, "Thanks to my losing streak. But it shouldn't take too long. Why do you ask?"

"I was thinking about heading into town and maybe seeing about petitioning the Council myself. I know it will likely be a dead end, but sitting on my hands is chafing where it hurts."

"I'll come," Helo said.

"Me too. Good thing I'm an early riser," Symon added.

"In spring maybe," Luca agreed, smiling at his friend. During the spring and summer months, Symon hardly slept. But he made up for it in winter and autumn when little could tempt him from his slumber. "I'll see you both in the morning." Luca nudged Nero again with his foot. The wolf opened one eye, nodded slightly in acceptance of the plan, and then closed his eye again.

Strolling back to his quarters, Luca's mind was spiralling with what Skylar had told him. He had joined the Guardians because he wanted to find a place where he belonged, a family. But now Luca was starting to question those he had trusted with his life. He felt sorry for Skylar, knowing that the centaur would place all of the blame on his own shoulders.

When Luca opened the door to his room, he was surprised to find the light on. He really must have been anxious when he had left. Wasting power was frowned on by the Guild, and those caught punished with extra chores. Opening the door wider, however, he found the culprit. Brax, a werewolf Guardian, was sitting in the room's one chair. Across from him, perched on the edge of his hammock, was a girl he didn't recognize. When they both turned to look in his direction, Luca saw that she was crying. Luca couldn't help but notice that she was also heavily pregnant. Her full, round belly poked out through the opening in her cardigan. Catching his shocked gaze, she pulled her cloak protectively around herself.

"Brax, what the hell?" Luca demanded. But before he could ask another question, the werewolf held one finger to his lips. Confused, Luca softly closed the door behind him. Standing and stepping past Luca, still not uttering a word of explanation, Brax locked the door. Throughout the charade the girl also remained silent, looking up at Luca with sad, amber-gold eyes. Unable to stand it anymore Luca growled, "Seriously Brax, I am in no mood for games. Either tell me what is going on or get out of my room."

"I'm sorry, Luca. We didn't know where else to go." Guilt flashed across Brax's face and then settled into resolve. "This is my daughter, Aeylin. She's pregnant, and we need your help to get her across the rift."

CHAPTER 2

"Daughter?" Luca asked, shocked, inspecting the girl. Now that he was looking, he could see similarities between the young woman perching precariously on his hammock and his stern friend. They both had the same almond-shaped eyes, although hers were much lighter in colour, and the stubborn line of her jaw definitely reminded him of Brax. Her hair, cut into a messy bob, was brown like her father's but in the lamplight, he could also pick out strands of copper and blonde. She was more delicately built than Brax, although her skin tone was similar, a pale brown sun kissed with freckles. "I didn't know you had a daughter. You never mentioned her." At Luca's words, the girl turned an angry look on her father, making Brax lower his eyes. Luca tried to hide a smile, not wanting to upset her, but this was all the proof he needed. Brax was not the type to bow down to anyone.

"Her mother and I aren't bonded, and I thought it would be better if no one knew. A Guardians' life isn't without its risks, and it kept her out of danger. Skylar knows, of course, but few others. I know we are friends, but I would rather it had remained that way. Now, well, I guess I have no choice," Brax explained, a hopeless look filling his eyes.

Luca's mind reeled at yet another secret that he had been too naïve to see. He wondered how many more were hidden within the Guild walls.

"I still don't understand. Why do you need my help, and why do you want her to cross the rift?"

"Aeylin wasn't born a werewolf, she was bitten like me. Bitten werewolves are not supposed to be able to bear children. When the full moon comes, it should have forced her to change, causing her to lose the child. Yet the full moon passed and she managed to resist the change. Another full moon comes upon us now, and she doesn't feel the urge that I can feel singing in my blood."

"But there are werewolf children. I know, I've seen them. Others have managed to have children without crossing the rift. There must be a simpler way," Luca countered.

"Never has a child been born to a bitten werewolf. Only those who are born themselves can birth live young. Those born as children of the moon can control when they turn. Those of us who are bitten cannot. When the moon calls, we answer," Brax said, his voice firm. Luca tried to think back, and as hard as he might, he couldn't ever remember seeing Brax in the Guildhalls during a full moon.

"Have you spoken to Skylar about this?" Luca asked

hesitantly, wondering if this would be another burden to add to the Commander's list of worries.

"No. Skylar cannot know. It would only put Aeylin's life in danger," Brax said with a scowl.

"Danger? Why? Skylar would never harm an innocent child," Luca said, jumping to the Commander's defence.

"Of course not. But the danger isn't from Skylar himself, but from the Council. Since the unicorn kidnapping things have been tense, to say the least. Skylar is under strict orders to report all rift crossings to the Ruling Council. If the Council find out Aeylin is pregnant, she will be killed. Two attempts have already been made on her life."

"But why would the Council care?" Luca asked, shocked.

"Because the father of my child is Kinnison, the pure born son of Tibarn. Should my child survive, our baby will be heir to the highest-ranking werewolf pack in Wundor." This time it was Aeylin who answered, her gaze boring into Luca's. She was trembling slightly, and tears continued to trickle down her face, but her voice was firm. "If it can be proven that a bitten werewolf can mate with a pureblood, and produce viable offspring, then it will lead to rebellion."

"It would mean civil war between the packs," Brax added in a low voice.

"So you are asking me to help you start a war?" Luca asked, his voice almost choking on the word war. Doing so would be a direct violation of his promise to Skylar. The Guardians could not be found to be going against the best interests of the Council, not with the turmoil that Skylar was sure they were in.

"No, I want you to help me keep my child," Aeylin pleaded. "Kinnison loves me. When the child is born, he will acknowledge our baby. Our union will stop the division between the bitten and the born. Kinnison won't let it start a war."

Luca shook his head. What they were asking of him was too much. He would never get the Council to approve Zara coming to Wundor if he went to war against one of its most influential members. Helping Brax and Aeylin would mean betraying Skylar's trust.

"I'm sorry, but I can't help you," Luca said. "You will have to find another way or find someone else who can help you. Surely one of your pack members can shelter you?"

"It won't work. Don't you think we've tried ..." Aeylin stopped Brax's words with a hand on his shoulder.

"There is no use in begging. Luca will not help us. We are just wasting our time." Standing, she put her arm through her father's. Shrugging, Brax unlocked the door and Luca watched the pair walk together slowly down the hallway.

"I'm sorry," Luca called out feebly, before shutting the door behind them. As the door closed with a loud click, he couldn't help but worry whether or not he had made the right choice.

The next morning Luca walked towards Lightfall with his

two friends. The day was lovely, a light breeze tempering the first flush of spring heat, so they had chosen to walk rather than take a horse from the stables or wait for a wagon. Nero, as was his habit, raced in front. He dashed off every now and then to chase some small animal that caught his attention. Luca had thought it best to dress casually, not wanting to give the impression that they were there on Guardian business. Plus the tunic and pants he wore were far more comfortable than the restrictive armour. Helo and Symon had followed his lead and, if anyone had not known them, they could have mistaken them for common creatures out enjoying the sunshine.

The only thing that darkened the day for Luca was his thoughts, which kept returning to Brax's request. He felt ashamed to let his friend down, but he could see no way around it without breaking his promise to Skylar. He was lost in his thoughts when he felt Helo's hand on his shoulder.

"You have been scowling all morning Luca. Are we not good company?" the elf inquired, one shapely eyebrow raised. Luca wasn't sure how to answer. He wanted to tell his friends about Brax's request, but the werewolf had told him about his daughter's situation in confidence. If he wanted to share the news around, he wouldn't have accosted Luca in his quarters and told him behind closed doors.

"Let me guess, you had a visit from a distressed were-wolf?" Symon asked, smiling.

"How did you know?" Luca asked, startled.

"After he saw you, he came to us. Wanted to ask us to convince you to help him," Helo explained. "He didn't give us all the details, just said that he needed to sneak someone across the rift. We declined, obviously," Helo said.

"He didn't tell you who needed to be taken across?" Luca asked.

"No," Symon shook his head. "He seemed very distressed about whoever it was though. I would have been willing to help him myself, but he said that he needed you; for your contacts. I assume he means Zara unless you have any other beauties hidden across the rift?" Symon raised one eyebrow questioningly.

"Afraid not, my friend. Not anyone who I would burden with you anyway," Luca teased, earning himself a punch in the arm.

"It is a shame we cannot help him, for Brax is not the sort of person to make such requests lightly," Helo prodded. "Are you able to tell us what has got him so worked up?"

Luca hesitated for a moment, but knew that his friends would not judge Brax unkindly for the news, nor spread word of Aeylin to others. If Brax had approached them, he must trust them.

"The help isn't for him. It is for his daughter."

"Daughter?" Symon and Helo exclaimed in unison making Luca laugh.

"Apparently. I didn't realise that Brax was a father, but you can see the family resemblance. "

"You've met her?" Luca laughed as his friends exclaimed again in perfect unison.

"Yes."

"Do tell us more. Is she good-looking?" Symon asked in typical fashion.

"Who is her mother? I didn't know that Brax was bonded," Helo asked.

Choosing to ignore Symon's question, Luca answered, "Brax isn't bonded to her mother. He didn't really go into a lot of details about their relationship, but I am not sure if he ever was."

"And..." Symon nudged Luca, refusing to allow his question to be ignored.

"She is quite good-looking," Luca replied, then added quickly when he saw a smile creep across Symon's face, "But she is committed to another."

"Married?"

"Well, no," Luca admitted. He thought about mentioning that she was heavily pregnant, but that would just raise further questions.

"Then, I will not give up hope."

Luca laughed at his friend's enthusiasm. They spent the rest of the walk to town laughing about what Brax's reaction would be to Symon becoming his son-in-law.

CHAPTER 3

The sun was reaching its midday peak when the party reached Lightfall. Despite it being the middle of a workday, the line of creatures outside the Council building numbered over two dozen. Scowling, Luca joined the end of the queue.

"I'm going to the Witch's Brew. Come find me when you have finished with this fool's errand," Nero muttered down the bond to Luca before stalking off in the direction of the tavern.

Guessing his intent, Symon added, "I think I might go and keep an eye on fuzzball," before hurrying after the wolf.

Watching them stroll away Helo said, under his breath so that only Luca could hear, "Want to place a bet on which one will still be standing by the time we get to the front of this line?"

Luca laughed. "Neither, at the rate at which this line is moving."

The creatures waiting in the queue were a mixed

bunch. Two goblins stood just ahead of Helo and Luca, grumpy looks on their faces for not having been able to bribe their way into a better position. In front of them, a fairy was fluttering up and down with impatience. Further ahead were centaurs, a minotaur, two vampires and a faun. A few positions back from the front of the queue, a large man was arguing with a young girl. Knowing it to be impolite to listen in, Luca tried to ignore their conversation. But, as the man's harsh words turned into snarls, causing the child to whimper, Luca started to move forward. Before he had made it two steps, Helo put a restraining hand on his arm.

"Don't get involved. You will only make it worse," Helo warned.

"He looks as if he is about to tear that poor child's throat out. She is terrified, and someone has to stop him."

"Remember that you are not wearing your armour. He will not see you as a Guardian keeping the peace, nor appreciate you interfering in a matter that doesn't concern you," Helo cautioned.

"Well, I can't just stand here and do nothing. Wait here and hold our place in the queue." Luca strode up the line towards the pair. On closer inspection, he could see that the girl was shaking. The bearded, dark-haired man held her firmly by the wrist, clearly hurting her as she tried to pull her arm out of his grasp. Her pale blue eyes were wide with fright, made all the bluer by the dark purple bruise which circled the left one. From the end of the line, the man's deep voice had appeared little more than a growl, but as he approached, Luca could make out the harsh words.

"You are coming with me. You belong to me now," the man growled at the child.

"Please, I just want to go home to my mother," the girl pleaded, her eyes filling with tears.

"Let her go!" Luca demanded, grabbing hold of the arm that held the child captive. With a snarl, the man turned to face him, and Luca could see the sharpness of his fangs as he bared them. He thrust the arm Luca held out with such force that Luca stumbled and had to take a step back to maintain his balance, but he didn't loosen his grip on the werewolf's arm.

"This is none of your business, elf. Unhand me now before I have you arrested," the man snapped.

Luca saw that the coat the werewolf wore was embroidered with a ruby red rose on a full silver moon, the symbol for the Bloodrose Pack. It was one of three werewolf packs situated within the borders of Lightfall. The snarling man was a pureblood werewolf and, as indicated by the blood-red rank slides adorning his collar, a sergeant to their Alpha. Luca guessed that Helo must have recognised the werewolf, and wished he'd been blunter in his warning. Yet the child was still innocent. Releasing his grip on the werewolf's arm, Luca took a deep breath and tried another tactic.

"I doubt that your mistress would be pleased to find you harassing children." Of the twelve werewolf packs in Wundor, the Bloodrose was the only one ruled by a female. Rumour said that she had killed the previous leader, her mate, by tearing his throat out with her teeth. She had managed to hold her position ever since.

"Who do you think ordered me here to register the

brat?" the werewolf sneered. The child, sensing a defender, tried to hide behind Luca but her tormenter was having none of it. With a hard yank, he pulled her to his side. The child let out a scream of pain as her arm was almost ripped from its socket.

"What do you mean register her?" Luca demanded.

"As my property, you ignorant elf. The brat belongs to me," he added, looked disgustedly down at the girl who was still crying. "Personally, I would happily leave her to starve on the streets, but my mistress has other ideas."

"Why don't you let her go home to her family?"

"Because her family doesn't want her." The werewolf spat, making the girl cry even harder. "They threw her out when she changed the last full moon. Apparently, she killed her grandmother, and now they don't want anything to do with her. Her own mother can't even look at her."

"I didn't mean to do it. I don't even remember doing it. I just want to go home," the girl pleaded.

"Well, you can't," the werewolf snapped.

Before the intervention could progress any further, a male fairy, dressed in the gold uniform of the Ruling Council, hovered through the doors, calling "Next".

"Finally" the werewolf grumbled.

Looking at the pair, the fairy, his face perfectly composed as if he didn't notice or care about the sobbing girl, said, "Please join the queue by the yellow door for Registrations." Pulling the girl along, the werewolf half dragged, half carried the child through the open doors. Luca went to follow them, not happy with the result of the confrontation, but the fairy blocked his way.

"I'm sorry, but the regulations state no more than two creatures per application. You will have to wait here for your friends."

"They are not my friends," Luca answered.

"Then you will need to join the back of the line. Have a nice day." Not waiting to see if his instruction would be followed, the fairy floated back into the Council building.

It took over an hour for Helo and Luca to reach the front of the line. The whole time Luca watched the doors, waiting for the werewolf and the child to come out again. Perhaps he could offer her shelter at the Guild, find her work in the kitchens. Or ask Brax if his pack could foster the girl, before reminding himself that Brax had enough on his own plate. Luca's hands kept clenching into fists as he imagined what he would do to the werewolf if he had harmed the girl further.

"There is no point in getting all worked up about it. There is nothing you can do," Helo said, trying to calm his friend.

"There has to be. Surely there must be some law about biting someone so young. That little girl couldn't have been older than nine."

"Each race has the right to set their own laws. You know that the Ruling Council cannot interfere and, there-fore, neither can we. If they did, it would lead to outright war between the races."

"But what about her own race? The girl wasn't a werewolf before she was bitten; surely it was the Council's duty, or ours, to protect her."

"You are right, she wasn't. But the first time she turned and was called by the moon, she fell under werewolf law. She became the property of her sire, the one who made her. A guess it is a loophole which lets them get away with it." Helo's tone was matter-of-fact, typical of an elf.

Seeing the child reminded him of Brax's daughter, Aeylin. Luca had never given much thought before to how Brax had become a werewolf. He knew he wasn't one of the creatures who chose to be bitten to change into something stronger than their original form or to heal from a fatal disease. He now wondered if it had been as horrific an experience for him or his daughter. Had Aeylin been as young as that girl when she was bitten? No wonder Brax was so desperate to protect her now.

Reaching the front of the queue, they were greeted by the same fairy that had dismissed Luca earlier. He gave no outward sign of recognition, his face a blank mask of politeness.

"How may I assist you?" he asked, his voice a high lilt.

"We would like to make an appointment to petition the Council," Luca answered politely, trying to prevent his frustration from showing.

"Personal or business matter?" The fairy inquired.

"Personal."

"Very well, please take this," the fairy held out a small, bright crystal ball the size of a plum. "When it is your turn to meet with the scheduler, it will glow red. When it does, make your way through that door," the fairy pointed to a sapphire blue door through the entry behind him, "with haste. You have fifteen minutes to enter. If you fail to do so within the assigned time frame, you will have to line up again. Do you understand?" The fairy looked at Luca, who nodded. "Good." The fairy turned about to leave when Helo stopped him.

"I have a question." The fairy half turned, clearly eager to move on to the next person. "How long are we likely to have to wait?"

"Around two hours at the moment. We seem to be processing them quite quickly today," the fairy said proudly.

"What is the range on the device" Helo indicated the bright ball.

"The device will notify you regardless of your location. You are only limited by your ability to return within the fifteen-minute window. Failure to do so will result in your having to start the process again. I would, therefore, highly recommend that you remain here and wait with the others," the fairy answered primly. When no follow-up question was forthcoming, the fairy floated away.

"Please tell me that I don't have to stand here bored for two hours," Helo begged Luca.

"Do you have a better idea?" Luca asked. The idea of standing around inside and bored on such a lovely day was unappealing.

"I do, indeed." A smile spread across Helo's face. "I thought we could visit Brina."

CHAPTER 4

Walking past Dulcie's Delights, Luca contemplated purchasing another bag of stars for Zara. Marx had reported how pleased she'd been to receive them and wanted extra next time for himself. But he thought he might find something different in Brina's shop. He was sure that the fire witch would help him select a unique and thoughtful gift. Despite only spending days together, his sister and Zara had quickly become friends. Brina constantly pestered him for updates on the petition to the Council. She had even offered to act as a witness of Zara's good deeds.

Pushing open the door of Callidus, Brina's shop, the tiny bell rang loudly, announcing their presence. Brina was seated at one of the cauldron fires, the two chairs opposite her occupied by a pair of pixies. Each pixie stood on their chair, the extra height allowing them to see into the steaming cauldron. Not taking her eyes off the bubbling contents, Brina held two fingers above her head, letting Luca know that she would be free in a couple of minutes. Weaving their way through the tables, Helo and Luca settled themselves into comfortable armchairs at the back of the room. Helo reached for the tarot cards spread out on the table, intending to shuffle them to keep himself occupied while they waited.

"I wouldn't do that if I were you," Luca warned, halting Helo's hand inches from the cards. "Brina doesn't like people touching her cards without permission. Plus," he added in a cheeky tone, "You'll give her access to your future. Who knows what she might see?" Blushing, Helo pulled his hand back, settling back into the chair, his eyes wide. It was apparent to everyone, Brina included, that Helo was deeply enamoured with the fire witch. Despite knowing that she tended to date females, he still held out hope. Luca felt sorry for his friend, and a little guilty for teasing him. It was fortunate that Symon was still in the Witch's Brew, for he would have teased Helo mercilessly.

"Sorry about the wait," Brina apologised, coming over. Leaning down, she kissed Luca's cheek and then leaned over and gave Helo the same warm greeting. As her ruby red hair cascaded over Helo's face, Luca watched his friend inhale deeply. He would have to talk to his sister about not encouraging his friend. Brina would never intentionally be cruel, and Luca was sure she was unaware of the real depth of Helo's affection. Taking the empty chair between the two males, Brina settled herself and picked up the scattered cards. Expertly shuffling, she asked, "What brings you two here on such a lovely day?"

"We came to petition the Council regarding Zara," Luca answered.

"Finally. How did it go?" Brina asked, hopefully.

"We are still waiting to make our petition," Luca held up the bright ball. "Had two hours to pass so thought we would come to bother you," Luca winked at her.

"You joke, but I am glad you did. Business is slow, and I could use the distraction. I've only had two customers in the shop today. Those two," she indicated the two pixies who were still huddled around the cauldron, "and a young woman who left shortly before you arrived."

"What are they here for?" Helo asked.

"They are trying to have a child but are having no luck. I am brewing something that should help, I hope, but you can never be sure. Conceiving a child is as much by the will of a Goddess as by nature, and my magic won't always help." Brina watched the two pixies with a thoughtful look on her face as she added, "Ironic really. My first customer was here because she wished to terminate her pregnancy."

"Terminate? Why would anyone want to do that?" Helo asked, startled. Brina looked at him, shaking her head.

"You shouldn't judge others too harshly. I understand that for elves, children are precious and rare, and the idea is sacrilege. But for other creatures, sometimes they feel it is their only choice. The child might be deformed, or they might be poor and the baby another mouth they cannot afford to feed. It could also be the result of a non-consensual coupling. So they come to me looking for help." Brina sighed deeply. "Unfortunately, in some cases, as with this woman, there is nothing I can do."

"Why, what was her reason?"

"She did not say. She was distraught and clearly

wanted to keep the child, yet something was forcing this horrible choice on her."

"Is that why you refused to help her? Because you thought that she should keep it?" Luca asked.

Brina was outraged."I did no such thing. The choice is hers to make, not mine. I couldn't help her because she is a werewolf. If the Council were to find out, I would lose my livelihood if not my life." Brina shook her head sadly. "Instead, I merely gave her something to help her sleep."

"Werewolf?" Luca asked horrified. Dreading the answer, he asked, "What was her name?"

"She never told me, she seemed very worried about her privacy." Seeing Luca's concerned look, Brina asked "What is wrong, Luca? You look like you have seen a ghost?"

"Can you describe the girl? Please, Brina, I need to know."

"Perhaps a foot shorter than you with dark hair cut to just above her shoulders. She was wearing a bulky black coat which barely concealed her full belly, so I didn't catch her features, but I will always remember that she had the most beautiful almond-shaped, amber coloured eyes."

"Is that Brax's daughter?" Helo asked. Lost for words Luca could only nod.

"Brax's daughter?" Brina questioned, confused. "I didn't know that Brax had a daughter."

"No one did. But Brax came to me last night asking for my help. She's pregnant, and that pregnancy has put her in grave danger. No wonder she was looking for a way to end it."

Brina's face suddenly paled. Grabbing Luca's hand in a tight grip she demanded, "Who is Aeylin's mother?"

"I don't know. A witch I think Brax said, although it sounds like they are no longer together." At his words Brina went even paler.

"You have to stop her," Brina demanded, her voice sounding panicked.

"I thought you said it was her choice," Luca said, confused. Brina's grip on his hand was so hard it hurt.

"Luca, if you are right then she is not a pureblood werewolf. She was very ill-advised to ask me for something to end her pregnancy." Luca looked at his sister, confused, not understanding why she was so frantic suddenly. "Luca, think. As a bitten wolf she cannot control her change, if she wanted to lose the child, she only had to wait for the full moon. She would be called to change form, and the child she carries would not survive. I am surprised that the pregnancy has progressed this far." Luca nodded slightly, still not seeing the problem. "But the sleeping draught I gave her was for a pureblood werewolf. If she takes it, especially in her fragile state, it will kill her."

"Shit. We have to stop her." Luca jumped to his feet.

"What about your appointment?" Helo asked.

"The appointment can wait. We'll have to send word to the Witch's Brew. Nero and Symon will wonder where we have gone and we may need their help. I just hope they are still sober enough to not slow us down."

"I can tell Nero and Symon," Brina offered. "But please hurry and find the woman."

Giving his sister a brief but tight hug, Luca headed for the door, Helo following close at his heels. They were halfway down the street by the time Brina locked the shop, the witch heading towards the Witch's Brew to find the others.

CHAPTER 5

Helo and Luca sprinted towards the Guild, muscles burning from the strain as they pushed themselves to their limits. Sweat ran down Luca's forehead, forcing him to wipe away the falling droplets before they blurred his vision. He had held hope that they would find someone on the road to offer them a lift, but luck was not on their side. All thoughts of his petition to the Council were forgotten. His one focus was to find Brax and warn him about Aeylin's intentions. He tried to push away the dreadful thought that Brax might not be at the Guild, or that Aeylin had returned home to her pack. They were within sight of the Guild when Luca felt Nero brush his mind.

"We are coming," the wolf informed him. The wolf's use of "we" meant that Symon was with the wolf and since he was able to bond-speak, the two weren't too far behind. Luca was relieved; if they needed to split up to find Brax the larger the group looking, the better. Luca was dreading that he might need to inform Skylar of the situa-

tion, to call others in to help search and, in doing so, break Brax's confidence.

"Open the gates," Helo yelled when they came within range of the high stone walls of the Guardian Guild. The elf's voice was calm and didn't sound at all breathless. Luca envied his stamina. His elven bloodlines granted him increased endurance and speed, but he would never be a match for a full-blooded elf.

The minotaur on guard duty looked as though he was about to object, then he must have seen the urgency in Luca's face for, a moment later, the massive Guild gates started to open. Luca could have sworn that they had never moved so slow before, but then again usually the Guardians were in a rush to get out not in. Stopping just inside the gate line, Luca took a moment to catch his breath. Helo, breathing normally, faced the minotaur and demanded, "Where is Brax?"

"Brax? I believe he is in the stables. What is the matter?" Not stopping to answer, the two friends raced towards the stables. Luca was glad they were on the ground floor; his aching muscles would not appreciate him galloping upstairs. Shoving their way past a pixie who was busy sweeping the hallway, they pushed open the main door to the stabling area.

"Brax!" Luca shouted. The heads of four horses poked out of the stalls, followed quickly by the concerned face of Brax, a shovel in his hand.

"Brax, where is Aeylin?' Luca asked, watching the werewolf's eyes widen at the question.

"In my quarters. Why?"

"We need to speak to her urgently. She is about to do herself harm," Helo explained.

Without another word, Brax dropped the shovel and sprinted out of the loose box towards the nearest stairwell. Like Luca, Brax's quarters were located in the accommodation block on the second floor. Luca and Helo raced after him.

Reaching the door, Brax tried to open it only to find it locked. Patting his pockets, he shook his head when he couldn't find his key. Locked doors were not usual practice for a Guardian and Brax's key, like Luca's, was probably on his table inside the room.

"Aeylin? Open the door," Brax called, but there was no answer. He tried again. "Aeylin, it's me, Brax. Open this door at once." Still nothing.

"I'm sorry Brax, but I need you to move," Luca said, before stepping back and throwing his full weight against the door. If it had been warded with magic, brute force wouldn't have worked, but wood and metal were no match for Luca's strength. The door opened with a crunch as the lock gave way. The light from the open doorway revealed the form of Aeylin lying in Brax's bed. For a dreadful moment, Luca felt his heart stop. They were too late. Relief washed through him, however, when seconds later Aeylin raised her head off the pillow, wiping the sleep from her eyes.

"What the hell is going on?" Aeylin asked, her voice still groggy. "What does a woman have to do to get some sleep around here?" Her eyes widened as she took in the three figures frozen in the doorway. Relief made Luca laugh at her question, earning him a scowl from Aeylin.

"We thought you were dead," Luca said.

"What?" Gasped Aeylin and Brax in unison.

"I think perhaps we should sit down and explain," said Helo, looking down the hallway at a pixie who had been passing along the hall and paused to check out the commotion.

"Good idea. Come in," Brax said, moving to sit on the bed next to his daughter, who was now sitting up.

Luca moved to the other side of the small room, facing them. Helo attempted to move the now broken door back into place to give the party some semblance of privacy. However, every time he released the door, it started to swing inwards. With a sigh, he positioned the door and then rested his back against it, using his body to hold it in place. Luca tried to think of a subtle way to broach the subject with Aeylin but couldn't. So, taking a deep breath, he said, "Aeylin we went to see Brina today. She told us about your visit."

"She what? That is a total breach of my privacy. I could have her license for that!" Aeylin was outraged, anger adding fire to her eyes.

Luca held up a hand. "Firstly, it wasn't her fault. If I had not known of you or your situation in advance, then I never would have known that the werewolf she mentioned was you. Secondly, you cannot report her because what you asked her to help you with is illegal, but I guess you already know that. Thirdly, who are you planning to report her to? The Council?"

"What did you do?" Brax asked Aeylin, his brow creased with worry.

"That is none of your business," she answered harshly.

Luca was unsure if she was talking to him or to her father, but the girl's lack of foresight was starting to grate on his nerves.

"It is my business. You didn't tell Brina the whole story and she rightly assumed that you are a pureblood. If you'd given her the slightest hint that wasn't the case, she never would have given you the sleeping draught. I don't want to see my sister arrested for causing you to overdose and kill yourself," Luca answered, his own anger rising to match Aeylin's, unconsciously curling his hands into fists. His hands relaxed, and his anger cooled slightly as he took in the look of guilt which flashed across Aeylin's face. Clearly getting Brina in trouble had not been her intention.

"You were trying to end your life?" Brax asked in a low voice.

For a moment Aeylin didn't answer. Then slowly, looking at her father, she said in a hollow voice, "No, but if I was, would you truly blame me? This child will destroy Kinnison's relationship with his father. This pregnancy has done nothing but bring danger to you and my pack, in fact every bitten wolf. I thought if I could end my child's life then everyone would be safe." As she spoke, she rubbed her hand protectively over her belly as if attempting to shield the unborn child from her terrible confession. She sighed deeply. "But Brina wouldn't give me anything to end the pregnancy. She said I was too far along and it could kill us both. Instead, she offered me something to help me sleep. I was going to refuse it, but then I had a stupid, crazy idea." Aeylin looked at Luca, her gaze steady. "Since you would not help me cross the rift, I worked out a plan to cross without your help. I thought that I could use the sleeping potion on the guards around the rift. If it is powerful enough to knock out a werewolf, then I am sure it would be strong enough to knock out a few Guardians."

"You have to admire her courage." Nero's tone was full of admiration, his comment letting Luca know that he was outside the door, listening and standing guard.

"You can't truly believe that you could have pulled off a stunt like that all by yourself? Do you have any idea what the punishment would have been if you were caught?" Luca asked. The girl had courage, but her common sense was severely lacking.

"Whatever the punishment is, could it really be worse than what the pureblood packs will do when they find out? They will kill me. If I were caught and locked away, at least I would be safe. What choice did I have?" Her final words were muffled as Aeylin tried to hide the sudden onslaught of tears by burying her face in her father's shoulder. Brax wrapped a protective arm around his daughter, gently stroking her brown hair. Looking up, he met Luca's gaze with one of shock and confusion.

Luca was torn. He hated to see anyone in trouble like Aeylin clearly was, and the look of silent pleading in Brax's eyes was almost enough for him to change his mind and agree to help. But in doing so he would risk any chance Luca had of seeing Zara again or reassignment to Rosa Brook. He looked at Helo, hoping his silent friend would have a solution. But the elf just looked at him, mouth quirked in a slight, knowing smile. The tension in the room increased, the silence broken only by the sound of Aeylin's sobs.

"I'm game to help if you are, mate. It'll be an adventure," Symon's deep baritone boomed from the other side of the door, startling everyone. It broke the tension as first Helo, then Brax and finally Luca started to laugh. Looking up, wiping her eyes with the back of her hand, Aeylin asked,

"Will you help me?"

Luca gave her the only answer he had, with no choice but to be resigned to whatever fate had in store."We all will."

CHAPTER 6

The party of seven (Brina demanded to be included) sat around the table in the back of her shop. It was another quiet day, which worked to their advantage as there were no patrons to overhear their plans. They had decided that it would be best if they didn't meet again in the Guild. It was bad enough that they had drawn unwanted attention with the broken door, but trying to fit seven of them into one person's quarters would have been impossible.

Aeylin sat on the sofa next to Brax, drinking a cup of tea which Brina had assured her would aid in relieving her aches and pains and reduce the swelling in her ankles. Helo and Luca had claimed the stools, with Nero at attention by Luca's side. Symon sat on one of the armchairs, knowing that even in his two-legged form, his bulk would threaten a stool's structure. He had offered his lap to Brina, but she had declined, pulling up a chair from a nearby table. Once everyone was seated, Luca started to tell them the plan that had been forming since the day before, when he had found out about the sleeping potion.

"There are two things that we need to consider. The first is how to get Aeylin across the rift without anyone finding out. The second is what to do with Aeylin once she gets into the human world. If we don't think of a believable tale for Marx, he will come storming back across the rift to inform Skylar."

"Marx?" Aeylin asked. "As in the werewolf Marx?"

"Yes, that's him. Is that going to be a problem?" Luca said, ready to add it to the already growing list.

"No. In fact, I think it might work in our favour. Marx is like me. He's not a member of my pack, but he was bitten not born. He has no loyalty to the purebloods."

"He may," Brax admitted, "have an issue going against Skylar's orders."

"Then we need to convince him that by protecting Aeylin we are working in the best interests of Skylar and the Guardians," Helo said, making it sound simple.

"I think I should be the one to stay with Aeylin, once we cross the rift," Symon offered. Luca looked at the bear shifter suspiciously. "Don't you trust me near Zara, Luca?" Symon gave him a toothy grin followed by an evil chuckle before settling into a more serious countenance. "It will have to be me. Helo can't pass for human even under a glamour, he's too rigid, and Brax will need to stay here to help us get back. Skylar is watching you too closely not to miss you, and staying will only put your petition and reassignment in jeopardy. I can pass for a human, albeit an extremely handsome one, if I have to. If need be, send Nero to keep me company."

Luca nodded slowly; it had never crossed his mind to send Symon, but his friend's offer made sense.

"If he gets out of line, I'll bite him," Nero promised. Symon wouldn't be able to talk to the wolf, not being bonded as Luca was, but Luca felt confident that Nero would let his thoughts be known. A grumpy wolf was hard to ignore, and he felt a stab of pity for Symon. Luca was a little surprised that Nero seemed so happy to be going back to the human realm. Perhaps he was missing his television fix.

"But you've never been across the rift," Luca noted, concerned how his friend would react to the strange environment.

"Which is why you will come with us," Symon said smugly. "You can settle us in and then return with no one the wiser."

"That still leaves us having to find a way for the four of you to cross without anyone noticing," Helo said.

"I might have a solution," Brax offered, and then he flushed slightly as he added, "But it isn't very honourable."

"Spit it out. It's for a good cause," Symon said, while Aeylin squeezed Brax's hand in encouragement.

"Well, it was actually Aeylin's sleeping draught that gave me the idea." He smiled at his daughter proudly. "I am rostered for the night watch tomorrow. Caster is meant to be watching with me but if he were to fall ill suddenly..."

"Then I could take his place," Helo finished, smiling at the werewolf. "But how are we going to make him fall ill?"

"I think I can help with that one," offered Brina. Walking over to the tables of potions, she selected a small, clear vial. Handing it to Brax, she said "Give this to Caster. Rich elves use it to detox their systems, from top to... bottom." She gave him a suggestive wink.

"Gross." Symon cringed.

"But effective," said Brina.

"Alright, so we have a plan. If we aim for when everyone goes into supper, there should be no one around to see us. Plus, the darkness will help hide our movements. Aeylin, Nero, Symon and I will cross the rift. I'll set you three up in the farmhouse and then return here. Time moves slower in the human realm so I should be able to safely stay for a few hours and return to Wundor before dawn the following day," Luca said.

"*That won't allow you time to visit Zara*," Nero noted. Luca sighed. Despite every part of his being wishing he could see her, his reunion with Zara would have to wait.

"Are we agreed? If anyone wants to pull out, now is the time to do it. We won't hold it against you." Luca's gaze met each of his friends as they all nodded solemnly.

"Aeylin and Symon, pack what you will need, but only the essentials. Whatever you take must be easy to conceal and carry. Don't worry about food, bedding, or comforts. The farmhouse will have extra hammocks. Clothing might be an issue," Luca frowned as he took in Symon's size. Even in two-legged form, he was both taller and broader than most humans. In a small town like Rosa Brook, it would be a struggle to find garments to fit his muscular frame. "Symon, pack at least three changes of clothes. Luckily the weather should be warm so you won't need winter layers or bulky jumpers. Aeylin, we should be able to find you suitable clothing in the town.

Or possibly order it online and have it delivered," Luca mused.

"Online?" Aeylin asked, confused.

"Using a computer to place the order so that the shop will send it to you," Luca explained.

"Computer?" asked Brax. "Is there no pixie post?"

Luca sighed. *Good thing I am going with them. This lot would not survive one day alone in the human world. Imagine their reaction to cars?"* Nero chuckled at the thought. Symon and Aeylin were in for a shock. It was one thing to hear tales of such things, but to actually see them was something else entirely. Luca remembered his own reaction the first time he had held a mobile phone. He had tried to make the call with the handset upside down.

"How long is a werewolf pregnancy?" Brina asked.

"It depends. When a bitten werewolf conceives a child with a non-werewolf, then the gestation period will be the same as for the mother. For pureblood wolves, I'm not really sure. This," Aeylin rubbed her hand on her belly, "Wasn't something I ever expected to happen to me. I don't know how long it might take to bring my child to term."

"If my memory from my study at the Witch's Academy serves me right, for purebloods, it depends on what form they were in at the time of conception. Since you and Kinnison are both werewolves perhaps it will work the same way," Brina surmised. "Pardon my bluntness, but what form were you in when your child was conceived?"

Not looking in her father's direction as sudden heat flushed her cheeks, Aeylin locked her gaze with Brina's. In a voice barely above a whisper, Aeylin admitted, "I'm not sure. Kinnison and I first met and coupled in wolf form, he thought I was like him, but we have also coupled in two-legged form. It could be either."

"So we could be looking at 9 months or 76 days, am I correct?" Brina asked. Aeylin nodded.

"Let's hope like hell, it's the latter!" exclaimed Symon. "I don't have enough leave to cover 9 months and I have no idea how to be a midwife."

"How long have you and Kinnison been a couple?" Brina asked.

"Just over 4 months."

"Then, looking at the size of your belly, I would be willing to wager that your child is in wolf form. Even if you had conceived early on, your pregnancy would not be as advanced as is it now if you carried a two-legged child."

"Thank the Goddess for that!" Aeylin exclaimed. "I feel like I am going to pop as it is. I couldn't imagine having to be this big and clumsy for so long." Brax squeezed his daughter's hand, and Brina's lips twitched, trying to hide a smile.

"What if a full moon occurs while we are in the human realm? Will that affect Aeylin?" Symon asked. He had gone slightly pale, and Luca wondered if his friend had bitten off more than he could chew by volunteering.

"The moon here in Wundor doesn't call me to change. Surely I won't react to a mere human moon," Aeylin answered confidently.

"Tell her she is wrong. I may not be a werewolf but the call to howl at the human's moon is as strong as it is here under Wundor's," Nero said, his tone in Luca's mind projecting his worry. Luca could well remember Nero howling at the

moon, joined by barking dogs from one side of Rosa Brook to the other. This was definitely going to make their mission more complicated. Relaying what Nero had told him, he watched as Aeylin's confidence crumbled and fear began to fill her eyes. Luca was grasping at the right words to comfort her when Helo spoke.

"Do not fret, Aeylin. We have promised to protect you, and we will. If that means sneaking you through the rift four times or a hundred, we will do it. If we have to rotate who looks after you, we will do it. You are no longer alone in this." To the elves, children were both precious and rare, and Helo was taking this duty seriously. Brina, seated next to Helo, reached out her hand and took hold of one of his. While the witch and the elf had differing opinions on a mother's right to terminate her pregnancy, on this matter they were in total agreement.

"Thank you, Helo, and to all of you," Aeylin said. Pushing his doubts aside, Luca joined the others in smiling reassuringly at the girl.

CHAPTER 7

Luca waited in Brax's quarters with Symon, Aeylin and Nero, listening for the signal that the way was clear for them to pass through the rift. Brax had managed to sneak the potion into Caster's food a few hours before. Luca felt sorry for the minotaur, who had been emptying his bowels for the past thirty minutes. The reaction had been so violent that Caster had been swiftly moved to the healers' quarters, under Celeste's supervision. Hopefully, the talented fairy wouldn't suspect foul play or order a quarantine, which would throw an obstacle into their plans for an empty courtyard. Once it was reported that Caster would be unable to perform his guard duties that night Helo had made himself handily available. It had been no challenge to convince Skylar to let him take the sick minotaur's place.

The supper bell had sounded a short while ago, calling all Guardians to gather in the hall to fill their bellies. Once the coast was clear, Helo was supposed to come and collect them. Luca could feel an ache starting to throb in his temples as the tension built, waiting for the alarm to sound. Looking at the others, he saw that they were also reacting badly. Aeylin had her trembling hands clasped firmly in front of her belly, and her jaw was clenched. Symon was holding an apple, which he kept rolling back and forth between his hands. Every time it moved from one to the other, he would make a little click with his tongue. Lying on the floor, Nero watched the apple's movement, and Luca could sense the wolf's temptation to reach up and snap it out of Symon's hands.

All four creatures jumped at a light tapping on the door.

"Who is it?' Symon called, deepening his voice in a weak attempt to mimic Brax's.

"It's Helo, Symon. The path is clear. Come now," Helo answered, chuckling at Symon's attempt. Aeylin, Luca and Symon each collected a large pack. Luca's contained Symon's clothes, as he would not need his own, plus a few surprise treats for Nero. The deer antlers in the human realm just weren't the same as the ones the wolf loved from Wundor. He wanted to thank the wolf for volunteering to be Symon and Aeylin's guide in the unfamiliar world.

Opening the door quietly, Luca looked around the dark hallway. He could see no one, but the hairs on the back of his neck stood to attention as if eyes were upon him. Signalling the others, he followed Helo down the stairs to the courtyard. The group waited in the stairwell while Helo went on ahead, resuming his guard position next to Brax at the rift's edge. After a quick word with the werewolf, the two Guardians motioned the party forward.

They were halfway across the courtyard when a voice suddenly called out, making them all freeze. "And just where do you think you are going?"

Luca's fears had come to pass. Celeste had discovered their foul play. Turning, he faced her, the fairy greeting him with a stern look. He returned it with a sheepish one.

"*Gode fen,* Celeste," Luca said, trying to resist the urge to look away.

"If I didn't know better, I would think that you four are sneaking through the rift, despite Skylar's orders for you to stay here and keep your nose clean." Celeste shook her head at Luca. He should have guessed that the meddling fairy would know that he was under house arrest. "I am also guessing that one of you is the reason I have a very sick minotaur lying in one of my beds feeling very sorry for himself."

"That was my fault, don't blame Luca," Brax volunteered, looking abashed.

"Hmmm, so you are all guilty. Are you going to tell me why this is so urgent that you would break our commander's trust?" Celeste demanded.

"I'll accept the blame and tell you everything, I promise. But first can we please do it somewhere a bit more private?" Luca pleaded. He felt very exposed out in the middle of the courtyard.

"Come with me to the healers' quarters," Celeste ordered.

Turning to the others, Luca instructed, "Go on ahead without me. I'll follow as soon as I can."

"No way, my friend. All for one and one for all and all that," Symon argued.

"I'm not letting you take the fall for this by yourself," Nero added, tone firm.

"I'm not the mission. Aeylin is, and the plan was never for me to stay. This might be our only opportunity. Go, and I'll follow or," with a side look at the scowling fairy, "If I am detained, Brax or Helo will send word. Look after Aeylin like we promised," Luca pleaded. If all four of them went with Celeste, it would risk raising suspicions, and their plan would fail. He had a much better chance of explaining the circumstances to the fairy alone.

"Fine, but if there is no word within an hour then I am coming back," Nero agreed grudgingly before stalking towards the rift. Symon only nodded while Aeylin mouthed a silent thank you. With Symon's hand on Aeylin's back to support her, the two followed the wolf, stepping through the rift and disappearing.

Luca turned to Celeste, who looked utterly puzzled at what had just occurred. Scowling at Helo and Brax she said, "Don't think you two are out of hot water with me just yet," before turning on her heel and heading towards the stairs, her blue wings fluttering wildly in agitation.

"Good luck," Helo said to Luca, no doubt glad he wasn't the one who would have to face the annoyed fairy.

"I'm sorry for getting you into this. If someone needs to take the blame, then it should be me," Brax offered. "You can wait, and I can go."

"No, I'll go. Celeste has a good heart. She will understand." With one last nod to his friends, he headed off after the fairy.

45

CHAPTER 8

E ntering the healers' quarters, Luca's nose was
assaulted by the smell of vomit and his ears by
the sound of a loudly snoring minotaur. Guilt
washed over him as he looked at Caster sprawled across
one of the beds. His skin had taken on a pale green tone,
and he stunk. He was an innocent victim in their plan,
and Luca knew he would have to think of something
extraordinary to repay him for the hurt they had caused.

"I hope you feel awful looking at the results of your
handiwork," Celeste scolded. "Poor guy was a fountain of
awful when he came in. Nothing I gave him would
work." She pointed to the nearly full bucket of vomit
next to the bed. "I have emptied that three times already.
I don't even want to think about what the contents of his
bowels have done to the plumbing. The pixies will have
your skin when they find out, it will be a nightmare to
clean up."

Luca felt his face flush."I'll empty the bucket Celeste,"
he promised.

"Yes, you bloody well will. But first, tell me what the hell is going on."

Luca looked over at Caster. The minotaur's eyelids fluttered in time with his snores. Noticing his look, Celeste said, "Don't worry about being overheard. I finally managed to work sleeping magic on him. He will be out for hours." Luca wondered how to begin. He needed Celeste to understand the severity of the Aeylin's situation. Before he could think of the right words, Celeste surprised him with a question of her own.

"You said your mission was to protect Aeylin, who I am guessing is the pregnant werewolf that Symon and Nero were trying to hide from me. Why would a pregnant werewolf need to be protected? And why would sending her to a strange realm be better than having the Guardians protect her?"

Luca wasn't too surprised that Celeste knew Aeylin was pregnant despite the loose cloak she wore. The healer's magic granted her the ability to recognize changes in those around her, often detecting an illness before the sufferer felt the first symptoms. Luca was relieved he wouldn't have to try and convince her, or somehow show proof. Deciding that, sometimes, the simplest explanation was the best, he said, "Aeylin is Brax's daughter." Celeste would be able to sense a lie, and this one fact formed the basis of their involvement.

But Celeste surprised Luca when she scoffed, "Adopted maybe. But when her pureblood family finds out she is missing, we will all have hell to pay." She obviously thought he was dodging the truth, but Luca's next words would shatter that misconception.

"No. Aeylin is his blood daughter. Her mother is a witch. Aeylin wasn't born a werewolf," Luca said, his tone leaving no room for doubt.

"But that's impossible," Celeste said hesitantly. "Bitten werewolves lose their babes before they have a chance to show. She looked to be close to full term."

"We don't know how, or why, but you saw the truth with your own eyes."

Luca could almost see the thoughts dancing through Celeste's mind as she tried to find a reason for the impossible. He waited, letting her work through the possibilities on her own, interested in finding out what conclusion the healer, with all her extensive training, would come to.

"Who's the father?" Celeste inquired.

"Kinnison, the pureblood son of Tibarn," Luca said simply. Celeste gasped.

"So, a bitten werewolf carries the child of the heir to the most powerful werewolf pack in all of Wundor," Celeste mused. "I can see why she is scared. That baby could change everything for the werewolves. But why take her through the rift?"

"Two attempts have already been made on her life. Her pack can't protect her. If she stays here, the Council or the pureblood packs will find her. She can't stay in the Guild as Skylar will be honour bound to report her presence. The human realm is the safest place for her," Luca informed her.

"What happens if the moon in the human realm is stronger than ours and forces her to change? Do you know their cycle?"

"She has managed to resist the change here. We are

hoping she can do the same in Rosa Brook. I don't know the exact cycle, but if it doesn't work, or the pull is too strong, then we will need to bring her back in a hurry and suffer the consequences." Luca hoped he sounded surer than he felt. Without the others there to boost confidence in the plan, all his doubts were coming to the surface.

Celeste thought for a moment. "So you intend to bring her back after the child is born?" Luca nodded again. "Do you know what form the baby takes?" Luca shook his head. "You need to find out. Either form will have its own complications. A two-legged form will mean a more prolonged pregnancy."

"We know. We think that it is a wolf, based on how quickly her belly is expanding, but we don't know for certain," Luca said, excluding the fact that the guess was his sister's. If this turned out badly, he didn't want her involved.

"A wolf pregnancy may be shorter, but it is hazardous to the mother. Without the right medical aid, there is a chance that the baby will kill its mother before it can live on its own. Her two-legged form is not designed to with-stand claws and fangs slashing her from within, and she cannot change form at will like a pureblood."

Luca's eyes widened in horror, a vision of a baby clawing its bloody way out of Aeylin's body flashing in his mind.

"I will help you in any way that I can," Celeste added, making Luca let out a breath of relief. "I see why you have made the choices you have, and for this mission to be a success, you will need me. But why have you not told Skylar?" Celeste asked, perplexed.

For a moment, Luca thought about confiding in Celeste the burdens Skylar already faced, his fear of a spy within the Guild. The fairy was loyal to Skylar and would support him no matter what, but, once again, the secret wasn't his to tell. "Brax made us promise not to. Skylar would be sworn to inform the Ruling Council, and Tibarn would not be happy should he find out."

"True," admitted Celeste, although the look she gave Luca made him feel she knew that there was more. "For now, then, we must continue to keep this a secret. I am assuming that you are not planning to stay on the other side?"

"No. Only Symon, Aeylin and Nero will stay. The plan was for me to return once they were settled."

"Hmmm. I can send you some supplies which will help Aeylin to cope with the pain. But first, we need to find out what form the babe takes. We also need someone qualified to monitor her on that side. Zara mentioned that she worked with animals in her world. Would she or one of her friends be able to provide the medical care Aeylin will need?"

"No. I don't want Zara or her friend involved. It's too risky," Luca said firmly, though his heart stuttered at the idea of seeing Zara again. He had put her in danger once, he refused to do it again.

"Well, you will need to find someone to help her. If you do not, there is a high chance that neither mother nor child will survive." Celeste opened one of the three draws in her desk and pulled out a clear crystal vial, the size of Luca's pinkie finger. Holding it in her hand, she focused her magic on it until it glowed a brilliant blue. From a nearby tray, the fairy selected a small silver-wrapped package. Handing both to Luca, she said, "You need to take a sample of Aeylin's blood. In the package, you will find a needle and tube. Take enough to fill the vial. If it turns pink, the embryo is in the form of a two-legger. If it turns black, the baby is a wolf. Either way, the task ahead of you will not be easy, but it is always better to be prepared."

Unsure what to hope for, Luca placed the vial and package into his pack.

"Now go, cross the rift. Make sure you return before first light tomorrow, or there will be hell to pay. Come see me when you do, and let me know the outcome." Luca hugged the fairy, feeling more hopeful now that the healer was in on the plan. As he turned to go, she called out "Oh, and if you see Zara, give her my love." Luca only nodded in response, unable to get words out past the lump in his throat.

CHAPTER 9

"Is she going to tell Skylar?" Brax asked Luca the second he stepped out of the stairwell and into the dark courtyard. The werewolf fidgeted from one foot to the other, and even Helo looked ruffled. Waiting, uncertain of the outcome, while Luca spoke to Celeste had not been easy on either of them.

"No, she is not. She is going to help us." For a moment, he debated telling Brax about Celeste's warning about a wolf baby, but decided he had enough to worry about. Once they had a definite answer, he would let the werewolf know. He was sure he had made the right decision as Brax's face relaxed into a grin.

"Told you, you had nothing to fear from Celeste," Helo said, brushing over the fact he too has been worried.

"I know. But it seems as if more and more people are being involved and I feel responsible for getting you all into this. I cannot express how grateful I am to each of you."

"Well, your thanks will have to wait. I need to get across the rift before Nero comes back and starts throwing his grump around."

"Go," Helo said, and then surprised Luca by grasping him into a tight hug. The elf was not usually one to show the strength of his feelings in public. "I'll see you soon, my friend. Watch yourself," Helo said, releasing him.

For a second, Brax looked as if he also intended to hug Luca but at the last moment he changed his mind, holding out his hand instead. Luca shook it firmly. Then, before the situation could get any weirder, he stopped further words and stepped through the rift.

No matter how many times he passed through, the sensation of being battered by the rift was a shock. He had only half regained his bearings, taking two steps to steady himself, when instead he almost stumbled over Nero's still form.

"What took you so long?" The wolf demanded, having no sympathy for Luca's aftershock.

"I wasn't that long, there was no need for you to wait for me. Celeste is going to help us. Where are the others?" Luca asked.

"We have a situation, and I thought you would appreciate the warning." Being soul bonded to Nero, Luca could usually interpret the emotions that flowed down their telepathic bond. The worry mixed with humour which he felt pouring forth from the wolf put Luca on edge. Nero could have communicated the warning from the farm-house, yet for some reason, he had chosen not to.

"What's wrong?" Luca asked, heart racing in fear that

Marx was about to come charging towards the rift. Perhaps Nero was there to prevent the Guardian from reporting them to Skylar. But the three words that drifted down the bond made Luca's heart race even faster.

"Zara is here."

The past two weeks had felt like a lifetime for Zara. Each day she had woken overcome with a single thought: the hope that it would be the day that Luca would return. The team at The Haven, not aware of the situation or why her moods could change so quickly, tried their best to distract her. They kept her busy at work, and in the evenings dragged her out to the cinema or stayed up late playing card games or watching television. Each day she would spend time in the morning with Karen, baking cookies or pies. In the afternoon, she would disappear, taking the baked goods with her, Bronson her only companion. She would always be edgy before she left and come home a little sadder than the day before.

Today she carried chocolate cookies in a paper bag, choosing to walk instead of driving to the farmhouse. The weather was beautiful, and she had managed to escape her duties at the vet practice early. If Luca wasn't there, she wouldn't stay long, returning before it was dark. George had planned a family dinner and, despite everything else, she was looking forward to it. Max had asked her if Luca would be coming; keen to show off his prowess in cards again. She hadn't been able to give him an answer. Part of her felt silly being so disappointed after only two weeks.

Yet knowing that almost two months would have passed in Wundor only worked to increase her doubt. Apart from the gift of Dulcie's star candies, she'd had no word from him.

Marx wasn't able to tell her much either, though she didn't think that he was doing it deliberately. Over the past week, she had grown fond of the werewolf, who was a sucker for baked goods. He had discovered Nero's collection of "Teen Wolf" DVDs and had become fascinated by them. Often Zara would stay and watch an episode or two with him, happy for the distraction and to feel that little bit closer to Luca. Marx was constantly pausing the show to marvel at the cars. He seemed to be becoming a motorhead. On the previous visit, Marx had begged Zara to open the bonnet of her car so he could check out the motor. She'd thought about teaching him to drive, considering it a way to thank him for the kindness he showed her, but was hoping there wouldn't be time.

Reaching the locked gate, she was surprised not to find Marx already there. The werewolf's keen senses usually informed him early of her coming, and she always found him waiting for her there. Perhaps he was patrolling the back fence of the property.

"Marx," she called, cupping her hands around her mouth. Nothing. She called again, this time louder. "Marx, it's Zara." Still nothing. Strange. She looked down at Bronson, who was sniffing at the gate post, whining softly.

Zara considered her options. She could leave and come back later, perhaps after dinner, or try walking the fence's perimeter and maybe catch sight of Marx. Or, maybe, she could try and jump the gate. The gate wasn't too high, reaching to her elbows, and even with the barbed wire edging the top, jumping it shouldn't be an issue. But if the magical wards were activated, she would be thrown back with a very nasty shock. Marx had warned her that the wards would detect her as human and use their full force to repel her.

Gingerly she held out a hand and touched the top of the metal gate, careful to avoid the sharp spikes of the barbed wire. The steel felt cold under her hand but not alarming. She couldn't feel anything unusual. Taking off her short-sleeved jacket, she laid it across the top of the gate. The paper bag of cookies she gently threw over the gate, where it landed in the soft grass at the bottom of one of the gum trees.

"Here goes nothing. Wish me luck," Zara said to Bronson, who looked up at her with agitation. Taking a few steps back, she ran towards the gate, grabbed hold of the top metal bar through her jacket and, using her forward momentum to her advantage, threw herself over, feet first. She landed safely on the other side, a wide grin on her face. The wards must have been disabled. She heard Bronson bark.

"Come on, boy, you can do it," she called to the dog. Following his mistress' path, he ran back towards the road before turning and sprinting towards the gate. At the last moment, he leapt, soaring over the gate to land, skidding, at Zara's feet. Leaning down, she patted the top of his head, ruffling his ears. "Good boy."

Grabbing her jacket off the gate, she was disappointed to find a couple of tears in the back from the barbed wire.

Putting it on, she decided she didn't care. That had been the biggest adrenaline rush she'd had since returning home through the rift. Picking up the cookies, glad to see they hadn't suffered any damage from their landing, she followed Bronson towards the farmhouse.

CHAPTER 10

*Z*ara had walked three-quarters of the way down the gravel drive leading towards the farmhouse when she caught sight of Marx, hurrying in her direction. He looked anxious, and she felt guilty for breaking his trust. "Marx, I'm sorry. I know I shouldn't have jumped the gate, but ..."

"Never mind that now. It's no matter. But you have to go," Marx said, grabbing her arm and attempting to turn her back in the direction she had come.

"What, why?" Zara asked startled. "Has something happened? Is Luca okay?"

"Yes, yes, he's fine. But you can't be here right now." Holding tightly to her arm, Marx started walking swiftly, pulling her with him. Zara almost stumbled, trying to keep up. Shoulders tense, eyes darting, the werewolf looked agitated. Bronson, not happy to see his mistress being poorly treated, started to growl.

"Marx, what's wrong?" Zara asked. She had never seen Marx act this way, and it was starting to scare her.

"Nothing. You have to go. You're not supposed to be here." Zara was about to demand an explanation when Marx froze, caught off guard by the sound of Bronson, who had stopped growling and was now barking loudly. The dog's ears were pricked, and he was staring intently at the farmhouse. "Damn, I forgot about the dog," Marx grumbled.

Zara gazed around, trying to work out what Bronson was getting so worked up about. She couldn't see anything that looked out of place. Without warning, Bronson shot off into the trees behind the farmhouse. About to call for him, Zara's shout died in her throat when Bronson's bark was answered by the yipping greeting of a wolf. A yip Zara recognised as Nero's. Pulling her arm free of Marx's grip, she sprinted towards the farmhouse.

"Zara, wait," Marx called half-heartedly, guessing correctly that she wouldn't follow his command. Zara didn't stop. Her heart started to race, her mouth went dry, and a feeling of giddy joy rushed through her as she ran. If Nero was here, then Luca must be. She wasn't sure why Marx had been trying to keep her from him, but she wasn't going to let him. She had to see Luca.

Coming around the trees, her feet skidded to stop so fast that she almost fell. Bronson stood in front of Nero, joyously barking as the wolf greeted him with greater restraint. Standing by the black wolf wasn't Luca but a ginormous black bear. Behind the bear, her body half-hidden by his vast bulk, was a woman Zara didn't recognise. She was trembling, one hand holding onto the bear's fur. As Zara watched the woman's face changed from healthy brown to ashen, and her eyes rolled back into her head as she fainted. Before anyone could catch her, she fell to the ground, her whole body racked with spasms.

As the woman hit the ground, three things happened almost instantaneously. The first was that Bronson stopped barking. The second was that the black bear shimmered, there one moment and the next replaced by a very tall, very muscular dark-skinned man. The third was Zara's legs started working again and, before she knew she was moving, she was at the fallen woman's side. "Symon cushion her head. Make sure her mouth is clear and that she hasn't swallowed her tongue," she instructed, not sparing a moment to greet the bear shifter. "Nero lay on her legs." The wolf did as he was told. "How far along in her pregnancy is she?" Zara asked, taking hold of one of the woman's hands and checking for a pulse. She found it, rapid and erratic, and started to count the beats in her head.

"We don't know," Symon admitted.

Zara lightly placed both hands on the woman's swollen belly. She was about to ask what the woman was, because something about her hinted that she wasn't human, when the woman's shaking suddenly stopped. For dragging seconds, nothing happened, then Zara felt the shove as a tiny hand or foot kicked her from inside the woman's belly. She gasped and suddenly, unable to stop herself, giggled. She had never felt a baby kick before.

About to look at Symon, to tell him about the kick and to find out what the hell was going on, Zara's gaze was instead caught by a pair of extraordinary golden, almond-shaped eyes. The woman, eyes wide but clear, smiled hesitantly at Zara. Licking her lips and swallowing, she asked in a husky voice, "Does anyone have a glass of water? My mouth is so dry."

Despite the pregnant woman claiming that she could walk perfectly fine by herself, Symon had picked her up and carried her into the farmhouse. The female werewolf, slightly shorter than Zara and slim despite the bulk of her pregnancy, looked even more fragile in Symon's tree-trunk arms. With surprising gentleness for one of his size, Symon laid Aeylin onto the sofa inside the house. Marx, following the party inside, grabbed a blanket from one of the bedrooms and draped it over the woman. Zara, rifling through the cupboards in the small kitchen, found a jar of honey. She scooped two teaspoons into a glass of water, stirring until it dissolved, and handed it to Aeylin. Unnoticed by the others, Nero had disappeared.

"Thank you," Aeylin said, taking the glass Zara offered her. She took a small sip and sighed contently. "Honey water, just what I needed."

"Celeste once told me that honey water was almost as good as magic," Zara said, smiling reassuringly at the woman.

"Ah, you must be Zara. My father told me about you; worst kept secret in the Guild, the human who crossed into Wundor," Aeylin said with a smile.

"Like we could keep such a beautiful secret to ourselves," Symon countered, smiling broadly at Zara. "It is good to see you again." The large man enfolded her into a bear hug, and she squeezed him back tightly. It was easy to see why a bear had been his final shifter form.

"You too, Symon. But why are you here?" She wanted to ask where Luca was but didn't want to be too forward or hurt Symon's feelings by letting him think that she wasn't glad to see him.

"What, are my charms not enough for you?" Symon asked with the grin, making Zara smile and some of the tension dissolve. His smile faded into something more serious as he added, "Because of Aeylin," introducing the woman on the couch. "Creature politics have made it impossible for her to stay in Wundor, so we are planning to hide out here for a while."

"Marx wasn't expecting you?" she guessed, aware of the werewolf scowling from the corner of the room.

"Indeed, I was not," Marx confirmed, his tone harsh.

"Well our visit was a little unexpected, and of the utmost urgency," Symon explained, looking slightly abashed. "When Luca comes, he can explain everything, I promise."

"Luca is coming?" Zara couldn't keep the note of excitement out of her voice. At the mention of his name, her heart had started to beat faster, and butterflies swirled in her stomach. For a moment, she wondered if she was going to faint.

"Indeed I am," came a rich caramel voice from the doorway and Zara spun, almost falling in her eagerness, to find Luca standing there. She had thought about their reunion so many times, promising herself that she would be demure; to show that she had been patient and that being away from him had not been torture. But at the

62

sight of him, tall, blonde, and smiling so warmly at her, Zara forgot all her promises. She ran to him, and he caught her up in his arms. For a second he held her so tightly she couldn't breathe and then he was kissing her. His kiss was hard and passionate, chasing away any doubts that he had forgotten about her. She kissed him back just as fervently, sending him that same message, that he was hers and she was his.

CHAPTER 11

A not-so-subtle cough from Marx made Zara pull very reluctantly away. At the sight of Luca, all thoughts of the others being in the room had disappeared. Facing them, she realised that their public display of affection had probably embarrassed the others, but found she hardly cared. They could have had an audience of a hundred, or even a thousand, and she still would have greeted Luca with the same level of enthusiasm. Meeting Marx's disapproving glare with a steady gaze, Zara defiantly held on to Luca's hand. Nero, who had returned to the farmhouse with Luca, stepped forward to stand at Zara's side. Out of the corner of her eye, Zara noticed Symon seat himself on the sofa next to Aeylin, sheltering her from Marx's scowl.

"While Zara may be overjoyed to see you, Luca, I am not. I had the impression that you are under strict orders to remain in Wundor. Have those orders changed?" Marx inquired, his tone portraying his obvious doubt.

"Not exactly but I won't be here for long. I'm just here

to help these three settle in, and then I'm leaving," Luca said. Zara's heart dropped at his words, and she squeezed Luca's hand tightly. Luca squeezed hers in return, but didn't meet her pleading look, his gaze never breaking from Marx's. "The reason we are here has nothing to do with me, or Zara, or the Guardians. The consequences of this mission are far greater, and we need your help. Aeylin needs your help." Marx's eyes flickered to the woman on the couch and his sharp gaze softened for a second.

Pushing her advantage, Aeylin said, "We may not be part of the same pack, Marx, but what we are doing affects all werewolves."

Zara tried to stifle a gasp. Aeylin was a werewolf. It explained the strange, not-quite-human feeling she had gotten when she touched the woman.

"My duty is to the Guardians and to my pack," Marx countered. "I will not risk my position in either to aid a fugitive."

"Are you blind, Marx?" Symon asked, making Marx growl. The tension in the room increased, and Zara felt Nero's rough fur brush up against her leg as the wolf stepped closer to her side. "Aeylin is no fugitive. She is pregnant! You know what that means."

"You think I'm fool enough to fall for this trickery? I know that Aeylin is a bitten werewolf like me. She cannot bear a child," Marx spat back at Symon. Suddenly, Aeylin was on her feet. She held herself rigid, and Marx must have been blind indeed to ignore her huge belly.

"Look at me Marx. This is no lie that I am carrying. I am the blood daughter of Brax. I am a member of the Dawnfall pack. The father of my child is Kinnison, the only son and heir of Tibarn. I am carrying a living child inside and, Goddess help me, even if it kills me, I will bring my child into this world. As a Guardian, and as a fellow werewolf, you are sworn, on both blood and honour, to protect those in danger, are you not?" Aeylin demanded. Marx could only nod in response, words failing him.

"Then you will aid me, and my protectors, while we remain here in the human world. Because to send me back is to sign my death warrant." Again, Marx nodded. Aeylin took a deep breath as if to say more on the subject, but the words never came. Her eyes rolled back in her head as she collapsed backwards. This time Symon caught her before she could hit the floor and moved her to the sofa, laying her head in his lap.

Letting go of Luca's hand, Zara ran to Aeylin. Falling to her knees next to the sofa, she laid her hands on Aeylin's belly, reassured to feel a strong kick. Not quite sure what to do next, she followed her intuition, reaching up to cup the werewolf's face in her hands.

"Aeylin? Can you hear me?" She asked in a gentle voice. She watched as a blush began to slowly creep across Aeylin's white cheeks. As the paleness faded away, Aeylin took a deep breath and opened her eyes. "Are you okay?" Zara asked, her brow creased with worry.

Aeylin blinked rapidly for a few seconds then slowly nodded. "I think so. One moment I was fine and the next everything went black."

"If I had to guess, I think all the arguing," Zara shot a dirty look at Marx, "slammed down your blood pressure, making you pass out. But without the proper equipment, I can't be sure. If you will stay here and lie quietly, I'll go to The Haven and grab a few things that will help you." Standing, Zara looked at Marx who stood stiffly against the far wall, his arms crossed. Some of the bravado had faded from his expression and Zara thought she caught a glimmer of regret in his eyes. "Marx, will you help her? You've told me about your family, and I know how much you love them. Imagine if Aeylin was Hali?"

At the mention of his daughter's name, Marx's shoulders slumped, and Zara knew she had won. She felt a little guilty for using his family loyalty against him, but she knew he would do anything for them.

"I won't report you to Skylar," he agreed, begrudgingly, "but I also won't lie for you. If Skylar finds out, I will tell him the truth." Zara smiled at Marx.

"We can't ask for anything more. Thank you, Marx," Luca said.

"Yes, thank you," Aeylin added. "My intent in hiding here was to protect my baby, I never meant to get all of you in trouble."

"We manage to get ourselves into enough trouble without you," Symon laughed, "So, don't you worry about us. We can look after ourselves. You need to look after yourself and the baby. Zara will find something to help stop you fainting, and you'll be good as new in no time." Zara couldn't help but be pleased with Symon's faith in her, she just hoped she wouldn't let them down.

"I'll be back as soon as I can, I promise," Zara said, standing and heading towards the door. Catching Luca's eye, she motioned for him to join her on the porch. After a quick scan of the room and a reassuring nod from

Symon, Luca followed, closing the farmhouse door behind him to give them the feeling of privacy.

"Will you be here when I get back?" Zara asked the moment the door was closed.

Luca looked at the position of the sun, which had just passed its midday peak and nodded. "Yes, I will be here until sunset, then I must return. I'm sorry, I can't stay. Things are... complicated in Wundor at the moment," he said, brow furrowed. "The Ruling Council seems intent on turning a blind eye to what happened here. They keep postponing the trial. Skylar is worried that there may be darker forces at play." Luca looked crestfallen, and Zara wished there was a way that she could help.

Stepping forward, she wrapped her arms around his waist and said, "Oh, Luca, I am so sorry." She laid her head against his chest. "Is there anything I can do to help? I've been scanning the newspapers for mentions of the goblin, but so far nothing has made the news."

"What!" Luca exclaimed, startled. He pushed her back, grabbing hold of her shoulders and looking into her eyes, his gaze serious. "Zara, you cannot get involved in this! It is too dangerous. Don't go looking for them. It is bad enough you plan to bring us medical supplies. Trust me, if I could think of another solution, I would, rather than getting you involved in this mess," Luca's voice was firm, his tone commanding.

"I'm not an idiot, Luca. I can take of myself," Zara said, hurt by his lack of faith in her. She was about to tell him that she would have reported any news to Marx, but Luca interrupted before she had a chance.

"Don't be naïve, Zara. A fragile human is no match for a werewolf or a goblin."

"This fragile human did just fine rescuing Wysh on my own, thank you very much," she threw back at him, temper rising. "I didn't need to wait around for you to rescue me. If I had, I would still be waiting, since you were ready to throw us away without a second thought." Her voice rose higher, anger disguising the hurt she still carried.

"I was trying to protect you," Luca countered, his voice rising to match hers. "You were taken in by the magic, caught up in your fairy tale version of my world from your childhood. You were oblivious to the danger. I never should have put you in harm's way."

"I don't need you to protect me. Go if that is what you want, return to your precious Wundor. But I am going to help Aeylin whether I have your permission to or not."

Without another word, Zara turned on her heel and, leaping down the porch stairs, sprinted down the gravel drive, leaving Luca, mouth open, staring after her.

CHAPTER 12

Watching Zara sprint away tore Luca apart. He fought down the urge to chase after her. He knew he had been an idiot talking to her that way. He'd practised what he would say so many times in his head, but not once in his imaginings had it ended like this. He could kick himself. Rather than go back into the farmhouse and face the others, he decided to sit for a while on the porch swing. The gentle rocking movement soothed his agitation and reminded him of the last time he had sat there. When he had said goodbye to Zara. When she had promised to wait for him. It had all seemed so simple then. He would go back to Wundor, bring the drug dealers to justice, and then return. The Ruling Council would have no choice but to allow her to return with him, not after she saved Wysh's life. But nothing had worked out the way he had thought.

He heard the door open and turned to see Symon standing there, a bemused look on his face. Slipping through the gap between Symon's legs, Bronson raced after Zara, pausing only seconds to give Luca a dirty look. It was clear whose side of the argument Bronson was on. Luca wondered if the others agreed with the dog.

"Can I sit?" Symon asked, gesturing to the empty seat beside Luca.

"Depends, have you come to make fun of me? Because I'm not in the mood right now," Luca warned him.

"Nope, no teasing. Just thought you might like a friend to talk to." Symon sat next to Luca and for a few minutes they sat in comfortable silence, the only sound the creaking of the swing as it rocked gently back and forward, and the voices of the birds singing in the gum trees. Symon took in a deep breath, "It smells different here. Fresher than the Guild, for sure, what with no horse manure tainting the air or scents of leather and metal, but still different. I wasn't expecting that. To be honest, I'm not sure what I was expecting," Symon admitted.

"Getting homesick already?" Luca asked.

"No, just find it strange, is all. I've never been through the rift before, and I guess I imagined it would be the same as home but in a different place. Like Bell Haven is different from Lightfall. The layouts of the towns are different, but in essence, they are the same. But here, even the air smells different." Symon laughed. "Am I making any sense?"

Luca tried to think back to his own first impression of Rosa Brook. It had been three years since he had first been assigned to the farmhouse and in that time this world had lost most of its strangeness. He's discovered that humans weren't that different from the inhabitants of Wundor. They ate, slept, worked, raised their children, fought wars and made love. They lived the best way they knew how.

"I guess I just don't notice the differences anymore," Luca admitted.

"I think that is why Skylar chose you for this posting. You've always been good with change. With fitting in with your surroundings. You make your home wherever you go, like at the Foundling Home or when we first joined the Guild."

"But I had Brina at the home, and you, Helo and Nero at Lightfall. I didn't have to do it alone."

"True. You and Nero are lucky that way. You have each other now; you never have to be truly alone. But Zara, well, she's had to deal with the fact that her's isn't the only world in existence, and that magic is real, all while falling for someone who isn't even human. Plus she has to keep it a secret from everyone she knows and loves, to protect a world that hates her. I think, all things considered, she's been amazing."

"You're right," Luca agreed with a sigh. "I've acted like such a fool."

"Hey, don't be too hard on yourself. There is no rule book for situations like this one. I know you just want to protect Zara, but that girl is tough, trust me. She can take care of herself. Also, the one thing women in both worlds have in common is that the stronger you tell them not to do something, the more determined they become to do it."

Luca laughed, letting the tension of the argument fade away. "Truer words have never been spoken, my friend." Nudging Symon's shoulder with his own, he added, "Thanks."

"Ah, what are friends for? Now if you have done moping can you come inside? It may be daylight here, but my head still thinks it is night and I think Aeylin would sleep better in a hammock, don't you?"

Smiling, the two friends headed into the farmhouse.

Zara didn't slow down until she reached the boundaries of The Haven, bending over clutching at the stitch in her side. As her breathing slowed, so did her temper, and she started to regret acting so rashly. Instead of proving she could help, she'd acted like a child, running away from the fight instead of standing her ground. He was going to think her such a fool. Now that she was starting to calm down, she could think rationally and admit that Luca had only been trying to protect her. After the events in the barn, where she had almost died, she couldn't really blame him. There was a darkness to his world, a kind Zara had never experienced before. But there was also light, and magic, unicorns and friends, and she wasn't about to give those things up without a fight. Most of all, there was Luca, who made her whole being tingle. She had to make it right, assuming he was still at the farmhouse when she returned. She was startled out of her reverie by a bark. Bronson was bounding through the field towards her. Stopping at her feet, he barked again and then cocked his head to the side, waiting.

"Come on, boy, let's hurry," she said, starting to run towards The Haven, Bronson following at her heels.

The practice had finished for the day, and George had

shut the clinic, barring any emergencies, so the team could share a family dinner. Checking her watch, Zara guessed she had just over an hour before everyone was due to arrive. Karen would already be in the kitchen. Hopefully, she would be able to sneak via the back through the yard and into the clinic without being seen. Zara felt bad deceiving Karen and for pilfering supplies for Aeylin, but there was no other choice. She had promised both Skylar and Luca that Wundor would remain a secret. She would leave a note to explain that she was going to miss dinner and make her apologies in person later, after she had helped Aeylin and made things right with Luca.

Grabbing a handful of dog treats from the storage shed, Zara used them to bribe the dogs milling in the dog run into silence. Instead of barking hysterically at the sight of her, their usual greeting whether she was gone for hours or minutes, they happily munched on the treats. Taking the opportunity, Zara headed for the clinic, grabbing one of the baskets they used at the farmers' market from its place by the door. She tried to think about what she would need. A stethoscope was a must. So were heat packs, cold packs, a thermometer and bandages. She was hesitant on what affects the medications might have on a werewolf. She wished she could ask Emma.

She was putting two bottles of sterilising solution into the basket when a tap on her shoulder made her scream and jump a foot off the ground. Spinning around, she saw Josh and Emma standing there. Emma looked stern, and Josh was trying to match the look but failing badly. The corner of his mouth kept twitching. Zara felt her cheeks flush with heat.

"What do you think you are doing?" Emma demanded.

"Nothing," Zara stammered. She tried to push the half-full basket behind her with her foot, but with a quick movement, Josh leaned down and swiped it up.

"Doesn't look like nothing to me," Emma said, flipping through the contents of the basket. "Where are you taking these supplies?"

"I can't tell you," Zara moaned, refusing to meet Emma's frosty stare.

"For the last two weeks, ever since you spent the night with Luca, you have been acting strange. Actually, worse than strange, secretive. You disappear without letting anyone know where you are going. You jump every time there is a knock on the door. You won't tell us what happened that night." Emma let out a deep sigh and shook her head. "Frankly I'm concerned and hurt. We thought we were your friends."

With every word of Emma's accusation, Zara felt cold stabs of guilt shoot into her heart. She didn't know what to say, but she tried to apologise, "I'm sorry. I truly am. But I made a promise ..."

Emma cut her off before she could say anything else.

"Yeah, well I am making you one now. I promise that you are not leaving the premises again without me. I will follow you even if it is at three o'clock in the morning. Whatever is going on, whatever the big secret is, enough is enough. We are your friends Zara, and we care about you. Whatever danger you're in, whatever this is, we are in. All the way."

Zara looked to Josh, who said, "Ditto. I'm with Emma on this, and with you. We both are."

Looking at her two friends, Zara felt her heart swell with love and pride. She had felt so alone these past two weeks, and it had torn her apart, not being able to share everything with them. They were her family. She could trust them with her secret. Smiling broadly, feeling happier than she had in weeks, she said, "Alright. Help me gather the last few things I need and then come with me. It's easier if I show you. I don't think you'd believe me otherwise." Both Josh and Emma looked perplexed but said nothing. Zara quickly gathered the things she needed. Meanwhile, Josh wrote a note to George and Karen, letting them know that all three of them wouldn't be there for dinner as they had been called away for an emergency.

Josh offered to drive, and they all piled into his car, including Bronson who refused to be left behind. Josh was hesitant about taking the dog, but Zara pointed out that if they didn't take him, the collie would just race across the fields and likely beat them there. What she didn't mention was that she didn't want to give Luca notice that they were coming. She was terrified he would cross the rift to avoid her before she got a chance to apologise. They drove in silence, no one quite knowing what to say. Zara tried to guess how her friends would react to the news that they lived a handful of miles from a portal to another world.

"Turn here." Zara pointed to the driveway leading to the farmhouse. Jumping out, she was relieved to find that the gate was unlocked. Marx, or Luca, must have left it open in anticipation of her return. She pulled it open wide, then closed it again after Josh had driven through. She was about to climb back into the car when she froze, startled, as a scream of pain, coming from the direction of the farmhouse, pierced the air.

CHAPTER 13

The moment that Zara was inside the car, the passenger door barely closed, Josh, hit the accelerator and sped towards the farmhouse. As they reach the driveway leading to the porch, he slammed the brakes so hard that the car fishtailed on the gravel before coming to a skidding halt. Emma, Zara and Josh leapt from the car and raced to the front door, Zara carrying the basket of supplies clutched tightly in her hand. She opened the door to find Symon, Nero and Luca crowded around the sofa. Aeylin, fists clenched and curled into the fetal position, was writhing in pain on the couch. Her eyes were closed tight, and she was whimpering. Luca looked up and caught sight of Emma and Josh. She expected him to be angry, to reprimand her. Instead he exclaimed, "Thank the Goddess, you are back!"

Zara rushed to Aeylin's side as the distressed werewolf let out another terrified howl. Sweat beaded her forehead, and her swollen belly shuddered as if it was about to tear itself apart.

"What happened?" Zara asked.

"We don't know. One moment Aeylin was lying on the sofa, and we were talking about moving her to a bedroom, the next she let out a scream and collapsed. We haven't been able to get a word of sense out of her. We had no idea what to do." Luca looked towards Emma, who stood frozen in the doorway, "Can you help her?"

For a moment, Emma said nothing, her eyes wide, gaze frozen on the large black wolf standing next to Aeylin's head. Zara realized she should have warned Emma about Nero. In the safety of the farmhouse, Nero hadn't bothered to glamour himself. None of the party had. Zara was about to reassure Emma when she watched the vet give a little shake of her head, then moving her gaze to Aeylin, take a hesitant step forward.

"I'm a vet, not a doctor," Emma said. "I'm not sure that I'll be much help."

"Aeylin is a werewolf if that makes a difference?" Luca asked, not having time to ease Emma into the world of creatures. Emma gulped and for a second looked as if she was about to take a step back when she stopped herself.

"A werewolf?" she stammered.

"Afraid so."

"Is he the father?" Emma asked, pointing to Nero. Symon let out a laugh but stopped when Luca glared at him.

"No. Nero is all wolf. You've actually met him before. You saved his life." Emma's eyes widened, and she looked to Zara for an explanation.

"Long story, too long to tell now. Just think of Nero as the black dog that escaped."

Emma's eyes widened even further, but she nodded slowly. Stepping closer to the sofa, leaving Josh still frozen in the doorway, she knelt next to Zara, making sure not to have her back towards Nero. Hesitantly, she held out her hand and placed it against Aeylin's forehead then quickly pulled it away as if burnt. "She is boiling. I'm guessing this isn't normal?"

"No, it is not. We tend to run a little hotter than most two-leggers but not that hot," Marx answered from the kitchen, where he stood watching the proceedings from a distance.

"Are you all werewolves?" Emma asked, not quite managing to keep her voice from trembling.

"Nope, I'm a shifter, and Luca is a half-elf," Symon said, tone matter of fact. Emma swallowed, and then gave a slight nod of her head. Zara could tell that she was over-whelmed but her urge to help others was overtaking her fear, at least for now.

"I need to examine her. Zara, help your friend, see if you can get her to roll over onto her back. I can't see anything with her curled up like that," Emma instructed.

Reaching out, Zara stroked Aeylin's bare arm sooth-ingly, while in a low voice she murmured, "It's okay Aeylin. I brought friends who can help you. Don't be scared." As Zara continued, the werewolf's trembling began to calm, the spasms that wracked her body slowing and then stopping. With a gentle push, she guided Aeylin so that she rolled over onto her back. Luca took Aeylin's legs, stretching her legs into a more comfortable position, and started to massage her feet. Josh, having taken hold of his own fear, appeared with a damp cloth in his hand, and with a smile of reassurance laid it across Aeylin's forehead. Zara pressed her palm against Aeylin's belly and felt a reassuring kick which made her smile, then another and then a third one. Thinking she had imagined the third, she placed both hands on either side of the protruding belly. Zara felt four distinct movements as each of her palms were hit twice in quick succession. Unable to hide her surprise, she gasped.

"Is something wrong with the baby?" Aeylin asked, brow furrowed with worry, trying to sit up from the couch.

"No, I don't think so. The baby feels strong and healthy, it's just..." Zara cut off what she was about to say at a stern glance from Emma, "I felt it kick."

"Kicking is an excellent sign," Emma reassured Aeylin, "It means that the child is active and healthy."

"Emma, we need to determine the form of the child. Celeste gave me a tester kit, but we haven't had a chance to try it yet. We need a sample of Aeylin's blood. Can you take it?"

"Sure, but I don't think we brought the right gear with us," Emma said.

"It's alright, Celeste made sure I was prepared." Luca collected his pack from where it lay against the wall and rummaged through it. He pulled out the glowing blue vial and the silver-wrapped package. He passed both to Emma, saying, "We need to take enough blood to fill the vial. The tools to extract it are in that package." Emma unwrapped the silver package to find a small cloth and a golden tube the length of her forearm.

"There's no needle?" Emma asked.

"No need," Luca explained, "Just hold one end of the tube near a vein, and it will automatically insert. But before you do that, wipe the area with the cloth. It will both disinfect it and act as a painkiller so that Aeylin won't feel anything." Picking up the cloth, Emma scrutinized it, rubbing it between her fingers and sniffing the fabric. Taking Aeylin's arm with one hand, she swabbed the curve at her elbow where the blue line of a vein could be clearly seen under the woman's pale brown skin. Josh moved forward to stand at Emma's side, ready to assist. He picked up the crystal vial and held it steady while Emma pushed one end of the golden tube through the membrane cap on the vial. Then while Josh held it upright at floor level, to assist the blood in flowing, Emma held the other end of the tube near Aeylin's vein. Emma's eyes widened as the tip of the tube sharpened into a point and slipped, unaided, smoothly into her skin. Instantly, bright red blood began to flow into the vial.

"Wicked," breathed Josh as the tube extracted itself from Aeylin's arm once it sensed the vial was full. "We need one of those for The Haven!"

"Celeste's magic isn't evil," Symon said defensively, "Her magic is only used for good."

"What?" Oh ..." said Josh, understanding dawning. "No, man. Wicked is a human expression. It means that something is cool." Seeing Symon's blank look, Josh tried again. "Amazing? As in I think the magic tube is amazing." Symon smiled broadly.

"Magic is wicked, man," he said. Immediately the whole group burst out laughing. Even Marx struggled to hold back a chuckle.

As the laughter faded, Zara's attention was caught by the vial, still in Josh's hand.

"Hey Luca, what does it mean when the vial turns black?"

CHAPTER 14

E ven though Brina had predicted that the child Aeylin carried was a wolf, the vial's confirmation had a sobering effect on the party. At Zara's question, all eyes in the room flicked firstly to the now black bottle and then to Luca. Aeylin, who was holding Zara's hand, suddenly squeezed it so tightly Zara gasped. Looking guilty, Aeylin quickly let go. Zara rubbed her hand, trying to get the blood circulation flowing to remove the red finger marks.

"It means that the child is a wolf, and that changes things," Luca answered, voice sombre. "Aeylin can't remain here, it's too risky."

"It is a far greater risk for me to return," Aeylin argued.

"You don't understand, Celeste warned me of the risks. Since you can't change into a wolf, there is a high chance that the child will tear itself out of you. Both of you could die." At his words, Aeylin's face crumpled, and she began to sob, her chest heaving. Worried that she would push herself into another panic attack, Zara took hold of her hand once more.

"It's going to be alright," Zara reassured the scared werewolf, hoping that she spoke true. "Emma will be able to help you."

"Skylar will not be happy when he finds out more humans are being involved in creature matters," Marx said grumpily.

"He won't be upset if he doesn't find out," Zara countered. "Plus Emma is Aeylin's best chance on this side of the Rift."

All eyes turned to Emma, Zara's and Aeylin's full of hope while others clearly showed that they doubted the human's capability. But the party from Wundor didn't know Emma like Zara did. She had watched the vet perform miracles, bringing animals thought lost back from the brink. Emma also wasn't one to shy away from a challenge, especially when a baby was in danger.

"Well, a wolf is more my forte than a human child, that's for sure," Emma said. "But this circumstance is definitely unusual. I'm not going to make any promises, but I will do all that I can. Before any decisions can be made, we need to know if Aeylin can be properly cared for here. I would like to run some tests and then perhaps," she looked thoughtful for a moment, weighing the different options in her head, "maybe give acupuncture a try. We need to find a way to manage your pain levels, and I don't know how our medicines would affect you or the baby." Turning to Josh, she instructed, "Can you please grab the medical kit out of the trunk of your car. I'd like to take a sample of Aeylin's blood and have it analysed at The Haven. There are also additional supplies I am going to need if you can fetch them? I'll make you a list."

"Emma, you can't run the blood tests, this has to stay a secret," Zara said.

"I know it does, and I guess I can understand why you kept it from us. You weren't wrong when you said no one would believe the truth without seeing it themselves, but I think we can do this one off the books. Assuming you are alright with that?" She looked to Luca, who nodded. "Good. Also, it would be handy to have blood samples of anyone who might be compatible, just in case the need arises that we have to do a blood transfusion. I hope it won't come to that, but better to be safe than sorry."

"Marx would be the best match, being a werewolf," Luca looked at Marx who was standing, arms crossed, in the kitchen, "and I might be compatible. My blood is half witch, and Aeylin was born a witch before she was turned." Emma nodded.

"I guess that makes sense." As if witches and werewolves were a normal part of life. Zara was so proud of her, and Josh, for the way they were both handling everything.

"I don't know ... "Marx said.

"Please," Zara begged. She couldn't understand why Marx was being so standoffish about helping Aeylin. Over the past two weeks, she thought she had come to know the werewolf quite well. He didn't seem to have anything against her, and was usually warm and welcoming. She thought they had become friends, but now he was acting strange. Perhaps he was still angry that Luca and the others had crossed the rift without permission. "I know it is asking a lot, but we need your help."

"Fine, I'll do it." Marx agreed reluctantly. "But if Skylar finds out, this is on you not me."

"Thank you," Aeylin said. "My pack will be in your debt." Marx simply nodded. Josh did as instructed, and came back from the car carrying a large black duffle bag. Opening it, he pulled out the first aid kit and blankets. From the outside pocket, he pulled out a notebook and pen.

"Are my acupuncture needles in there?" Emma asked.

Josh shook his head, but Zara piped up, "There is a set in the basket. When you two decided to tag along, I thought they might come in handy."

"Good thinking." Holding up the golden tube, Emma asked Luca "Will this work with one of my vials?"

"It should."

Opening the first aid kit, Emma pulled out a sample bottle. Inserting one end of the tube through the stopper, she once again held the other near the vein in Aeylin's arm. As before, the tube inserted into the vein with no effort or pain. "I really need to get myself one of these," Emma murmured. Once Aeylin's sample was safely stored, Emma disinfected the tube and then took samples from both Marx and Luca. She labelled each bottle with the initial of the donor's first name, nothing else, and slid them into the plastic bag marked hazardous. Giving them to Josh, she took the notebook and scribbled a list of things she wanted him to pack.

"Bring these, but only if you can do so without raising suspicion." Emma looked at her watch, "I'm guessing you'll get back to The Haven just before family dinner. Put the blood on to run, and then you may as well stay. If anyone asks, Zara and I are still with our emergency patient. Make up some story to cover for us. I am going to stay a while and try out some acupuncture on Aeylin. Once everyone leaves, come back and collect us." Turning her focus to Luca and Aeylin, Emma said, "We should have the results by tomorrow morning."

Luca scowled. "Can't they be done any faster? I need to leave by sundown."

"I'm afraid not. Can someone bring word to you? Once we know what our options are, then we can make an informed decision. If no one is compatible, then I would have to agree with you, Luca. The safest option will be for Aeylin to return home."

"Agreed," said Luca, looking at Aeylin, "If no-one here is a match, then Symon and Nero will escort you back to Wundor." He sounded almost relieved.

"And if one of you is, we stay," Aeylin said, voice firm. "Agreed?" Luca's shoulders sagged slightly in defeat.

"Agreed."

CHAPTER 15

J osh had departed thirty minutes ago, after giving
    Zara a tight hug and a whispered, "This is so cool,
    thank you for telling us." Emma, having retrieved
    her acupuncture kit from the duffle bag, had set
herself to work, and now Aeylin's forehead, arms and
belly were covered in the tiny needles. While Aeylin
found the process fascinating, the sight made Symon
freak out. It turned out that the huge bear shifter had
been hiding a severe fear of needles. When Marx said he
was going to check the farm's perimeter, Symon hastily
volunteered to accompany him. Fresh air and a chance to
stretch his legs had also appealed to Nero, who followed
to two out. Whether they intended to do so or not, this
allowed Luca and Zara the opportunity to finally be alone
together.

Taking Zara's hand, Luca gently pulled her in the
direction of his bedroom, and she followed, a little hesitantly. She fretted that they were going to get into another
fight. Fighting with Luca was the last thing Zara wanted

to do. She expected him to reprimand her for involving Emma and Josh, but she knew that she had made the right call. As he opened the door and led her into the room, Zara got ready to argue on her friends' behalf. She was surprised and pleased, therefore, when the first words Luca spoke after closing the door were, "I'm sorry Zara. I had no right to push you away."

"You were only trying to protect me," she admitted. Since Luca seemed willing to admit his faults, she could try and acknowledge his good intentions.

"Yes, but I was a fool. I promised you after last time that I would never push you away again. Then what's the first thing I do? Can you forgive me?"

"Can you forgive me for telling Emma and Josh? I know it wasn't my secret, but they caught me grabbing the supplies. They said that they wouldn't let me go without them. I was so scared that you were going to leave and I've been so alone." Zara could feel tears threatening to fall.

"Oh, Zara, I am so sorry, truly. I never thought about what a toll keeping such a secret might take. You did the right thing. Emma is the best chance we have of saving Aeylin and her baby, and Josh is... well... Josh. They're your best friends. If you trust them, then so do I." Reaching out, Luca took one of Zara's hands in his large, strong one. He pulled her close, using the thumb of his free hand to wipe a tear from the corner of her eye. Looking down, gazing into her eyes, he said, "Zara, I never could have left without seeing you again. These past months have been hell for me. I have missed you like you have stolen part of my soul. Everything seems empty without you." He pulled her closer, letting go of her hands so that he could wrap his arms around her waist. Reaching up, Zara slid her arms around Luca's neck, running her fingers through his blond hair. She felt him shiver in response. "I have done everything I could to come back to you."

"And now you are here with me, and that is all that matters," Zara said and, unable to resist the urge any longer, reached up and kissed him. At first, it was a gentle hello after time away, but then the passion began to grow. Zara explored Luca's mouth with her tongue, taking in his sweet taste, recommitting to memory every part of him. As the kiss deepened, she ran her fingers through Luca's hair, and then slowly started caressing down his neck, the curve of his shoulder, and then his broad arms. Her fingers left a trail of goosebumps everywhere they touched. While she moved down his body, Luca's hands moved up hers. From her waist, they climbed their way up her spine until both hands were entwined in her hair. The shivers of pleasure which ran across her skin made every cell tingle. Her body, pressed so close she could feel his heartbeat, was warmed by the heat which radiated off him.

Like a slow dance, Luca gradually stepped further into the room, towards the hammock, leading Zara. She went willingly. As they reached the hammock, Luca released her hair and, reaching down, gripped her under her buttocks, lifting her up in one smooth movement so she could wrap her legs around his waist. She moved her hands, clasping them around the back of his neck, holding tight as he leaned back, and together they fell, as one, into the hammock. Not designed to hold two, it rocked wildly from side to side like a ship caught in a storm, the bolts connecting it to the walls letting out an alarming creak. But Zara hardly noticed, caught up in the feeling of Luca underneath her, lost in their ever-deepening kiss. Luca's hands were now on her back, roaming underneath her shirt, sending flames roaring across her body. She felt like she was burning up, her skin boiling. Breaking the kiss, she pulled her body off Luca, not quite to a sitting position but enough to allow her to lift her purple t-shirt off over her head. She smiled as Luca gasped, grateful she had chosen to wear lace that morning instead of her usual sports bra.

"You are so beautiful," Luca told her, eyes wide and roaming every inch of her. Her skin tingled everywhere he looked like it was a physical touch, and she felt him grow even harder beneath her. Reaching one hand down, planning to help him with his own shirt, but the movement proved too much for the hammock. Zara let out a startled scream as with a spin, the hammock dumped them both onto the floor.

"Ouch!" Zara exclaimed, rubbing at her elbow, which had taken the brunt of her weight. Rolling over, she looked at Luca, who was rubbing his head. He looked so funny, his hair a ruffled mess, that Zara started to giggle. Luca caught her eye, and suddenly they were both laughing so hard that tears poured from their eyes. A handful of minutes passed, with both of them clutching their stomachs and taking gasping breaths around the laughter, before they got a semblance of control. Managing to sit up on his knees, Luca crawled over so that he was behind Zara, and wrapped his arms around her. He held her tightly against him, kissing her tenderly at the point where her neck met her shoulder.

"I love you Zara, more than you could possibly know. But right now, I don't think that the first time we make love should be in a hammock with a pregnant werewolf in hearing range."

Zara wished that he was wrong, but had to admit that Luca was probably right. Imagine if Nero had tried to communicate with Luca when they were in the middle of things. She had to stifle a giggle at the thought, not wanting to set them both off again. Luca stood and offered Zara a hand to help her up. Zara grabbed her t-shirt from where it had fallen and put it on. She ran her fingers through her dark locks, straightening the tangles. Seeing Luca's ruffled hair, Zara had to resist the urge to reach up and try and tame his curls. If she did, then her barely held restraint would vanish.

"You might want to do something with your hair," she said, taking the safe option.

Together they exited Luca's bedroom, holding hands, but stopped short when they reached the living room. Aeylin was sitting up, acupuncture needles still sticking out of her head in all directions, and the look she gave Luca and Zara told them plainly that she knew exactly what had just happened in the other room. Her smirk was matched by Emma's, who gifted Zara with a wink, causing her to flush. Luca squeezed Zara's hand. Looking up at him, she noticed that the top of his ears had turned a deep shade of pink. It made her smile to not be the only one feeling embarrassed to be caught in the act. Looking out the window, they saw that the sun was heading towards the horizon. Zara felt her stomach sink, knowing that her time with Luca was drawing short.

To distract herself she asked, "How about we put on some dinner? I am sure that everyone is starving," and, making their escape from the knowing looks, Zara and Luca headed to the kitchen.

CHAPTER 16

S earching through the cupboards in the kitchen, Zara found a packet of spaghetti, a couple of cans of diced tomatoes, and two brown onions which had seen better days. She wasn't much of a cook, but pasta with a tomato sauce was simple enough. She wondered if they had anything similar across the rift. Grabbing a block of cheese out of the fridge, Zara handed it to Luca to grate while she took out a large saucepan from the cupboard, filled it with water, added a dash of salt, and put it on the stove to boil. Dicing the onion, she threw it into the pan to brown, and added the canned tomatoes.

Every time Luca walked past her, whether to find the grater or stir the pot, he would stop and caress her back-side or kiss the back of her neck. For her part, she couldn't resist the urge to pinch his perfect rounded buttocks and laughed when it made him jump. It felt so good, the two of them acting so domestic together. She knew she had a silly grin on her face, and found that she didn't care. She loved Luca and, somehow, everything was going to work out.

There weren't enough matching plates to feed six, so they used the breakfast bowls as well. As Zara laid them out and started dishing out cutlery, she sent Luca to find Marx, Symon and Nero, who still hadn't returned. Even if they were at the very edge of the farm's perimeter, Luca wouldn't have to go far to contact the wolf. As Luca closed the front door behind him, Emma stood from her seat on the sofa and headed over to the kitchen to give Zara a hand.

"So ... things seem to be going well between you two?" Emma prodded.

"Yes, yes they are," Zara said, smiling more broadly than she had in weeks.

"It is good to see you happy. You had me worried about the way that you were acting. But Zara ... is it smart falling for a guy who's a ..." Emma stumbled, not sure precisely what Luca was.

"A half-elf, half-witch and Guardian to boot?" Zara asked with a laugh. She'd spent many nights while they were separated, staring at the ceiling above her bed, trying to work out the answer to that question. So she answered Emma with the only conclusion she had been able to draw. "Smart, probably not. But I think I've fallen too hard to get out unscathed now." Grabbing a handful of grated cheese, she sprinkled it on the spaghetti as she added, "Oh, Emma, I wish you could see Wundor. It is beyond belief, like everything you thought impossible is suddenly possible. All the bedtime stories from your childhood suddenly made real. But as amazing as it is, the whole time I was there, the thing that seemed the most impossible, was that someone like Luca existed and that, against all the odds, he seems to love me as much as I love him. And I guess that is worth fighting for."

"Wow," Emma sighed, "Here I was looking for a fairy tale prince, and you beat me to it. I'm happy for you Zara, truly. Even jealous, maybe. But can I offer one piece of advice? Make sure you–"

Before Emma could finish her sentence, the quiet of the farm was shattered as a deep, commanding voice suddenly bellowed, "Luca. I know you are here. I command you to come out this instant and bring the werewolf with you!"

Zara felt her heart drop as she recognized the voice of Skylar, the Guardian Commander. *Shit.* Throwing down the cheese, she sprinted for the door.

"Emma, stay here with Aeylin. Don't come out unless I call for you." Without a backwards glance, Zara raced through the door, looking for Luca. She jumped off the porch, not pausing to take the stairs. She wanted to call out for Luca, but knew that would only make matters worse. The others must have heard Skylar's command, his voice had boomed so loudly that galahs had taken flight and were calling their disapproval at being disturbed. If the group were in the back paddocks, she wouldn't be able to reach them before they got to Skylar. She was not going to let Luca be escorted through the rift, never to return again.

She ran up the gravel driveway heading towards the gate, eyes scanning in all directions looking for three two-leggers and a wolf. In a low tone, she called for Nero, guessing that of the four, the wolf's hearing would be sharpest. When a large, black form came galloping out of the trees towards her, she had to hold back a cry of welcome.

"Where are the others?" she asked the wolf in a low voice, not for the first time wishing that she shared the telepathic bond. The wolf cocked his head in the direction of the barn then turned and took a few loping steps in that direction. Nero looked over his shoulder as if to say, "Are you coming?" Not needing to be asked twice, she ran after him. They met up with Symon, Marx and Luca when they were halfway between the farmhouse and the barn, faces sombre. Zara ran to Luca, who held out his arms and she threw herself into his embrace. His arms wrapped around her, holding her tightly as he whispered into her ear,

"I'm sorry, Zara. I thought we had time to say a proper goodbye."

Leaning back, looking up into his dark blue eyes, she said, "Don't think you can escape me that easily. I'm coming with you to face Skylar."

"You can't, you will just make it worse," Marx informed her.

"Butt out Marx, this has nothing to do with you," Zara answered, scowling at the werewolf. "This is between Luca and me. If Luca wants me with him, then I will be there." Looking up at Luca again, suddenly less confident, she asked, "You do want me to come with you, don't you?"

For a moment, Luca hesitated, and Zara felt her heart drop. Maybe he didn't trust her, or perhaps he was trying to protect her again. She let out a breath of relief as he said, "I do. If we tell Skylar why we came then having you there might help. He'll know that we have support in this world. And, perhaps it is selfish, but I also want you there for myself. I'm tired of having to face things without you." Zara smiled up at him, and her hand gripped in his, the group headed towards the rift. They hadn't gone far when Nero's ears suddenly pricked. In an instant, he was a blur of black fur, racing in the direction of the farmhouse.

"Shit!" exclaimed Luca, breaking into a run, dragging Zara along behind him as she tried valiantly to keep pace. The others followed, the look of sudden concern spreading across Symon's face making Zara's anxiety levels peak.

"What is it?" She asked the group, but no one answered. As they raced around the right-hand side of the farmhouse, Zara was confronted with what had caused the commotion. Emma stood, feet wide and hands on hips, giving the centaur Commander a piece of her mind.

CHAPTER 17

Standing up, spine straight, the top of her head barely reaching the centaur's shoulder, Emma stood staring, unblinking, at the Commander of the Guardians, giving him a piece of her mind. Instead of cowering in fear at the sight of the enormous half-man, half-horse, who was stamping his dinner-plate-sized hooves, Emma had switched into what Zara referred to as protection mode. She had once watched Emma stand up to a group of bikies who had been abusing a dog. Then it had been five to one, and Emma had come out victorious. Zara felt a moment's pity for Skylar.

"How dare you come here, demanding for Aeylin to leave, throwing her back into danger, causing her to have an anxiety attack when she is heavily pregnant?"

"I am –" Skylar tried to interrupt her tirade.

"I don't care who the hell you are!" Emma shouted. "You could have chosen to approach in an easy, friendly manner. Instead, you came booming in here, throwing your weight around and scaring the living daylights out of all of us!"

Zara could have sworn she saw a look of unease cross the usually grounded centaur's face. Behind her, she heard Symon mutter under his breath, "Emma is wicked." She was pretty sure he didn't think her friend was evil. Deciding she needed to intervene before things went further and Emma said something she couldn't take back, Zara stepped forward and closed the distance between them. Luca, who still held onto her hand, came with her and stood at her side facing Skylar, Nero stepping in front to guard them both.

"Emma, it's okay. I'm sure that Skylar didn't mean any harm," Zara said smoothly. Looking up at the centaur, whose eyes were wide, "Plus I'm pretty sure the information that Aeylin is pregnant is news to him."

"Thank you, Zara. It is a pleasure to see you again," Skylar said, dipping his head slightly in her direction before turning a harsh gaze to Luca, "Although I wish it were under better circumstances and with my authority. As I was trying to tell this human, I had no intention of scaring Aeylin. I am here on behalf of Kinnison, who failed to mention that she was pregnant."

"Kinnison sent you?" Aeylin asked, stepping out of the trees where she had been hiding.

Turning to her, Skylar said in a softer voice, "Indeed. He has been in my office for the past hour demanding to speak to you. I told him that you had returned to your pack, as Brax had informed me. You can imagine my surprise when he said that he had visited them only to find no sign of you. If Helo had not gotten wind of the situation and made the wise choice to let me in on your deception, I am sure that by now Kinnison would have torn the Guild apart looking for you. As it is, if I do not return with you shortly, I am sure that all hell will break loose."

Aeylin's bottom lip began to tremble, and her voice was a little unsteady as she said, "I cannot return. If I do, my life will be in danger."

"Yes, your father told me of the circumstances. I only wish that he had taken me into his confidence sooner. I give you my word, as Commander of the Lightfall Guardian Guild, that no harm will befall you or your child while you are within my care."

"But what about the Council?" Luca asked, surprised. Skylar sighed.

"What other choice do I have? It would seem that it is my destiny to remain at odds with the Council for now. Though I wish there were another way, our first duty as Guardians is to protect the people of Lightfall, not to answer to the Council."

"There is another way: Aeylin could stay here," Emma offered. "Kinnison could join her."

"No, that is not an option. It is bad enough that Luca, Nero and Symon are here without my informing the Council. They cannot stay, only Marx, who is officially assigned to this post. Now come, we must return."

"I'll grab my medical kit, and I'll be right with you," Emma said.

"No. You and Zara must remain here," Skylar ordered his tone almost apologetic. "I cannot risk two humans crossing into Wundor. The uproar it would cause if you were to be found out is not worth thinking about."

Zara was trying to think of something to say to change Skylar's mind when Aeylin beat her to it. "In the past hours, these two humans have saved my life not once, but twice. I need them," Aeylin exclaimed.

"Celeste is more than capable of taking care of your medical needs. She has experience with werewolves," Skylar countered.

But Aeylin crossed her arms, standing firm and played her trump card. "If Emma and Zara don't go, neither do I. Then you can return and explain to Kinnison that you chose to leave me, the werewolf carrying his heir, on the other side of the rift." Zara looked at Aeylin and smiled gratefully. The werewolf smiled back.

Skylar looked between Aeylin, Emma and Zara. All three met his gaze full on. Skylar shook his head and then, looking at Zara, he said, "It would seem, Zara, that you are making a habit of saving creatures from a world which isn't yours. As such, I also grant you the Guardians' protection." Looking to Emma, he added, "Since both Aeylin and Zara appear willing to vouch for you; I extend that same offer to you. But know that if the Council discover you then more heads will roll than just mine. You must both keep your heads down and obey every order I or one of my Guardians give you, without question. Is that understood?"

Both girls nodded solemnly, the reminder of danger darkening their victory.

"Good."

CHAPTER 18

Zara and Emma had no time to talk about what was happening. Skylar was agitated, stomping from one hoof to another, tail swishing. He allowed them fifteen minutes to pack their belongings. Emma quickly bundled everything into the duffle bag. Symon grabbed his pack and Luca shouldered Aeylin's, which they'd had no chance to empty. Looking at the servings of spaghetti and sauce going cold, Zara searched the drawers for plastic wrap. Finding nothing, she scooped the contents of all the meals into the pot she had used to cook the pasta and, putting the lid on top, placed it into the fridge. She wasn't sure if Marx would eat it, but felt wrong to have the meal go to waste.

"What should I do about clothes?" Emma asked.

"I wouldn't worry, I'm sure Celeste can help us out with spares." Zara decided not the mention the magical closet that produced outfits to meet any need a person could have. Emma, a lover of fashion, would either adore the convenience or hate not being able to browse and choose for herself.

Looking to Aeylin, Zara noticed that the werewolf was trembling. Concerned that she was going to faint again, she asked, "Aeylin, are you feeling okay?"

"Fine, truly, just nervous about seeing Kinnison."

"Are you afraid of him?" Symon asked.

"No nothing like that. Kinnison would never hurt me. It's just..." she bit her lip "the last time I saw him we didn't part on the friendliest of terms."

"In what way?" Luca asked. "Sorry I don't mean to pry, but it would help if we had some idea of what we are walking into."

"When Kinnison found out that I was pregnant, he wanted to announce it to all of Wundor, he was so excited. The first person he wanted to tell was his father, but I was scared..." More lip biting. "And I told him no. That I wanted to wait until after our child was born. He hadn't even told his father that he was courting someone like me and, well, Kinnison is naïve when it comes to the world around him." Aeylin blushed furiously at her words, and her eyes reflected the guilt she felt for speaking ill of him. "He's grown up the heir to the mightiest pack in Wundor. His father sits on the Council. All of his friends are purebloods. He doesn't see the animosity that exists between the bitten and the purebloods. But I do." At these words, Aeylin's lip started to tremble violently, and her eyes began to brim with tears. She wiped them away angrily with the back of her hand before they had a chance to fall.

"You had every right to be scared. Look at what happened to you," Symon said in a gentle voice.

"I know. I just hope that Kinnison understands and isn't too angry at me for running away from him."

"I am sure that once you tell him everything that has happened, he will understand. But for now, we had better go before Skylar decides to break down the door."

Together the group left the farmhouse and came upon Skylar speaking quietly to Marx. The werewolf looked tense, standing at attention, arms rigid behind his back. He kept nodding his head as if agreeing to something. Zara couldn't hear what Skylar was saying, but Nero lay, playing innocent, under a nearby tree. No doubt the wolf would give Luca a blow by blow of the conversation later.

"Are you ready?" Skylar asked, breaking off the conversation as they approached.

"Yes," Luca answered for all of them.

"Are you sure you want to come?" Skylar asked, directing the question to Emma and Zara. Zara looked at Emma, who gave her a sharp nod.

"We are," Zara said, taking hold of Emma's free hand and squeezing it.

Turning on his hooves, Skylar walked four steps and then disappeared. Emma gasped, her jaw dropping open. Zara barely held back a gasp of her own. She knew that the rift was there, but she had never actually watched anyone go through it. Seeing them suddenly vanish into nothing was a little unsettling. Symon went next, offering his arm to Aeylin, and together they followed Skylar, disappearing into the rift. Nero was next, one moment there and the next gone. Luca came and took hold of Zara's other hand.

"You ladies ready for this?"

Zara nodded, smiling broadly up at Luca. Turning, she saw Emma take a deep breath and then step forward. It was only as the three friends stepped through the rift that is suddenly occurred to Zara that they hadn't left a note for Josh.

CHAPTER 19

Brax and Celeste greeted them as they stepped through the rift. Brax's face was creased with worry, and sweat beaded his forehead, while Celeste's turquoise wings fluttered in agitation. Emma fell, the unexpected shock of their journey forcing her to her knees, but Zara grabbed her under her arm before she could hit the sand.

"Sorry, I should have warned you," Zara apologized to Emma.

"A heads-up would have been nice," Emma gasped, still trying to catch her breath.

"Where is Kinnison?" Skylar demanded of Brax.

"He's waiting in your office. Helo is with him. He's trying to keep him calm, but I don't think he's having much luck. You have been gone for over an hour." Brax informed them.

"I forget how slow time moves in that world. Never-mind, it can't be helped now. Celeste," Skylar turned to the fairy, "I need you to take Zara and Emma to the healers' quarters and hide them. Kinnison cannot know that two humans have crossed with us into Wundor. Glamour them before anyone else has a chance to spot them." Celeste motioned to Zara who stepped towards the fairy, Emma and Luca following. "Not you, Luca. You and Symon need to come with me to face Kinnison. Aeylin too." With a smile at the girl, he added, "Hopefully, your charms can sweeten his mood." Aeylin glanced anxiously at Zara and Emma. Based on their last meeting, her presence was as likely to anger the pureblood werewolf as calm him. Before anyone had a chance to say anything Skylar was cantering off in the direction of his office, the others having no choice but to follow. With a last glance at Luca and a small smile of encouragement, Zara followed Celeste towards the courtyard stairs, which would take them to the healers' quarters.

Luca's group had reached the landing outside of Skylar's office when they were affronted by the sound of something smashing against the floor. Skylar pulled open the door, Luca positioning himself so that he could see the cause of the noise over the centaur's broad frame. A stone pitcher, once filled with golden ale, was shattered into pieces on the floor, its contents spilling onto the woollen rug. Helo sat in one of the two wooden chairs, his back arched away from the angry werewolf who was snarling at him, a mere handbreadth away from his face. The elf's eyes were wide, and the knuckles of his hands white where he gripped the arms of the chair.

"I don't want any more ale. I want to see Aeylin. Now!"

Kinnison demanded, his words coming out as a barely human growl.

"Stand down, Kinnison," Skylar ordered, his voice firm, not showing a trace of fear. At his words, Kinnison turned to the centaur. His face was a deep crimson, and the air rippled with the waves of heat coming off him. He looked as though he would change form at any second.

"Do not order me about, Skylar. You know who I am and who my father is. If you don't tell me where Aeylin is this moment, then I will bring the full force of the Blood-moon Pack down upon your Guild."

Luca was unsure how far the power struggle would have escalated if Aeylin had not chosen that moment to say, voice soft and stuttering slightly, "It's alright, Kinnison, I am here." The effect of her words was like a bucket of water thrown onto a fire. The heat faded from Kinnison's body, which had been rigid, and relaxed instantly. As Skylar stepped aside to let Aeylin through, Kinnison spotted her, rushing to embrace her. Luca was about to leap forward, ready to protect Aeylin from harm, but pulled himself back as he watched her step forward and let herself be cradled in Kinnison's arms. Aeylin's delicate build, sun-kissed pale skin and brown hair were a perfect contrast to Kinnison. Luca had never been formally intro-duced to the heir of the Bloodmoon Pack, but it was clear, looking at him towering over Aeylin, that he had inher-ited his looks from his father. He was tall, almost as tall as Symon, and his hair was the colour of fire, a vibrant red which fell in waves around his head. Red hair was rare for a werewolf, and it was why Tibarn's Pack had chosen the name Bloodmoon. Kinnison's skin was a dark copper, his body gracefully muscled, and his eyes, which had softened upon seeing Aeylin, were the colour of emeralds.

"Oh, my love, my sweet, are you alright? Is our child alright?" Kinnison asked Aeylin, his eyes roaming over her.

"Yes, thanks to these two," Aeylin gestured to Symon and Luca, "and a few others. They saved me and swore to protect me. And our child is fine. Here," she reached for Kinnison's hand and placed it on her belly. "Wait ... wait ... there, did you feel it?" At her words, Kinnison's eyes had widened, and a smile of absolute joy spread across his face.

"Is that our baby?"

"Yes. That is our little wolf," she answered, smiling up at him.

"Forgive me for brushing away your concerns. I should have listened to you. Brax and Helo both tried to tell me about the danger you faced, and I am ashamed to say I did not react well." Looking around the room at each of the Guardians surrounding them, he said, "I think I owe you all thanks for caring for Aeylin." Looking down at the ale, which was still spreading across the now ruined rug, "Skylar, I believe that I also owe you a new rug." Luca didn't think it possible for a werewolf to look sheepish, but the expression on Kinnison's face was definitely close.

"That would be nice," Skylar said, the corner of his mouth twitching.

"I think you should get a healer to look you over," Kinnison said to Aeylin, one hand still on her belly, the other wrapped protectively around her shoulders. "Then we should be off."

"Off where?" Aeylin asked, puzzled.

"To my father's house, my home. Your home now." At the mention of his father Aeylin's body stiffened, and a frown creased her forehead.

"No, Kinnison. I told you that it is not safe for me there," Aeylin said, her voice firm.

"It's alright, my love. I have told father about you and about your pregnancy–"

"What!" Aeylin cut in, her face flushing with sudden anger.

"It's alright. Father is happy for me, for us both. He said that if this is what I want, and it is, then he will not stand in my way. He is preparing rooms for you at the castle. We are to stay there until the child is born, and once that happy moment occurs, we will be bonded." Aeylin looked doubtful, still holding herself stiffly in Kinnison's embrace. "Don't you trust me?" Kinnison asked, his eyes wide and pleading.

"Yes, but..."

"Then trust me now to take care of you. Family means everything to my father. He will see that no harm comes to you."

"I will send four of my Guardians with you to ensure your safety," Skylar offered. From the tone of his voice, it was clear that he also doubted the sincerity of Tibarn's offer. The werewolf member of the Ruling Council was not known for his soft treatment of bitten werewolves.

"There is no need," Kinnison said. Then looking at Aeylin, who still seemed apprehensive, "But if it will make Aeylin feel better, then I thank you, and accept your kind offer."

"I also want Luca, Symon and," Aeylin paused for a moment before adding, "My two new friends, if they are willing, to come with us. Emma is a healer, and Zara saved my life."

"I don't know if that is wise," Skylar interrupted, but Kinnison brushed off his comment.

"Aeylin may bring whoever she wishes. There is more than enough room at the castle for everyone. I will send one of my wolves ahead to let father know to prepare rooms for them."

"I need to collect my things," Aeylin said.

"Do so and then meet me outside. I have a carriage waiting for us. You and your friends can sleep inside. If we leave now, we should arrive in time for evening meal tomorrow night." Leaning down, Kinnison kissed Aeylin deeply, and she kissed him back just as hard.

As they all turned to leave to make their preparations, Skylar called, "Luca, wait. I need to have a word with you."

Symon paused to wait for his friend, but Luca, thinking Skylar might wish to talk about the spy, told him to take Aeylin to the healers' quarters and let Zara and Emma know what was going on. With a shrug Symon left, leaping down the stairs two at a time to catch Aeylin, Helo following at a more sedate pace.

"Close the door, Luca," Skylar instructed. Luca did as he was told, and then faced his Commander. "What were you thinking, taking a pregnant werewolf across the rift? I never took you for a fool, but that choice was pure idiocy."

"I'm sorry, Skylar," Luca said, hanging his head so as not to see the look of disappointment in Skylar's eyes. "But there didn't seem to be any other option."

"There are always other options. You could have come to me, for starters."

"I thought it best not to involve you. With everything else that you are dealing with at the moment, I didn't want to burden you with this."

"So instead you crossed the rift without my knowledge or authority, you gave one of your fellow Guardians a disabling dose of food poisoning, and now you have brought the wrath of the highest-ranked werewolf pack down upon us. I am well within my rights to strip you of your rank for this."

Luca looked up, startled. He knew it had been a risk, but he didn't think that Skylar would ever take things that far. Surely he could see that Luca's heart, if not his head, had been in the right place.

"I am giving you one last chance to prove your loyalty to the Guardians. You will escort Aeylin to the castle, you will not let the two humans out of your sight, and as soon as the child is born, you will bring Zara and Emma back here. They will both be sent home. This action has made it clear to me that when it comes to Zara, you do not think straight. You cannot be relied upon. It is time for you to choose between her and your place here as a Guardian. Now that the attention of the Ruling Council is focused on us, you can no longer have both." Skylar sighed, and his tone softened. "I am sorry, Luca. But in this case, there truly are no other options. The role of Guardians in Wundor is hanging by a thread. I will not let everything we are be put into jeopardy by the desires of one."

Luca felt his heart sink all the way to the soles of his feet, but he nodded.

"Yes, Skylar. I understand."

"If Aeylin had not requested you I would consider sending Helo in your place. There is enough tension in this endeavour as it. But that will just lead to further drama and upset. So go, do your duty and remember the before all else you are a sworn Guardian," Skylar ordered. Then, in a softer voice, he added, "Enjoy what time you have remaining with Zara."

CHAPTER 20

Zara perched on one of the empty patient beds, peering through a gap in the curtain, watching for Luca. She knew that Symon, standing guard outside the healers' quarters, would let her know at first sight of him, but she was worried about what was taking him so long. On the bed next to her lay Aeylin, dress rolled up and naked belly exposed while Celeste examined her. Emma watched, eyes wide and mouth open, as blue light glowed above her, forming into the shape of the baby wolf. The sights caused Aeylin's eyes filled with happy tears, and she clasped Emma's hand.

"Zara, you have to see this!" Emma exclaimed. Turning from the window, Zara had to admit that the sight was astonishing. The blue light formed a perfect three-dimensional image of the wolf. The pup's eyes were closed, and its tail was tucked between its hind legs. Perfectly pointed ears and small padded feet would twitch every few seconds as if the pup was dreaming. As Zara watched, Celeste rotated her hands, and the image moved, spinning the wolf slowly, so they had a clear view of all sides. As the fairy turned the image so that the pup appeared to be laying on its back, the gender became obvious.

"Congratulation Aeylin. You are carrying a healthy boy," Celeste announced, making Aeylin cry even harder.

"I'm so happy, I don't know why I'm crying like this," Aeylin said, trying to stifle her tears.

"Pregnancy hormones," Emma and Celeste said in unison, making Aeylin laugh through her tears. Zara laughed too, after the stress of the past hours it was wonderful to share in this happy moment.

"What did I miss?" Luca asked, startling all of them. Jumping up from the bed, Zara threw her arms around him and kissed him before answering.

"Aeylin is having a boy."

For a moment Luca's gaze darkened, so quickly that Zara almost thought she imagined it, and then he said lightly, "Congratulations, Aeylin. I am sure that Kinnison will be delighted."

"I cannot wait to tell him." As Celeste released her magic, Aeylin pulled down her dress and sat up. Swinging her legs off the bed, she looked ready to rush off to find Kinnison.

"Wait," Luca said, making her pause, "before we go, we need Celeste to place a glamour on both Zara and Emma. We can't have Kinnison, or especially Tibarn, suspecting that they are human."

"No need, already done," said Celeste with a warm smile at Emma.

"Can't you tell?" Emma asked, her voice a little disappointed.

Zara laughed. "Luca won't see your glamour, Emma. He knows the truth, and he has seen you without it. But it will work on strangers, I promise," Zara reassured her friend. Emma still looked doubtful, causing Zara to try to recall if she had looked as uncertain the first time Celeste had glamoured her.

"I think you both look lovely as you are," Symon said. "I always thought there was something unusual about Zara's pointed ears the first time we met. She didn't seem composed enough to be an elf."

"Thank you, Symon, I think," Zara said.

"From Symon, that is a compliment," Luca said. Looking at him, Zara thought the smile that followed the comment looked strained. There was also a crease between Luca's brows which hadn't been there before. Reaching for his hand, she squeezed it. The pressure of keeping them all safe must be wearing on him.

"I have also given Emma a bag of medicines to add to her own that should help Aeylin when the labour starts. If you need me send Nero to fetch me, and I will come with all haste," Celeste offered.

"Thank you, Celeste," Luca said, gratefully.

"Yes, thank you," Aeylin added, kissing the fairy's cheek.

"You are welcome, young one. Your baby is healthy and strong. Just remember to also take care of yourself. I wish I could come with you but my duty is here."

Looking around the room at the two humans, Symon, Luca and Nero, Aeylin said with a smile, "That's what I have my friends for."

The inside of the carriage was spacious, and Kinnison had outfitted it with blankets and furs to make it as comfortable as possible for the three women. Aeylin claimed one of the seats, Emma had taken the other, and Zara made a nest for herself on the floor. With the curtains drawn it was a little stuffy, but comfortable, and the rocking motion lulled Aeylin into sleep within minutes. Zara had expected Aeylin to tell Kinnison about the baby being a boy straight away, but she had not. Perhaps she was waiting for them to be alone so they could share the joy in private. Zara wished she had a chance to pull Luca aside and find out what Skylar had said. Symon and Luca, together with three of the Guardians Skylar had assigned, were spread out around the carriage, protecting all sides. The fourth Guardian sat atop the carriage driving the horses. Nero's snores filtered through from his chosen position next to the driver.

Zara's eyes were closed, and she was on the edge of a dream when Emma's voice whispered to her out of the darkness, "How do you deal with it?"

"Deal with what?" Zara asked, opening her eyes and turning to look up at her friend.

"All this," Emma made a circle with her hands, encompassing the carriage and everything around them. "Knowing that magic is real and there are fairies and werewolves and elves. How did you manage to keep all of this a secret?" Zara thought for a moment before answering.

"I don't know. At first, it seemed like a dream, like I

had bumped my head too hard, and it couldn't possibly be real. But then I got to know the people here, and I guess they aren't that different from us. Not really. Not in the way that counts."

"They seem pretty different to me," Emma admitted. "I wish I could perform even half of the miracles that Celeste can with a wave of her hands. Think of all the animals I could save."

"Even magic has its limits. After the forest fire, Celeste almost worked herself to death, and we had to fall back on honeyed water. When she used my strength to save the unicorn, it was too much, and I almost died." Emma suddenly sat bolt upright.

"You almost died!" she demanded.

"Um, yeah ... but Celeste saved me."

"Zara, I think you need to start at the beginning and tell me everything."

"It's a long story," Zara warned.

"We've got all night, and I am not the slightest bit tired."

So Zara started to tell Emma about her last trip to Wundor. About drinking the poisoned wine at the picnic, meeting Helo and Symon, and the witch's fortune at the Market of Stars. She never got as far as the forest fire before both women fell asleep, both dreaming of unicorns playing in a sunlit field.

CHAPTER 21

Zara woke with the taste of apples in her mouth. For a moment, she had no idea where she was. Morning light shone through the gap in the carriage's curtains, so bright it made her eyes hurt. Looking up, she saw that Aeylin was still curled up on the bench seat, but Emma was gone. Sitting up, wiping the sleep from her eyes, Zara pulled back one of the curtains, careful to make sure no light fell on Aeylin, and looked out of the window. The sun was above the horizon but had not yet reached its midday peak. She must have slept through the night and into part of the morning. From this vantage point, she could make out a surrounding of green, rolling hills. Animals grazed the pastures, not looking that different from the cows and sheep she had watched on the farms around Rosa Brook.

Looking at the gravel road passing below the carriage, she could see that they were moving at a steady pace, but thought she could probably exit the carriage safely without making too big a fool of herself. Carefully, trying to make as little noise as possible so as not to wake Aeylin, Zara moved so that she was in a crouching position. Undoing the clasp, she swung open the carriage door and stepped out. Her plan to make a smooth exit was foiled, however, when Zara miscalculated the low height of the roof. As she stepped out, she knocked her head with a hard thump, making her head spin. Blinded by the bright sunlight, she would have fallen had Luca not seen her danger and quickly dismounted his horse, grabbing hold of her shoulder to support her.

Wrapping his arms around Zara's waist, Luca asked, "Are you alright?"

"I'm fine if a little embarrassed. I had hoped to make a much more dignified exit," Zara admitted, laughing.

"If it makes you feel better, I don't think anyone else witnessed it, and I won't tell. You have my word as a Guardian," Lucas promised solemnly, though his eyes twinkled with mischief. This thought was proved quickly wrong, however, when the next moment a chuckle floated down from the driver's seat. Looking up, Zara saw the amused faces of the carriage driver, Falcon, and Nero.

"Sorry, Zara," Falcon, the aptly named bird shifter said, trying to stifle her laughter by covering her mouth with a hand, and disappearing once more from view. Nero, however, grinned widely at Zara, his long pink tongue lolling to the side.

Zara felt heat rush to her cheeks. Distracting herself, she asked, "Where are we? Where's Emma?" She looked around but could see no sign of her friend.

"We're about two hours away from Bloodmoon Castle; we've made good time. You will find Emma riding on the back of the carriage. Symon has been telling her all about his heroics, and yours," Luca added with a cheeky grin.

"What about the other Guardians? And where are Kinnison and his men?"

"Once Symon and I promised on our lives that Aeylin would come to no harm, Kinnison thought it best to ride ahead and let his father know that we are coming. His companions went with him. There are two spare horses tied to the back of the carriage if you feel like riding?"

Breathing in the fresh air, so crisp and lovely after the stuffy cabin, Zara was grateful for the offer.

"That sounds good. But where are Otto, Karn and Marika?" Zara asked, looking around for the other Guardians.

"Marika has cantered ahead and is scouting. Otto is about 2 miles behind us. I think he is trying to avoid me, and I honestly cannot blame him," Luca said, looking ashamed.

"Why?"

"Caster, the minotaur we inflicted with food poisoning, is his brother. He hasn't yet forgiven me for what Helo did to him."

"Ah, I see. What about Karn?"

"He is roaming around somewhere in those," Luca pointed to the tree line a few miles to the East, "making new friends." Karn was a dryad. "Don't worry, he is close enough to hear us if we shout for him, though I doubt we will have the need. We passed into Tibarn's lands half an hour ago."

"Tibarn controls all this?" Zara asked, her eyes widening.

"The Bloodmoon Pack does, and Tibarn is their Alpha. Since our carriage bears his emblem, no one would dare touch us for fear of drawing his wrath."

Zara looked at the carriage and noticed the emblem on the door. It had been dark when they had climbed in, and she hadn't had an opportunity to scrutinize it. Seeing it now made a cold shiver run down her spine despite the warmth of the day. The backdrop was a full moon, tinged with red. In front of it, the image of a black wolf. It had been painted in mid-attack, muzzle curled in a snarl with sharp, white fangs exposed. Its eyes were like rubies, and bright red blood dripped from its teeth. On its head, it wore a golden crown.

"Yuck," Zara spat, turning away from the disturbing image. Yet despite having her back to it, she felt as if the werewolf's eyes were boring into her, wanting to swallow her whole. She was startled out of these dark thoughts by Emma's voice, quickly followed by her smiling face poking around the end of the carriage.

"So you are finally awake? Symon has been telling me all about the unicorn you saved. I want to see a unicorn."

The next two hours passed pleasantly enough as Symon basked in the attention of an audience who hadn't heard all of his stories before. Zara had chosen to sit next to Emma, and the two girls almost fell off the carriage, they were laughing so hard. Towards the end of the journey, Aeylin woke, and Luca helped her down from the carriage so she could walk for a bit and stretch her swollen legs.

Jumping down, Emma took the opportunity to pull her blood pressure cuff out of the duffle bag and check Aeylin. She was relieved to see that the journey seemed to have had no ill effects on mother or baby. Next, she checked Aeylin's temperature. The thermometer was still sticking out from under a confused looking Aeylin's tongue when Marika came to let them know that the castle was in sight.

"The gates are open. We should reach the castle in fifteen minutes," Marika announced, tossing her golden mane to one side. Where Skylar's horse body reminded Zara of a broad-chested Andalusian, Marika's form had the classic lines of a high-bred Arabian. The blonde waves of her hair matched her tail perfectly. Her coat was the colour of butter toffee and her skin, beneath her golden tunic, a flushed pink. Her hooves were painted a pearl white which shimmered in the sunlight. Looking at her, Zara thought she seemed too delicate to be a Guardian, she looked like she belonged on the cover of Centaur Magazine, assuming that was a thing. Yet Skylar must have had his reasons for choosing her as one of the two female Guardians to escort them. Marika had been polite, if not exactly friendly, to both Zara and Emma when they had been introduced at the beginning of the journey.

"I'm glad. I am sure that Aeylin will welcome a chance to rest," Luca replied. Aeylin smiled her thanks awkwardly, the thermometer still protruding from her mouth. "Would you mind rounding up the others and letting them know?"

"No problem," Marika said, cantering off down the road behind them.

Emma took the thermometer from the werewolf and announced, "Everything seems normal, or at least I think it is. It hasn't changed at least, which I guess is a good sign."

The girls chose to walk rather than ride in the stuffy carriage, and the party ambled towards the castle. Marika had just caught up to them, Otto following in her wake, when they crested the hill. Before them lay the castle. Its grey stone walls stood five storeys high, with turrets facing every compass point, protecting the battlements. The Guardian Guild at Lightfall could have easily fit its entire floor plan within the outer walls over a dozen times. Two flags flew above the gate, each bearing the emblem of the Bloodmoon Pack, proclaiming that both Alpha and Heir were in residence. Outside the castle, on either side of the entry, waited two huge werewolves. The entire thing gave off a distinct vibe of power and control, and Zara thought there was nothing in the slightest bit welcoming about it.

"I have a bad feeling about this," Aeylin said, putting Zara's own thoughts into words.

"Remember, we are here for you. If you want to leave at any point, just say the word, and we are gone," Luca promised.

Zara reached out, and after taking Aeylin's hand, she squeezed it.

"Together?"

"Together."

CHAPTER 22

Despite their protests, Luca had thought it best for Aeylin, Emma and Zara to enter the castle from the safety of the carriage. It would give him, and the other Guardians, a chance to suss out the place. Falcon had exchanged places in the driver's seat with Karn, and now soared above the castle in her bird form. Otto and Marika flanked one side of the carriage; Luca, with Symon behind him, guarded the side with the door. All of them were on high alert. The carriage's curtains were pulled back, and three wary sets of eyes looked out, watching Luca for any sign of danger.

As they approached the gate, the larger of the two grey werewolves guarding it shimmered. In the wolf's place stood a tall, muscular man with a shock of white hair, cut into an unruly Mohawk. Claw mark tattoos ran from the front to back of the shaved sides of his scalp, almost a perfect match for the actual scars on his cheekbones. He was dressed in black leather pants and a sleeveless jerkin. The snarling wolf sigil was embroidered over his heart.

On the cap of each shoulder, two ruby-red moons were emblazoned, signifying that he was a general in Tibarn's guard.

"*Gode fen,* travellers," he greeted them, his voice rough and deep. "Tibarn is expecting you."

"*Gode fen* to you too, Quaritch," Luca greeted the werewolf, recognising him from the few times he had seen him guarding his Alpha at the Lightfall Council Building.

"Where is Aeylin?" Quaritch asked, trying to peer through the carriage's curtains.

"It has been a long journey, and she and her two companions are tired. I am sure they would be grateful for a chance to clean up before the introductions happen."

"Of course." Quaritch raised two fingers in the air. At his signal, a boy came running out of the castle, halting to stand at attention at the General's side. He didn't appear to be much older than eleven, and wore a thin band of iron around his neck. Unlike the General, his clothing was tattered and torn, his feet were bare. Meeting Luca's gaze for a second, the boy blushed and dropped his head, not raising his eyes from his feet again. Quaritch addressed the boy, seeming not to notice his strange reaction. "Myles, please escort Luca, Symon and the ladies to the rooms which have been prepared for them." Turning back to Luca, Quaritch added, "Kinnison requested that you be lodged in the castle. We have set up lodging above the stables for Falcon, Otto and Karn and a fresh stall for Marika." At his words Marika let out a snort and stomped her hoof. Quaritch's brow twitched as he added, "I advised Kinnison that they would be more comfortable there than staying in the castle. There are many stairs and narrow halls. I trust this will not be an issue?"

"It will be fine," Luca answered hurriedly before Marika had a chance to voice her disapproval.

"There will be a feast later to celebrate Kinnison's news and you are all invited. The ladies have rooms prepared for them in the East Wing, and yours and Symon's are in the West Wing near Kinnison's."

So Aeylin and Kinnison are not to lodge together. Not a good sign," Nero commented, his tone edgy. Luca gave him a curt nod in agreement. If Tibarn was happy about the union, as Kinnison claimed, then there was definitely something odd about his allocation of rooms. But it was too late to turn back now. Quaritch led the way through the outer gate and into the courtyard. Instead of taking them through the inner gate, he directed them down the Eastern side of the outer bailey.

"Next to the stables, you will find a staff entrance. If you do not want to meet Tibarn as you are, I would suggest you go in that way. Myles can direct you. When you are ready to come downstairs, Myles will announce you." With a stern look at Myles and a slight nod to Luca, Quaritch left them to return to his station at the gate.

Scanning the outer bailey, Luca counted over a dozen guards standing around. Surely having such a high number wasn't normal? Reaching the stables, Luca sent Otto ahead into the darkened barn to check for any danger. Falcon returned, landing with a flutter next to Symon as she changed form.

"It all looks clear," Falcon informed him, "Though if I

had to guess, more guards are mingling around than normal."

"Why do you say that?" Luca valued Falcon's opinion, and was keen to see if her reasoning matched his own.

"Every exit and entrance is guarded by a minimum of two wolves. Tibarn clearly doesn't want anyone getting in without his authority."

"Or anyone leaving," Symon added. Luca and Symon exchanged a worried look but, since they were already within the castle walls, they didn't have a lot of options.

Otto returned from his assessment of the stables, "All clear, nothing out of the ordinary." He gave the report to Luca without quite looking him in the eye. It made Luca feel a little nervous, but he guessed it was more due to poisoning Caster than that the minotaur was hiding something. Perhaps later, in the evening, he would find a moment to pull Otto aside and apologise. Try and break this tension which had built up between them.

With the others keeping an eye out, Luca opened the carriage door. Holding out a hand he helped Zara down, followed shortly by Emma and then, hesitantly, Aeylin. Zara and Emma blinked rapidly, trying to get their eyes to adjust to the sudden brightness after the darkness of the carriage. Aeylin, whose werewolf eyes quickly adjusted, stared up at the high walls of the castle, mouth agape. She stood so still that it worried Luca.

"Is everything alright Aeylin? If you are uncomfortable, we can leave."

"I just never realised that Kinnison was..." For a second she seemed stumped, trying to find the right words. Giving up, she instead gestured with her hands, encompassing the castle, the guards, the size of the place. "All this." Her voice became choked as she added, "Why would someone like him ever love someone like me?"

Meeting Zara's eyes over Aeylin's shoulder, Luca answered, "Because love chooses for us, and when you truly love someone nothing else matters. Not money, or rank and even," with a smile at Zara, "if you are from different worlds." Zara smiled at Luca, and the look made his heart stutter for a moment. "Come, let's go inside and find our rooms. When you see Kinnison, you can ask him yourself."

Luca, Symon and the girls bade their farewells to the others. Nero informed Luca that he would be staying in the barn and would join them later, wanting to snoop around. Part of Luca wished that Nero would stay with them. But as he headed through the door and under the arch of the walkway leading into the castle, Luca felt Zara's hand find his. Luca squeezed it, grateful for her presence. With her by his side, he could face anything.

CHAPTER 23

M yles met the party just inside the side door. As they followed him through the corridors and up the stairs, Zara was startled to notice that his shoulder blades and ribs could be seen through the back of his threadbare shirt. His pants, which threatened to fall with every step he took, were also ragged and held up by a piece of rope. His bare feet were dirty. Slowing her pace so that the others could pass her, she signalled for Luca. She waited for a gap to form before asking, "If Tibarn is so well off, then why does he allow his servants to wear rags?" She hadn't allowed for a werewolf's keen hearing, and the boy's step faltered slightly before he quickly righted himself and continued on. Luca held a finger to his lips, the answer to her question would need to wait.

At the bottom of a stairwell, a young girl waited with dark hair and large brown eyes. Dressed in clothing as ragged as Myles, her neck was also adorned by a thin metal ring. She smiled shyly at the group and dropped into a deep curtsy.

"This is Beth. She will show the ladies the way to their rooms in the East Wing. The gentlemen will need to come with me. You all will have time to change and rest before we come to collect you for the feast."

"*Gode fen,* Beth," Symon greeted the girl. Her only response was another shy smile.

"Beth doesn't talk," Myles said, apologising for her silence.

"Why?" asked Emma, guileless. Zara and Luca shared a worried look, already guessing the answer.

Myles hesitated for a moment before responding in a quiet voice, "Because she doesn't have a tongue."

The room Myles led Luca to was spacious. Luca's accommodation in the Guild could have easily fit within the walk-in robe. Yet, for all its luxury, Luca would have happily traded staying there for a night in his own room. The four-poster bed, covered in an opulent, scarlet, velvet bedspread and half a dozen pillows, was large enough that all six of the Guardians, including Otto with his horns, could have slept head to foot. Luca's pack and armour had been brought up, and sat on top of a polished wooden chest at the foot of the large bed. The scuffed canvas bag looked utterly out of place in all the surrounding opulence. Opening it, Luca quickly checked the contents and was both surprised and relieved that nothing appeared to have been tampered with.

The room was also furnished with a dragon-skin couch, and running his hands over the smooth scales Luca guessed that it wasn't a fake. It must have cost a fortune, dragons only shedding their skins once every 100 years, and yet Tibarn had it displayed in one of many guests' bedrooms. Luca wondered what other priceless treasures would be found within the castle walls.

Nestled between two enormous hardwood wardrobes was a door connecting his room to Symon's. He knocked sharply, and it was quickly opened by the bear shifter.

"I could get used to this," Symon exclaimed, clearly much happier with his surrounding than Luca was. "Shame that Tibarn doesn't have a daughter."

"If he did, I doubt he would be happy to have her bonded with you," Luca said, then thinking his words a little harsh he added, "Which would be his loss." Symon shrugged.

"For the best, I guess, as it would make Tibarn my master and, looking at the way he treats certain members of his pack, I doubt greatly that I would like it very much."

"I am going to report his treatment when we return to the Guild. Tibarn shouldn't be allowed to get away with this," Luca swore.

"I don't know if it will do you any good. Did you see the metal rings? They are Tibarn's property, and under werewolf law, he can treat them as he wants."

"Well, then the werewolf law needs to be changed!" Luca exclaimed.

"One day, perhaps, but not tonight. We need to change and then meet the ladies. I am sure that this place is giving them the creeps."

"This place is absolute bliss," Emma sighed, as she sunk into the pillows on the soft bed. Zara, lying on the bed next to hers, had to agree. Large windows flooded the bedroom with sunlight, dancing across the crystal chandelier and making the entire room sparkle. Soft white rugs covered the floor so it felt as if they were walking on clouds when they crossed them. Each of them had her own bed, with a canopy trailing shimmering sheer cloth to match each bed's pastel coverings. The walls were decorated with a beautiful mural of blooming flowers and plants. Zara wished she could take a photo for Karen, who loved flowers and was a total green thumb.

The ladies had all taken turns enjoying a long soak in the bathroom's deep porcelain tub. Spelled to give the user a perfect experience, each time it filled with water heated to the temperature they each liked best, with bubbles perfumed with their favourite scents. For Zara, the water was scented with rosemary and daisies. It reminded her of home, of herbs growing in the kitchen gardens, and the daisies Luca had once given her. Once dried off with towels as soft as petals, they had found dresses waiting for them, one laid out on each of their beds. Zara found a note on top of her dress from Kinnison, inviting her to join him at the feast. Emma's note contained the same words, but from the way that Aeylin blushed while reading hers, Zara guessed that her note included a personal touch.

They had taken their time getting ready, each doing the other's hair and gossiping like only girls getting ready for a party can. Emma, a magician with makeup, discovered pots of colour and coal for darkening lashes and happily applied a dash for her friends. For a time, all three were able to forget the craziness of the past few nights and just relax. Even the baby had stopped his urgent kicking.

They were startled, therefore, when a knock came at the door. Zara, who was ready, opened it to find Kinnison standing there. His red hair had been combed neatly back from his face, exposing his strong jawline and chiselled cheekbones. He was dressed in a dinner jacket the colour of dark cherries. Zara would have thought it would clash with his auburn hair, but it didn't, instead only making his green eyes sparkle and emphasising his copper skin, which was flushed with health. For a moment an image appeared in her mind, comparing Kinnison's grand appearance with Myles' poor one, but she pushed it aside. Now was not the time to stir up what was likely to be an awkward subject. She was here to keep her mouth shut and keep Aeylin safe. So Zara smiled warmly at Kinnison and said, "It is a pleasure to see you again. Aeylin is still getting ready. Would you like to come in and wait?"

"I would indeed, thank you, Zara," Kinnison said, giving her a slight bow. "Might I take the opportunity to say that you look wonderful in that dress?" The dress Zara wore was a pale sky-blue, and the fabric felt as soft as silk. Sleeveless, the bodice hugged Zara's curves and showed off her bosom to great advantage. At the line of her hips, it flared out, reaching almost to the floor, and swayed around her ankles with each step she took. Tiny stones, which looked to be blue opals, shimmered down the front of the bodice and glittered on the skirt like a waterfall. Zara had never worn anything like it.

"Thank you. Did you choose it?" Zara asked, wondering how they had guessed her measurements so perfectly.

"No, I'm afraid I can't take the credit. The wardrobes here are all spelled. Someone forwarded your settings from Lightfall."

"Ah," Zara said, remembering the cupboard in Celeste's quarters and guessing that the fairy must have thought ahead. "Don't tell Emma or you might find yourselves short one wardrobe in the morning." Kinnison laughed, his laughter sincere and hearty and not at all princely, and Zara found herself liking him even more for it.

"What are you two laughing about?" Emma asked. Zara turned and saw that both Aeylin and Emma were dressed and ready. Emma's dress, a similar style to Zara's but in sunshine yellow, showed off her brown skin and made her hazel eyes appear almost copper. Beside her, Aeylin was dressed in pale pink satin, with short sleeves capping her shoulders and a lace ribbon circling under her ample bosom, before flowing out in chiffon which did little to hide her baby bump. The colour made Aeylin look like a sweet princess, but the look she directed at Kinnison was anything but innocent. Looking at Kinnison, Zara noted that his mouth was agape, his eyes full and staring, at a complete loss for words. He looked as if he wanted to ravage Aeylin right there, in front of Emma and Zara. Stalling the inevitable, Zara looped her arm through Kinnison's.

"Which way to the feast? I am sure that we shouldn't

be keeping your father waiting." Kinnison nodded slowly, his gaze still fixed on Aeylin, and allowed Zara to guide him down the hallway.

CHAPTER 24

After calling in to check on the ladies' bedchamber and finding it empty, Luca and Symon followed Myles towards the main hall. Luca did not like the idea of being separated from Zara, and his head filled with thoughts of the trouble she could get in. As a Guardian, he barely understood all the rules that a werewolf pack was governed by. A human would have no idea how to navigate the dangers. As Myles led them closer to the hall, Luca could hear music and conversation beginning to float towards them. Instead of calming him, his anxiety rose with the increase in volume. Tibarn must have over fifty wolves stationed within the castle, not to mention the additional guests and pack members. How would he find Zara among them all?

But as he stepped onto the landing and looked down the sweeping stone stairway, his eyes found Zara instantly, and what he saw froze him in place. She was surrounded by three of Tibarn's most ferocious wolves, but instead of snarling at her they were all smiling broadly. Onyx, one of Tibarn's most powerful Generals, was laughing. Zara was facing away from him so Luca couldn't tell what she was saying, but her shoulders shook with tiny tremors indicating that she too was sharing in their humour. Her dark hair had been swept up into a braid which cascaded into curls down one shoulder, revealing the long, smooth skin of her neck. His elf eyes picked out the tiny heart-shaped freckle which marked where her neck and shoulder met, and he was overtaken with the urge to kiss her there. He had been worried that she would be out of place but at that moment, dressed in a pale blue gown, looking like a princess and laughing with werewolves, she looked like she belonged. Like she belonged better than he did.

Sensing his thoughts as if they were a physical touch, Zara turned and caught Luca's gaze. As he started to descend the stairs to meet her, her eyes and smile brightened, taking in the sight of him dressed in his armour. Guardians tended to only wear their full armour in battle and for special occasions. They preferred the ease and comfort of tunics and pants, occasionally wearing a padded leather jacket when the need arose. Luca usually hated getting dressed up, but for once, he was glad. The steel breastplate had been polished so that it shined like silver, as had the shoulder and arm guards. Instead of leg greaves, he wore soft, black leather pants which clung to his muscular legs and matched the black leather straps which held the steel in place. A cloak of softest black and silver was draped across his shoulders, and almost perfect match to Nero's coat, symbolising their bond. Engraved on his breastplate, above his heart, was a picture of a burning flame surrounded by two circles, the emblem of the Lightfall Guild. As he strode towards Zara, her werewolf companions parted to let him through.

Luca stopped as he reached Zara and bowed low. Standing, he said, "You look beautiful, Zara." His words were simple, but Zara felt heat rush to her cheeks as she blushed, as much for the devouring look in his eyes as for the compliment. It caught her off guard and for a moment she wasn't sure how to respond.

"You wash up pretty nicely yourself," she said, her voice a little unsteady. "Skylar should order you to wear that more often." Her comment made Luca laugh and some of the tension of the moment dissipated. Zara was relieved. Watching him as he strode down stairs, Luca had looked like a knight from a fairy tale, and it had taken her breath away. Watching him, she had forgotten where she was.

"Skylar knows better. If he made us wear this all the time," Symon exclaimed, running one thick brown finger along the neckline of his breastplate as if it were choking him, "he would have a far more difficult time finding recruits. I signed up to help protect Wundor, not to be constantly choked to death." Despite his claims to hate the armour, Zara had to admit that the giant bear shifter made an impressive sight. The shining metal somehow made him look even larger than usual, and the blacked furred cloak gave him a carnal edge. From the corner of her eye, Zara could see Emma admiring both of the Guardians from a rear perspective.

A large gong sounded, drawing the guests' attention to Tibarn, who had risen to stand at his place in the centre of the head table. To his right sat Kinnison, smiling widely and nodding to his friends in the crowd. To his left sat Aeylin, eyes wide and hands protectively spread around her belly. Her whole body was tense, as if she would shatter should anyone touch her. Zara waved to catch her attention, but Aeylin was oblivious.

"Welcome, Bloodmoon Pack members and honoured guests, to my home." Tibarn's greeting was answered by the wolves stomping their feet and a howl which crossed the room like a wave. Zara didn't think it was possible, but she could have sworn that Aeylin's eyes widened even further at the sound. The girl was clearly terrified. She hoped that she wasn't about to fall into another fit. She tried to catch Kinnison's eye, to warn him, but the were-wolf prince was still smiling happily, oblivious to his mate's terror. She was about to weave through the crowd to go to Aeylin herself when Tibarn raised one hand, silencing the guests.

"I have invited you all here today as we have some exciting news to celebrate. My son Kinnison is shortly to become a father." Stamping and howls broke out once more, joined by shouts of Kinnison's name. Smiling broadly, Tibarn turned to his son and beckoned for him to stand up beside him. Kinnison happily obliged, his face flushed with pride as he took in the well-wishers. Tibarn put one arm around his son, holding him in a tight embrace, which Kinnison was quick to return. After a few moments, Tibarn released his son and shouted to be heard over the cheering guests, "Enjoy the feast. Let us all be merry at this great news."

On cue, servants, all wearing rings of steel around

their necks, hurried forward from their hiding places around the edges of the hall. Some carried large pitchers brimming with deep red wine or frothy dark ale, which was hastily poured into waiting tankards. Others brought large silver and gold platters, piled high with cut meats, savoury dishes and roasted vegetables. One tray, so large that it took four servants to carry it, held a whole roasted boar, its skin glistening with honey, an apple in its mouth. The guests started finding seats and filling plates. Onyx motioned for Zara to join him and his fellow wolves, but Luca grabbed her hand before she could agree. He pulled her towards a nearby table and sat her down next to him, wrapping one arm around her shoulders possessively. He met Onyx's gaze, and the werewolf gave him a slight nod before turning back to his friends.

Symon claimed the stool on Zara's other side, while Falcon and Otto positioned themselves on each side of Emma. Marika and Karn had chosen to remain in the barn, but the minotaur and shifter could not resist an invitation to enjoy the feast. Everyone tucked into their meals with gusto, the sumptuous food a luxury after the nutrient-rich but plain hardtack they had consumed on their journey. Servants continually passed the tables, filling their cups to the brim. Though Luca felt a twinge of unease at drinking while still officially on duty, it was overwritten by Otto smiling and laughing in his direction for the first time since they had left the Guild. Perhaps the minotaur was finally forgiving him. Smiling down at Zara, Luca was concerned to see that she was only picking at her food. Instead of tucking into the piles of roast boar, her silver plate only held vegetables and bread.

"Is something the matter?" Luca asked, concerned. The last time she had been in Wundor, Zara had not held back from all the culinary delights it had to offer.

"No, nothing," Zara replied, swallowing hard. Looking closer, Luca noticed that a bead of sweat had appeared on her forehead and her face was flushed.

"Why are you lying to me? I can see you aren't well."

"I'm fine, really. I just don't really eat roasted meat anymore. There's something about the smell ..." Zara reached for her goblet and took a large gulp of water. "Ever since my link with Wysh, meat just hasn't held the same appeal. Especially anything that has been roasted," Zara said, turning a little green at the word.

"Come," Luca said, holding out a hand for her. She took it, and he pulled her into a standing position. "How about we get away from all this food and find you some fresh air?"

"Are you sure? We aren't being rude? Surely you haven't had enough to eat?" Zara asked, hesitatingly.

"I'm sure. Everyone here will soon be too far into their cups to notice us."

"What about Emma?"

Luca looked to Emma, who appeared to have no complaints with her current environment. She was deep in conversation with Falcon about the increased healing benefits for a shifter when changing form. Symon was happily offering his bear experience, anything to share in Emma's attention.

"Emma is fine," Luca assured Zara.

"I'll watch her for you," Nero offered from his place under the table. Unlike the others, he had chosen not to

drink any of the plentiful ale but merely to avail himself of one of the boar's trotters. He munched on it while his dark eyes roamed the hall, watching everything, missing nothing.

"Nero will watch out for Emma," Luca said.

"Thank you, Nero," Zara said, bending down the stroke the wolf's ears. His only acknowledgement was a low rumble in the back of his throat and warm feeling which floated through his bond with Luca.

Taking Zara's hand, Luca escorted her through the maze of tables to the back of the hall. Spotting Myles, stationed near one of the archways leading further into the castle he asked for directions to stables. Myles pointed to a hallway, "Follow that to the end, turn right and then take your first left. At the end of that hall you'll find a door which will let you into the outer yard. Unless you want me to show you?" he asked with a knowing smile which made Zara blush.

"Ah, no, we'll be just fine. Thank you, Myles," Luca said and, wrapping one arm around Zara's waist, turned and headed out of the hall.

CHAPTER 25

Stepping into the outer bailey, Zara breathed in a large gulp of fresh air. Then another, chasing away the visions of smoke and fire which had filled her head. Inside, for a horrible moment, she'd thought she would embarrass herself by being sick all down her pale blue dress. Luca's offer had come not a moment too soon. Part of her felt guilty for making him leave, but mostly she just felt relieved. She breathed in another lungful of air, greedy for its crisp freshness. The night was cool, and the light breeze felt lovely against her warm forehead. Luca held her hand but said nothing, as though sensing her need to recalibrate. Waiting until her breathing had steadied, he suggested, "Should we go and check on Marika and Karn?"

"Sure," Zara agreed, noticing a nearby guard eyeing them suspiciously. They passed under the watchful gaze of another two guards before they reached the stables. She thought it a pity that they had to guard the walls and miss out on the celebration inside. Surely, with most of the Bloodmoon Pack inside, Tibarn wasn't concerned about anyone attacking them? Inside the stables they found Karn sitting on a hay bale, drinking a flagon of ale, froth caught in his leaf beard. He had obviously been enjoying the plates of food spread out around him; bits of roasted tomato had dripped down the front of his tunic. It made Zara wonder if all dryads were messy eaters. For her part, Marika daintily bit into a honeyed apple, leaning forward slightly so the sticky, golden coating wouldn't drip down her front. Spotting them, Karn inquired,

"Tired of the party already?"

"Just wanted some fresh air. I'm not really one for such lavishness," Luca answered, covering for Zara's unease. She squeezed his hand.

"Neither am I," Karn said. "Plus, too many wolves for my liking. Worried they would get drunk and piss on me by mistake," Karn added with a wink in Zara's direction. A sudden image filled her head of Onyx in wolf form, lifting his leg against a tree, and she struggled to compose herself so she didn't giggle.

"I would have liked to join the party, but unfortunately, Tibarn did not see fit to decorate his hall with suitable dining options for four-legged creatures of my stature," Marika said, her flicking tail the only sign of her agitation.

"He must be afraid that you would out-class him," Luca said, making Marika whinney slightly at the compliment.

As they chatted amicably with the two Guardians for a while, Zara felt the tension and the ache in her belly relax. Both Marika and Karn were vegetarians, so there was nothing here to threaten her composure. When a servant appeared at the door carrying another flagon of ale for Karn and a carafe of wine for Marika, Zara and Luca decided to take their leave. Saying goodnight to the others, they made their slow way back towards the door which would lead them into the castle. Zara did not want to go back inside and based on how Luca was dragging his usually agile feet, she guessed he didn't either. As Luca pulled open the wooden door, they were greeted by a sweet melody. Luca pulled her forward, but instead of heading down the hall, he guided her into a side alcove.

"May I have this dance?" he asked her, his smile barely visible in the dark corridor.

"I'd love that," Zara said. Lifting the hand that still held hers, Luca spun her in a circle, capturing her waist with his other hand as she turned to face him once more. Reaching up, she rested her free hand on his shoulder. The steel of his armour felt cold under her skin. Together, they began to sway in time to the melody, the skirt of Zara's dress swirling around them. Neither spoke, not wanting to break the moment as one song ended and another began. She had never been much of a dancer, but as Luca twirled and dipped her, she found herself enjoying the feeling of letting go, of letting him lead her. When the next song ended, Luca pulled her closer and kissed her sweetly on her forehead, then the tip of her nose, her cheeks and finally her mouth. As Zara leaned into the kiss, the cold metal of his armour pressed against her, making her shiver, but she didn't care. She would put up with far worse to keep on kissing Luca.

But he broke the kiss and began to plant tiny, light kisses along her neck, causing her to let out a moan. She felt his lips form a smile against her skin as he murmured, "I've wanted to do this all night since I first saw you in that dress." She was about to ask him what else he wanted to do to her when they both jumped, startled, as the door to the outer bailey opened and a servant, empty drink tray in hand, stepped into the corridor. The boy let out a panicked cry and dropped the dish, which banged loudly against the cobblestone floor.

"I'm so sorry. Please forgive me," the boy apologised, eyes full of fear. "I did not see you." Before Zara had a chance to brush off the apology, the boy knelt down at their feet, his forehead pressed against the hard stone. "I am so sorry, please do not tell my master. I beg you," the boy pleaded, his voice muddled with tears. His whole body shook, his clenched knuckles white. Where the back of his shirt rode up, exposing the flesh below, she could just make out the dark purple bruises which mottled his skin.

"The fault was not yours. You surprised us, that's all. But you could hardly have expected to find us here," Luca said kneeling, reaching one arm out to help the boy up. But as Luca touched him, the boy flinched violently. Luca looked up at Zara, brow furrowed and mouthed the words "You try."

"If anything, we are to blame. We shouldn't have been here, and we made you drop your tray. We promise that if you say nothing, then neither will we and this embarrassing incident will be quickly forgotten."

At first, Zara thought she would get no better reaction than Luca, but slowly the boy raised his head. With a trembling smile and in a barely audible voice, he said,

"Thank you, Mistress." Cautiously he stood, his still trembling legs barely holding his weight, and bowed to Zara. Grabbing up the fallen tray, he hurried off towards the hall, almost slipping on a flagstone in his haste.

The incident with the boy had thrown cold water on Zara's mood, but she still didn't feel like returning to the celebration. Seeing the lavish decorations in such contrast to the care Tibarn had for his servants made her feel sick. She was trying to think of somewhere else they could go when Luca, as if reading her mind, asked, "Would you like to come back to my room?"

"Please. I don't think I can face returning to the party."

"I think that I can find my way back without a guide, but we will need to pass though the hall. I'll also let Nero know, in case he needs us."

"I should probably check on Emma," Zara admitted, feeling a rush of guilt for abandoning her friend. Hand in hand, they walked into the hall. Tables had been pushed aside to widen the existing dance floor, and couples whirled around it, or in some cases stumbled, clearly enjoying Tibarn's hospitality. Zara spotted Emma dancing the Twist in a small group, which included both Symon and Otto, and laughed at the sight of the minotaur trying to copy her moves. All guilt over abandoning Emma fled. Her friend was more than capable of looking after herself.

Luca, gripping tightly to Zara with one hand, swiped a carafe of wine and two long-stemmed glasses with the other. Sticking to the edge of the hall, they headed towards the stairs, bolting up them in their eagerness to escape without notice. Laughing, they ran through the halls, up the three flights of stairs, and along the corridor to Luca's room with Zara holding up the skirts of her dress so that they didn't tangle about her feet. They reached the door of Luca's bed chamber, almost breathless. As Luca opened the door, Zara spotted the dragon-skin couch and flopped down onto it with a deep sigh. Luca bolted the door behind them and then checked that the connecting door between his room and Symon's was also locked. Filling the two glasses with wine, he passed one to Zara saying, "A toast. To finally being alone together."

Clinking her glass against Luca's, Zara took a sip of the wine. The cool liquid flowed down her throat, filling her mouth with the taste honey and summer melons. Looking at Luca, his gaze warm and enticing, she took another sip for courage. They had wasted too many opportunities, and something always seemed determined to keep them apart. This time, she was not going to let anything come between them. With one last sip, she stood and placed her half-full glass on the table next to the couch. Taking three steps forward, closing the gap between them, she claimed his mouth with hers. There was nothing subtle or gentle about the kiss this time; instead, it was hungry and demanding. Wrapping her arms around his neck, she pulled him to her, moulding her body to his. But the steel of his armour acted as a barrier, causing her to let out a groan of frustration. Letting go of the kiss, Zara started to work one of the straps which held the arm greaves in place.

"Are you sure?" Luca asked, his voice husky. Zara's only reply was to continue working. With Luca's help, she quickly had his arm greaves and breastplate off. Still not satisfied, Zara grabbed the bottom of his tunic and pulled it up over his head before throwing it on the floor at her feet. Stepping back slightly, Zara admired Luca's bare chest. She had only seen him this naked once, in the training yard when he had sparred with his friends. Zara had averted her eyes then. This time she devoured the sight of him. Luca's chest and arms were a glorious bronze from the time he spent sparring in the sun, their only blemish the star-shaped scar on his right shoulder and four claw marks which ran down his left side. A dusting of fine blonde hair covered his chest, which heaved slightly as he breathed deeply. There was not a single bit of fat on him, his chest and abdomen muscled to perfection. Drinking him in, Zara couldn't stop the moan that escaped her lips.

"Now you," Luca pleaded. The zip of Zara's dress was at the back, and for a moment, she struggled to undo it. Luca raised a hand, no doubt intending to help, but it froze in mid-rise as Zara undid the clasp and the dress shimmered down her curves to fall in a puddle at her feet. She stood naked, except for a lacy, strapless bra and the skimpiest of knickers. Suddenly embarrassed, knowing that her figure was not gloriously toned like Luca's, she covered her breasts and nakedness with her hands. But Luca reached for her hands, holding them out so he could have an unobstructed view.

"You are the most beautiful thing I have ever seen. I love you, Zara."

"I love you too," Zara replied, her own voice turning husky. Without waiting for an invitation, Luca picked Zara up in his arms and carried her towards the bed.

CHAPTER 26

The sunlight was just starting to filter through the window when Zara's eyes began to flutter open. She had been having the most beautiful dream. She had been dancing with Luca, under the stars in the unicorns' field in the Forest of Secrets. Wysh and Sateen had both been there watching. Coming awake, Zara stretched luxuriously and opened her eyes to find Luca looking down at her, smiling. The actual events of the previous night, even more enjoyable than her dream, came back to her. Feeling suddenly self-conscious, she grabbed the sheets, pulling them up to cover her naked body. She could feel the heat rush to her cheeks as she said, "Morning," making Luca smile broadly at her.

"Morning, my love. Would you care for something to drink?" Luca asked, pulling back the bedding and stepping out. Doing so revealed that he was still gloriously naked, and, nervous that words would fail her, Zara simply nodded. Though, as she watched him walk to the side table where they had left the half-full drinks the night before, she discovered she wasn't very thirsty. Instead, creeping up her body, from her toes to the slightly sore and sensitive area between her legs, to her tingling breasts, was hunger that only Luca could satisfy. All shyness gone, she sat up in the four-poster bed, letting her gaze roam down his back. Zara's previous experience with men had been with office workers or the occasional farmhand. They all paled in comparison to Luca, who spent hours on horseback and who could spar while hefting a massive sword with ease. His broad shoulders flowed down into a V, drawing her eyes to his firm buttocks. She smiled as she noticed the dimples that flashed at her as he walked. She had to fight the urge to jump out of bed and bite him. Having topped up both of their glasses, Luca turned and, catching sight of her expression, grinned wickedly at her, eyes full of mischievous intent. Putting down the drinks, Luca started striding back towards the bed, making Zara's heart pound rapidly, her blood vibrating in anticipation.

Luca was halfway to the bed when they were interrupted by a loud knocking at the door, making Luca freeze.

"Luca, open up!" Kinnison shouted in a frantic voice, continuing to bang the door. Zara pulled the bed covers up and slid down so she would be hidden, not sure if it was a good idea for Kinnison to find her naked in Luca's bed. Waiting only long enough to ensure she was fully covered, Luca went to open the door, then stopped short, realising that he was naked.

"Hold on. I'm just putting some pants on," Luca called out, eyes roaming the room to find the pants he had thrown in haste the previous evening. He spotted them, half draped over the armchair, and quickly pulled them on. Opening the door, his eyes widened at the sight of Kinnison. Gone was the elegantly-styled and well-dressed werewolf of the night before. Kinnison's red locks were dishevelled, and the shirt he wore had been done up in such haste that the buttons were not aligned correctly. The ankle-length pants he wore were stained with red wine, his feet bare.

"Luca, you have to help me. Aeylin is missing!" Kinnison exclaimed, pushing past Luca into the room.

"What do you mean missing?" Luca demanded.

"I went to her room this morning. The door was locked, and when I knocked, there was no answer. I assumed she must have been sleeping, I know that the party last night wore her out. But after five minutes of knocking with no answer, I became worried. I hunted down Beth and got her to let me in. The room was in shambles, the dressing table was knocked over, and two vases were smashed to pieces on the floor. There was also a large streak of dried blood." Kinnison's words came out quick and panicked, and his eyes were huge with fear.

"What about Emma?" Zara asked, no longer able to remain hidden. Her words made Kinnison spin in her direction, but he didn't seem overly surprised to see her there.

"I'm sorry, Zara, but Emma was also gone." Turning back to Luca, he pleaded, "You have to help me. I don't know what else to do. I left Beth on lookout at the door I didn't know who else to trust." Kinnison ran his fingers through his hair, making the red curls stand up in agitation. "If anything has happened to her, it will be all my fault."

Luca placed a comforting hand on Kinnison's shoulder.

"Go get Symon from the next room. We will all go with you. Don't worry, we'll find her." Kinnison nodded and without another word left them to dress, his fists pounding on Symon's door moments later.

"What do you think has happened to them?" Zara asked, voice trembling. She grabbed up her pale blue dress from where it still lay puddled on the floor. She was not looking forward to making the walk of shame back to her room, especially in the circumstances, but guessed that Luca's closet wasn't spelled like the one in her room. There was no need when the men travelled with their uniform. Finding her heels under the bed, she picked them up and sat on the dragon-skin couch to put them on.

"I honestly don't know. I didn't want to alarm Kinnison, but something else is worrying me. When he started his telling of the events, I tried to mind-link with Nero, but I'm receiving nothing. It's a total blank." Luca's brow furrowed with worry as he pulled a worn tunic over his head and stepping into his travelling boots, buckling them on. Pulling a knife belt out of his pack, he slung it around his waist. Wearing weapons inside Tibarn's castle could be perceived as disrespectful to the host, but at that moment, Luca didn't care.

"But Nero's alright, isn't he? You'd know if he was hurt?" Zara had been trying to tame her hair, it had come loose from its braid and stuck out at all angles around her head.

He hesitated for a moment before answering, "If he were dead, I would know, for my own heart would stop. But if he's injured, I would have no way of telling if he is out of range or unconscious. Communication through our bond only works when we are near each other."

Hearing the tone of worry in Luca's voice, Zara gave up on hair, going to him and wrapping her arms around his neck. "Perhaps the castle walls are blocking you? Like a mobile phone signal under a tin roof?" Luca looked puzzled at her example, but nodded slowly.

"Perhaps. But let's go and make sure."

Zara wanted to run to the ladies' bedchamber, but Luca held them all back, not wanting to draw anyone's suspicions. Until they knew what was amiss, the last thing they wanted was to raise the alarm. She struggled to keep her pace even and carefree. Surely anyone who looked at their group too closely would see the tension that flowed off them. Kinnison kept running his fingers through his hair, and it had started to look like a bird's nest. Symon's shoulders were tight, his stance stiff and his gaze kept roaming left to right, scouting for any signs of danger. From the look of concentration on Luca's face, she guessed that he was still trying to contact Nero and having no luck. The previous night, their giggling run back to Luca's room had seemed short, yet now she could have sworn they were walking for miles. Fear for Emma and Aeylin was forming a knot in her throat. If anything had happened to Emma, it would be all her fault, and she would never, ever, forgive herself.

As they reached the last landing, they caught sight of Beth standing outside the bedchamber. She was clearly terrified, but determined not to desert her post. Catching sight of them, she breathed a sigh of relief and held the room key out to Kinnison. "Thank you, Beth," Kinnison said, taking it from her as the girl stepped away from the door. Zara half expected her to make a run for it now that her guard duty was over, but it appeared that the girl's interest was piqued. As Kinnison turned the key in the lock and pushed open the door, Zara let out a gasp.

CHAPTER 27

Kinnison had not been exaggerating when he described the room as in shambles. Zara thought it looked like a tornado had erupted, hopping from spot to spot and leaving destruction in its wake. Stepping over the threshold, she almost slipped on shards of what looked like a teapot before Luca deftly caught her. Clothes and bedding were flung around the room. One of the pillows was slashed as though someone had tried to use it as a shield, and white feathers fluttered over the unmade bed like snow. A vase had been knocked over, and blue crystal shards sparkled on the floor. The dressing table had crashed to the floor, spilling the pots of colour, and smashing a bottle of perfume, so an overwhelming scent of roses flooded the room.

"Come in, quickly," Kinnison said, moving so others to get past him. Once they were all inside, including Beth, Kinnison locked the door behind them.

"Your nose is better than ours," Luca said, looking at Kinnison, "Are there any clues as to who is responsible?"

"I'm afraid not. I tried when I was in here before, but that perfume is so strong. It is making my eyes water and shielding anything I could usually sniff out."

"Alright, then we will all have to rely on our eyes. For now, we want to disturb the scene as little as possible. Fan out and stand against this wall," Luca indicated the wall behind them, "and take note of anything unusual. If you see anything, tell the rest of us."

Zara did as instructed, her eyes scanning the room. At first it was impossible to see past the destruction; there was too much for her eyes to take in. Her panic at what could have happened to Emma and Aeylin was making her heart beat loudly in her ears. For a minute, all she could do was focus on slowing her breathing. Suddenly something dark, hooked between the base and posts of one of the beds, caught her eye. She leaned forward, trying to get a better look. It was fur.

"Luca, there by Aeylin's bed, caught between the post and the base. Is that a clump of Nero's fur?" Zara asked, pointing. On agile elf feet, Luca tiptoed across the room to where Zara pointed, careful to avoid stepping on anything. Reaching down, he extracted the fur, rubbing it between his fingers.

"It is indeed, good spotting, Zara," Luca confirmed his voice sounding strained. He started looking around the bed for more clues.

Beth, who was standing next to Kinnison, suddenly tugged on his sleeve. When she had his attention, she pointed to the floor near where the dressing table had fallen.

"I don't see anything..." he said, confused. But Beth

continued to gesture frantically at the same spot. "Luca, I can't see anything, but Beth seems sure there is something over there by the dresser." Moving carefully over in the direction that Beth indicated Luca knelt down, balancing on the balls of his feet, and scanned the floor. His eyes froze on a droplet of red, half-hidden by one of the pots of colour. Dabbing it with his finger, he held it to his nose.

"Blood," he announced, "But I can't tell whose."

"I might be able to," Kinnison offered. "If you bring it close enough that I can block out the perfume." Luca did as requested, and Kinnison took a deep sniff. "Wolf," Kinnison answered.

"Are you sure?"

"Yes. And not a werewolf either."

"Nero," Luca said.

"One drop doesn't mean much. Only that Nero was here and that he fought," Symon said, trying to erase the worry that had clouded Luca's eyes.

"I know," Luca said, giving his friend a grateful smile.

"Look, there by the window!" Kinnison exclaimed. "More blood. I've got the scent for it now."

As fast as he could without disturbing anything, Luca headed for the window. At the hem of the curtain, Luca could clearly make out two perfect paw prints, marked out in blood. If he had had any doubt that the blood they had found was Nero's, it faded at once. Pulling back the curtain revealed a small puddle of blood which dripped slowly down the window sill. The window was unlocked and slightly ajar. Nero might be injured, but he was still alive when he had climbed out of the ground floor window. Luca's chest filled with pride and reassurance.

Nero knew how to take care of himself. The puddle was still wet, meaning that the escape couldn't have happened more than an hour ago. Kinnison must have only just missed them. About to call out his findings to the others, Luca paused. Leaning forward, he noticed that a bloody fingerprint had smudged the edge of one of the window panels. Whoever was with the wolf must have gotten his blood on them as they escaped. At least one of the girls was alive. No longer concerned about contaminating the scene, Luca called the others to join him. Kinnison quickly confirmed that the blood on the window sill and floor were Nero's and that Luca's guess had been right, that the fingerprint smudge on the window was made in Nero's blood.

"Alright, we need to find Nero and the girls before anyone else does. Until we know otherwise, we are going to assume that all three are hiding somewhere together," Luca said taking charge. "Beth, can you clean up all the blood? We don't want anyone else finding this and coming to the same conclusion that we have." The girl nodded and ran to the bathroom. She was back in a moment with an armful of towels. "The more sets of eyes we have searching for them, the higher our chances, and we have to find them before someone raises the alarm. I suggest we head to the stables and grab the others and then come up with a search plan." Everyone nodded. Luca half expected Kinnison to have an issue with his authority, but the werewolf prince kept his mouth shut. It was clear that he was in no fit state to make life and death decisions.

"I need to change," Zara said glancing down at her dress, the bottom of which was now covered in grime.

"Do it, but be quick. We want to be out of here as soon as Beth's finished cleaning."

Zara hurried to one of the wardrobes and grabbed the handle. She had expected it to open easily and was a little surprised when it didn't. Grabbing the handle with both hands, using her full weight, she pulled with all her might. With a loud creak, the door flung open, the force throwing Zara backwards and saving her from being squashed by the body of an enormous black werewolf which fell out of the cupboard, landing with a thump as it hit the floor. The shock made Zara scream, and Luca was at her side in an instant.

"What in all the hells!" Kinnison exclaimed.

"You know this wolf?" Luca asked.

"You all do. This is Onyx, he was flirting with Zara before you arrived at the feast." Zara remembered the tall general who had been polite and friendly to her and Emma while they had waited for the men to arrive. He had been attentive, but she wouldn't have described his demeanour as flirtatious. However, based on the way that Luca's arms tightened around her, she guessed that his opinion differed. "Do you think the attacker could have hidden him there?" Kinnison asked, doubtfully. Symon let out a snort of laughter.

"Don't kid yourself, Kinnison, you're no fool. The only way that Onyx could have gotten in this room was with a key. The lock wasn't broken, and there is no way the ladies would have let him in. He is the one who attacked Aeylin and Emma, likely on your father's orders."

"We don't know that for sure," Kinnison retorted, his natural instinct to defend his father overriding the facts before him.

"What we do know is that the girls are missing, and that is was a good thing that Nero was with them," Luca said.

"And that at least one if not both of the girls are alive," Zara said, relieved.

"What makes you seem so sure?" Kinnison asked, his tone changing from defensive to hopeful.

"Nero doesn't have opposable thumbs, and I doubt he could have manoeuvred Onyx into the cupboard and managed to close it all by himself," Zara explained.

"I think you're right. Let's work on the assumption that all three are alive. The sooner we find our friends, the better," Luca said, letting go of Zara so that she could go to the other cupboard for a change of outfit. Zara nervously pulled open the door, but this time it opened easily and contained no surprises. Inside she found a pair of black jeans, a black short-sleeved t-shirt and black runners. The cupboard must have decided that Zara needed something to sneak around in. Picking up the pile of clothes, she rushed to the bathroom to change out of her dress. By the time she was ready, Beth had finished cleaning up the blood around the window. The men had also made fast work of the room, putting the furniture to rights and tidying up the fallen bedding. Anyone who looked too closely wouldn't be fooled, but hopefully, if anyone glanced into the room, they wouldn't see anything to cause them to raise the alarm.

Beth led the party through the servant corridors to the

door which they had used to enter the castle the afternoon before, coming out just in front of the stables. They received a few strange looks from a handful of servants who passed them but, catching sight of Kinnison, they had asked no questions and hurried past, eyes down. Opening the door, Kinnison looked around for the guards, but Lady Luck was with them, and no-one was in sight. Quickly, they headed towards the stables, keeping close against the wall, so they were out of sight of anyone above. The stable was dark, and they paused, standing in a huddle, blinking while their eyes adjusted. Zara's eyes had only just started to focus when she heard Beth scream. As her own vision cleared she fought to swallow a scream of her own. Laid out on the straw floor were all four of the Guardians. They looked as if they had collapsed suddenly, limbs spread in odd positions. Karn, who had landed face first, was lying in a puddle of green blood. Luca rushed to him and turned him over.

"He's alive, but his nose is badly broken," Luca announced in a relieved voice. Splitting up, they raced to check the others, relieved to find them all still breathing. Not dead, just unconscious. The cause became apparent when Symon pointed to one of the stable cats sprawled out on the floor. It had come looking for scraps and gotten more than it bargained for.

"Who would do this?" Kinnison asked, appalled.

"Someone who wanted to keep them out of the way while they murdered Aeylin," Luca said, tone harsh. "I'm no healer, so I can't tell if the poison is lethal. I'm hoping, however, that they only intended to delay, not kill, these four."

"Makes sense since I am guessing these four were merely a complication. As it is Skylar is going to have a fit when he finds out," Symon said. "If they had been killed while on a diplomatic mission, Skylar would go to war."

"What? But it wouldn't lead to war if Aeylin was killed? She was under his protection?" Zara demanded.

"Don't get me wrong, Skylar would want to go to war over her death, but he wouldn't have the support of the other Guilds. One of our mandates is not to get involved in creature politics."

"We have to find Aeylin now!" demanded Kinnison in a panic. "I'm sorry about your Guardians, but I am sure that they will be fine."

"You're right, but I won't leave them here unprotected. Not while they're in no fit state to defend themselves," Luca stated tone firm. His brow furrowed as he tried to think of the best solution. "I think that Zara and Symon should remain here and try to wake the others. Kinnison, Beth and I will continue to search the castle. It will look less suspicious with just the three of us looking, and Beth," he smiled at the servant, "knows all the best ways to not be spotted. If we don't find anything within the next half an hour, we'll return and regroup. Agreed?" Luca looked at the others who all nodded.

"I'll watch over Zara, no harm will come to her," Symon added, clasping Luca's forearm.

"Thank you," he said, grateful for his friend's reassurance. Luca hated to leave Zara when they were all in danger. For Zara's part, she just stepped forward into his arms and wrapped her own around his waist. She held him tightly for a moment before reluctantly releasing her grip.

"Come back to me," she whispered.

"Always." Luca kissed her forehead before turning and making his way out of the stables, Kinnison and Beth following.

Zara watched Luca walk away and felt her heart tighten. To distract herself, she looked around for a bucket. Perhaps splashing the Guardians with water would help speed up the process of waking them. Seeing nothing, she decided to try the stables. Symon was moving the Guardians into upright sitting positions, propping them against bales of hay. Explaining her idea, he quickly agreed to help.

"I'll take the left side, you take the right one," he suggested. There were only a dozen stables, and it wouldn't have taken Zara long to search them all herself, but it appeared that Symon was taking his duty seriously. The stables were still quite dark and having company was comforting, so she chose not to say anything. The water troughs in the first two were empty, but when she opened the third, she found something unexpected. Crouched against the far wall, his eyes as large as saucers, was the servant boy Myles.

CHAPTER 28

As Zara stepped towards Myles, the boy scooted back into the corner, edging away from her. Halting, she asked, "Myles, what is wrong?" But the boy just shook his head. She guessed that he must have witnessed what had been done to the Guardians. She could think of nothing else which could account for his terror. Treating him as she would a frightened animal, she crouched down, so she was level with the boy. "Myles I'm not going to hurt you," Zara promised, but still the boy said nothing. Edging a tad closer she held up both hands to show that she was unarmed. Instead of asking further questions, Zara instead tried to reassure the boy. In a soothing voice, she told him, "It's okay, Myles. We know what happened to our friends wasn't your fault. You aren't in any trouble." As she continued to murmur, she watched the boy's hands relax their grip on his knees and his posture slowly straightened.

In a quiet voice, Myles asked, "Has he gone?"

"Has who gone, Myles?"

"Kinnison," he asked, voice barely above a whisper.

"Yes. He's gone with Luca and Beth to look for our other friends, the ones who are missing." At the mention of the missing girls, Myles gulped, sucking in a large lungful of air. Zara didn't think the fact that they were missing was a shock to Myles, more that Zara and the others knew.

"Myles, do you know where Aeylin and Emma are?" Zara asked, trying to keep the tension out of her voice. Myles hesitated for a second and then gave the barest of nods.

"Are they alive?" Another nod. This time Zara couldn't hide her relief and smiled broadly at the boy. "Thank you, Myles. I've been so worried. Can you tell me where they are?" Again, the boy hesitated, this time so long that Zara thought he wasn't going to answer. Then he said, voice low, "No, but I can take you there."

It took a lot of coaxing but eventually Zara managed to convince Myles to come out of his hiding place. Exiting the stables, she noticed that Symon had moved away and was sitting on one of the hay bales, splashing water from a bucket into Otto's face. Looking up, Symon said, "*Gode fen*, Myles. It is good to see you, my friend," his voice gentler than its usually honeyed burr.

"*Gode fen*, Symon," Myles greeted the bear shifter, managing the words with only a slight tremble in his voice. Zara smiled at Symon. With his keen ears, he must have overheard every word of their conversation and made the smart choice to wait and not startle the boy.

"Are they dead?" Myles asked.

"No, just knocked out. Look, Otto is starting to come

to," Symon said. It was true, the minotaur had started to snort and roll his head from side to side as if trying to shake off the fuzziness. "Your idea with the water was a good one, Zara. Do you two want to help me with the others?"

Each grabbing a bucket, Zara and Myles went to the aid of a knocked-out Guardian. Myles worked on Falcon, as the bird shifter was the least intimidating of the four. He delicately sprinkled water on her face. Now that Otto was starting to mumble, Symon moved on to Marika. He stood a few feet away as he splashed water on the centaur, knowing when she woke, she was likely to stand up in a rush and not be at all happy with her unexpected shower. Zara found a cloth draped over one of the stalls and, dipping it into the water, started to wipe the green blood off Karn's face. At first, the movement made the dried wound start bleeding again, but it quickly stopped as she continued to wash it. She thought that the new angle of his nose gave the dryad a jaunty air but guessed he would probably appeal to Celeste or one of the other healers to have it fixed.

Slowly, one by one, the Guardians gained full conscious, though all four remained a little groggy. Each confirmed that their last memory was breaking their fast that morning with food bought by a servant boy. Zara looked towards Myles, but the boy shook his head. Relieved that the four would suffer no permanent damage, Zara's concern redirected once again to her missing friends. "Myles, you said you know where Aeylin and Emma are? I need you to show me."

The boy nodded and started to turn in the direction of

the exit, when Symon stopped him, "Hold on a minute. You can't go alone, and we need to let Luca and Kinnison know."

"I'll fetch them," Falcon offered and within seconds she had taken bird form and was flying out of the stables, the gust of wind from her wings causing Zara's hair to blow across her face. Brushing it aside, she looked at Myles to find that the boy had gone pale, his legs trembling, and he had bitten his lip so hard that a single droplet of red blood dribbled down his chin. Stepping forward, Zara wrapped her arms around him, cradling his head. In return Myles wrapped his too-thin arms around her waist, squeezing so tight that it made Zara gasp.

"Myles, what is wrong?" Zara asked.

"Kinn-i-son is go-ing to pun-ish me," the boy managed to get out past chattering teeth.

"No, he won't," Zara said soothingly. "Kinnison is our friend, he won't hurt you." Zara hoped that she was right. She barely knew the werewolf prince, but he didn't seem the type to hurt small children. "I won't let anyone hurt you," she promised.

By the time Luca, Kinnison and Beth returned, Falcon flying in front, Zara had managed to calm Myles enough that he sat on one of the hay bales next to her, still clutching tightly onto one of her hands. He stiffened when the others entered but relaxed when he saw Beth enter at Kinnison's side. Unlike him, the girl showed no fear, her eyes wide and face flushed slightly with the excitement of the morning. Catching sight of Myles, Beth ran and plonked down next to him. She started to sign rapidly with her fingers. The others had no clue what her signals meant, but Myles clearly did.

Taking a deep breath, Beth smiling at him in encouragement, Myles turned to Kinnison and said, "I know where Aeylin is. I can take you to her."

No one wanted to be left behind, so the entire party of six Guardians, three werewolves, and Zara, followed Myles through the underground tunnels that led outside the castle. When Myles had first admitted that he was the one who helped smuggle Aeylin, Emma and Nero out of the castle through the tunnels Kinnison had scoffed, "What secret tunnels? If there were tunnels, I would know about them." Myles' eyes had met Beth's, watching the girl shrug then nod, before replying,

"I beg your pardon, Master, but you don't know this castle half as well as you think you do." His response made Symon roar with laughter, breaking the tension which had started to build. "I doubt there are many in the castle who knows, except the servants."

The castle had not always been owned by Tibarn and his pack. When the werewolf pack had claimed it, the purebloods had not lowered themselves to exploring all the tunnels and servants' corridors. But the bitten had.

"When you get punished for being late, you try to find every possible route to get anywhere in the castle," Myles explained. It had been the cook who had first discovered the tunnels leading out of the castle. He guessed that they had initially been used for trade and in times of siege.

They ran from the kitchens, under the castle and moat, and came up about a mile outside the castle grounds.

"If my father knew about this, he would be outraged. He would have made sure that the tunnels were sealed," Kinnison said.

"Then we better hope he never finds out," Luca replied, ducking his head to avoid a low-hanging beam. Whoever had built the tunnels must not have been very tall. Luca had come close to giving himself a concussion multiple times. Symon had taken the more comfortable option and changed into his bear form. Marika kept grumbling under her breath as cobwebs and dust fell into her golden mane. Zara was surprised that the centaur hadn't offered to stay behind, since she seemed to despise the dank and dirty tunnel so much. Marika seemed to be made of stronger stuff than her dainty appearance indicated.

"Myles, how did you know that our friends needed help?" Zara said, asking the question they had all been thinking.

"When Mistress Aeylin left the party and headed to bed, she wasn't feeling very well. Mistress Emma recognised me and asked if I would be kind enough to fetch Mistress Aeylin a cup of tea. She was so nice, even said please. I knew I wasn't meant to leave my post but, well, no one really takes much notice of us servants. I went to the kitchens, but when Cook found out about my errand, he wanted to make a good impression. As well as the teapot and cups, he loaded my tray with biscuits and cakes. I think that he may have saved my life by stalling me," Myles said, pausing for a moment in his story.

"But what happened next?" Kinnison asked impatiently, keen to find out what had happened to his beloved.

"When I reached the ladies' bedchamber, the door was ajar, and I could hear growling and loud thumping. One of the ladies was screaming. Both of my hands were full with the tray so I couldn't knock, but I managed to push the door open with my foot. I should have called for help, but I guess it worked out better for everyone that I didn't. As I opened the door, I saw that two wolves were fighting. Onyx had Nero by the throat, though in my fright I didn't recognise either of them at first. The thumping I had heard was Onyx banging Nero's head back and forward against the floor. Aeylin was on one of the beds, screaming and sobbing. I thought we were all going to be killed." Myles shivered at the memory and Beth, walking next to him, took his hand in hers.

"I dropped the tray I was carrying, and it hit the floor so hard it shattered, splashing me with hot tea. For a second I thought I'd wet my pants I was so scared. But the sound must have distracted Onyx because he paused in his attack and turned to look at me. His eyes were red, and he had blood in his teeth. I thought that I was a goner." Myles' voice was coming fast now in his excitement to tell the story, and the others strained to catch every word. "But then Emma grabbed one of the silver candlesticks from the bedside table and smashed it down on Onyx's head. You should have seen her. She looked like an avenging angel in her bright yellow dress, with her red hair flying out behind her. Onyx never saw her coming. The next moment he was down, crumpled on the floor."

"Emma knocked him out?" Luca asked astonished.

"She hit him twice more for good measure. I was ready to turn and run, but before I could Nero took hold of my arm with his teeth," Myles continued making Beth gasp. "He didn't hurt me or nothing," the boy reassured her, "Just dragged me inside and kicked the door shut behind me. Emma was busy comforting Aeylin who was all shaky and crying, but Nero clearly wanted to get everyone out of there. You know," Myles said, looking back at the group, "For an animal that doesn't talk he sure is good at getting what he wants across."

"We know," Symon and Zara said in unison, making Luca laugh.

"He picked up one of the sheets and started using it to wipe the blood off the floor. Would have been a funny sight had he not been bleeding so badly himself that he kept leaving a trail behind him."

"How badly hurt?" Luca asked.

"He has a cut across his eye, and on the back of his head, a gash along his throat where Onyx grabbed hold of him and his front right paw is cut up pretty badly."

"That explains the bloody footprints we found," Symon said.

"Actually, no, those were Nero's idea. He wanted to leave a false trail should anyone try to follow them."

"Clever," Luca said. Trust Nero to be level headed even when injured.

"So how did they escape?" Kinnison asked.

"I'll let the ladies tell you that story, they should be just up ahead." Caught up in the story, no one had noticed when the ground had started to slope slowly upwards. Looking ahead, Zara could make out a faint light coming through an opening. Knowing their friends were close, the group put on an extra burst of speed. Luca was the first to climb out of the tunnel's exit. He was surprised to find that it had been fashioned to resemble a natural cave opening. If someone didn't know exactly where to look, they could easily have missed it. Looking around, he could see no sign of the wolf or two women. Pushing out his thoughts, he called out to Nero.

"About time you got here," Nero's grumpy voice answered, making Luca smile.

CHAPTER 29

They found Nero, Emma and Aeylin resting near a cluster of trees not too far from the tunnel's exit. Aeylin sat with her back against one of the trees, her legs spread out in front of her. Nero stood next to her, his front paw held gingerly, pieces of Emma's yellow gown bandaged around his paw and throat. For her part, Emma stood in front, guarding them both, the silver candlestick she had used to hit Onyx clutched in her hand. Catching sight of Zara and the others, she dropped the candlestick and flung herself into Zara's arms. The two women clung to each other, the terror and worry of the past few hours flooding down both their cheeks.

"I'm so sorry, Emma. I shouldn't have let you come here," Zara apologised, holding Emma tight.

"It's not your fault. I chose to come, and I don't regret it, not for an instant. I was just so scared. We didn't know what had happened to you, or Luca or Symon. We thought that they must have sent someone to murder you. Myles didn't know, and Nero couldn't reach Luca."

"No one came for us, I guess we weren't their target. Luca blocked Nero when we were... busy. When he reopened the link, he couldn't reach Nero."

At the word "busy" Emma pulled back from Zara's embrace and looked her friend over in a suggestive way. Mindful of the sharp hearing of the others Emma mouthed "Details later," making Zara laugh. From the corner of her eye she saw Symon punch Luca's shoulder lightly.

"So, what happened? From someone who actually speaks," asked Symon, no longer able to hide his frustration. By the body language and eye signals passing between Nero and Luca, it was clear that the story was being passed through the bond. Zara watched Luca's face become a deeper shade of red and his jaw was clenched tightly shut. His anger made her own urge to hear the tale build.

"You tell them, Emma," Aeylin said, snuggling into Kinnison, who had seated himself beside her. His arm was wrapped tightly around her while his other hand gently rubbed her belly. "I don't think I can without starting to shake again."

"Okay, well, I guess I better start when Aeylin and I decided to leave the party. You two had disappeared," Emma winked at Zara, "and Aeylin was fading. Since everyone was distracted dancing, I thought we could get away unnoticed and sneak back to our rooms. We managed to reach the top of the stairs but stalled when we realised neither of us knew how to actually get back.

Luckily, Nero found us and used his brilliant sense of smell to guide us there." Emma smiled fondly at the wolf, who seemed to almost shrug at the compliment.

"On the way, we passed Myles. Aeylin looked a little pale, so I asked him to bring us some tea to help her sleep."

"Thank the Goddess you did otherwise we'd all be dead," Aeylin put in, with a smile at Myles. The boy ducked his head, his ears turning pink.

"All I did was drop the teapot. It was Emma who brought down the werewolf," Myles said, glancing at Emma, hero-worship in his eyes.

Shrugging off the comment, like braining a werewolf was nothing, Emma continued with her story.

"When we got back to the room, it was as we left it. Nero jumped straight onto Zara's empty bed and made himself comfortable but just in case I left the door unlocked. It was stupid."

"It wouldn't have made a difference if you had locked it. Onyx had a key, remember?" Aeylin pointed out.

"True, but I still feel like an idiot. Anyway, we had just gotten into our nightclothes, and I was taking off my makeup when the door opened. I assumed it was Myles but instead it was Onyx. Before I had time to even ask what he was doing there, he picked me up and literally threw me across the room, like I weighed no more than a feather. If I had hit the wall, he would have broken my back, but I landed on my bed. I still don't know if that was intentional or not. Either way, the fall was hard enough to knock the wind out of me. My head was spinning so bad it took me a minute to right myself. If Nero hadn't been there to stop him from reaching Aeylin, I hate to think what would have happened. Onyx definitely was not expecting Nero to be there."

Nero let out a snarl of agreement.

"Nero was amazing," Aeylin said, with a grateful look in the wolf's direction. "I just froze when Onyx started prowling towards me. I thought he was going to snap my neck with his bare hands. But he never even made it to the foot of my bed. Nero was on him like a black thunder-cloud and they both went crashing into the dressing table. I don't know which was louder, my scream or the sound of the mirror shattering. I think if Onyx had stayed in man form, the fight would have been over quickly, but before Nero could restrain him, he changed. They were both tumbling together so fast, a whirl of black and grey fur, so I had trouble working out which wolf was Nero and which was Onyx."

"I remember looking around for a weapon, and the only thing I could find was the candlestick. But even with it, I was too scared to interfere. I had as much chance of hitting Nero as Onyx." Emma explained. "Then Myles opened the door and dropped his tray. Both wolves froze for a second, and I thought to hell with this and just hit the wolf on top. I wasn't even sure it wasn't Nero," Emma admitted with a guilty glance in the wolf's direction, "but at that point, I thought we were dead either way."

"You did the only thing you could," Luca said, "Nero wanted me to tell you, and I agree with him. Although," he admitted, "good thing it was Onyx you hit."

"I wouldn't say Nero got away unscathed," Emma said, looking in wolf's direction.

"Nero's paw is in bad shape, and I'm worried about the

gash on his neck." Nero's answering growl was conde-scending as the wolf tried to shrug off Emma's concerns. But he wasn't fooling anyone with his nonchalance; anyone looking at him carefully could tell that his wounds were far worse than he was letting on.

"Well, once I confirmed it was Onyx, we dragged him off Nero, and then Myles and I shoved him in the cupboard. That guy is heavy, but Myles is way stronger than he looks," Emma said, smiling broadly at Myles, who blushed the colour of a ripe tomato. "We were going to escape through the window, but then Myles mentioned the tunnels, and here we are."

"So what do we do now?" Aeylin asked.

"Now we get the hell out of here," Symon said.

"Yes," Falcon said sarcastically, "Obviously. But how?"

"We can't go back to the castle, too high a risk of getting caught and trapped. How long do we have until someone notices we're missing?" Luca asked Kinnison.

"I'd say we have a couple of hours, maybe a little longer if everyone is hungover. But if we don't come down for food sometime soon, then they'll start to wonder where we are."

"We'll have less time if Tibarn sends someone to check if Onyx succeeded," Karn pointed out.

"Or if Onyx comes to," added Otto.

"Oh, I don't think there is much risk of that," said Emma smiling impishly. "When I realised I hit the right wolf, I gave his head a few more knocks for good measure."

"Either way, we need to get out of here. If we don't cross out of Tibarn's territory before he catches us, we are screwed. We'll have his entire pack chasing us," Symon said.

"Beth and I can cover for you," Myles suggested.

"No way. You two are coming with us," Emma said.

"They can't," Kinnison said. "They belong to my father."

"They belong to themselves. If we leave the children behind and Tibarn finds out they had a hand in helping us escape what will happen to them?" Emma demanded. Kinnison didn't answer, his silence an admission of shame.

"They will whip us, but we have to go back. If we leave with you, Tibarn will kill us," Myles said, taking hold of Beth's hand. The silent girl nodded her agreement.

"Can't the Guild offer them asylum?" Zara pleaded, looking at Luca. Luca hesitated for a moment before answering.

"Skylar can offer them sanctuary if there is proof that their lives are in danger. But the proof will have to be substantial. Guardians cannot interfere with the rules of creatures."

Aeylin nudged Kinnison, "Myles saved my life and the life of our unborn child. Surely as Tibarn's son, you have the power to help him?"

Kinnison looked down at Aeylin. His lips thinned, his jaw becoming rigid and his hand on her belly clenched. The others waited, letting him battle a lifetime of rules and pack obligations. Finally, with a slight nod, he made a decision. Looking up at Luca, he said in a firm voice, "I will vouch for Beth and Myles. They will be under my protection. If anyone asks I ordered them to accompany us."

"Thank you," Zara said, while Emma gifted him with a happy smile. Aeylin, for her part, reached up and covered his face in kisses. The look Aeylin directed at Kinnison was so full of pride that the werewolf prince relaxed and smiled warmly at them all.

"We need to travel fast," Luca said, taking command. "Marika, would you be alright to carry both Beth and Myles on your back?" Asking a centaur to carry riders was like asking a human to wear a saddle. Yet, without the slightest hesitation, the golden Guardian nodded her proud head.

"It would be my honour," she said, kneeling down on her front legs so that the two servants could climb onto her. Myles sat in front, Beth behind, clinging to his back. "You can put your hands around my waist, Myles, but please do not squeeze too hard," Marika instructed.

"Falcon, I need you to fly ahead and warn Skylar. Ask him to send help, to meet us at the border. It would be better if he didn't have to cross it. Let's not start a war if we can help it."

"As you wish. Travel safe," Falcon said. A moment later she was in the air, her wings flapping hard, flying in the direction of the Lightfall Guild.

"Kinnison, can you carry Aeylin?"

"Yes." With a kiss on his mate's forehead, Kinnison stood. The air shimmered, and a millisecond later, a large grey wolf took his place. Symon helped Aeylin to her feet and then lifted her up, so she sat behind the werewolf's shoulders.

"It won't be a comfortable ride for you; I'm afraid," Luca warned.

"I'll be alright. I've had worse, and the sooner we get away from here, the happier I'll feel," Aeylin said, grabbing two handfuls of Kinnison's fur. The werewolf reached around with his massive head and licked her leg.

"Symon, I am entrusting you with Zara and Emma. I'm hoping it won't be too much of a problem for you to carry them both."

"It'll be my pleasure," Symon agreed before shifting form. As Zara climbed onto his back, she added bear riding to her list of impossible things she never thought she would ever find herself doing. Emma jumped up behind her.

"It's just like the time we rode Hiccup back from the farmers' market," Emma laughed, referring to the underfed donkey they had saved from slaughter. Once again, Zara felt amazed at how well Emma was taking everything in her stride. She also hoped Symon never found out that she had compared him to a donkey.

"What about Nero?" Zara asked. The way that the wolf was holding his front paw she doubted he would be able to travel far.

"Leave me. I'll only slow you down. When you reach the Guild send someone to come get me," Nero told Luca, his tone grumpy and frustrated.

"We are not leaving you. That is not how this bond of ours work remember?"

"Maybe I can help," Karn offered. Zara looked at the stick-thin Dryad, thinking it kind of him to offer but unsure of what he could do. But as they all watched, Karn walked up to one of the trees, placing his open hand on the trunk and closing his eyes. For a moment, nothing happened. Zara was about to say something when the leaves above her head rustled as if in a strong wind. She watched, mouth open, as three of the trees sprouted branches, entwining them together. The limbs thickened and within minutes became branches.

"Watch out," Luca shouted as the entwined branches broke off at the trunk, falling to the ground. Symon jumped forward, almost dislodging his two riders, managing to avoid being hit by mere inches.

"Apologies for that," said Karn, who had moved to stand near Luca, "Trees don't really have an awareness of those that stand below them."

"Great work Karn," Luca said as he looked down on the wooden stretcher that the trees had made.

"I'll carry one end if you can take the other?" suggested Otto.

"Done. Nero, get on," Luca ordered the wolf. With a look of resignation, his body moving stiffly, the wolf manoeuvred himself so he was above the stretcher before collapsing with a sigh. Otto grabbed one end while Luca took hold of the other, and together they lifted the stretcher as if it weighed nothing.

"Wish it had been that easy when we found him on the doorstep of The Haven. Nero weighs a tonne," Emma whispered into Zara's ear. If Emma and Josh were the ones carrying him this time, they wouldn't have lasted a mile, let alone to safety.

"Right, let's go. We stick together. We'll stay near the trees and off the roads," Luca said and, with a last look back at the castle for any signs of alarm, he headed in the direction of the Guild.

CHAPTER 30

Luca knew he was going to end up with a twinge in his neck if he kept looking behind him, but he couldn't help it. The castle was now just a grey blur in the distance, yet he couldn't resist the urge to keep checking for some sign that their escape had been discovered. He almost wished that he hadn't sent Falcon on ahead. Almost. As much as her scouting would be an advantage right now, she was the only one who could reach the Guild in time to warn Skylar. Should they be caught, the Guild would be their only hope of getting out of this mess alive.

Looking around at the others, he felt his heart swell with pride. If he had to be stuck in a life-threatening situation, he couldn't have asked for a better team. Marika had claimed the position at the front of the group, her twitching tail the only indication that she was frustrated at having to slow her usual racing pace. Otto and Luca walked behind her, the minotaur not even breaking a sweat at carrying his half of Nero's weight. Luca was grateful that Otto seemed to have forgiven him for what they had done to his brother. This assignment had given him a new respect and liking for the stern Guardian. To their left strode Symon, ears pricked and nose lifted as he scented the air. While his eyesight was as good as any human's, in bear form his sense of smell was his real advantage. If there were threats anywhere in the woods, he would smell them before any got a chance to find them. On his back, Zara and Emma both scanned the surrounding area. The girls amazed him more with every experience. He never knew that humans could be so resilient and have so much courage. Instead of shaking in fear, they both looked ready to take on whatever came at them. Emma, he noted, still clutched the silver candlestick in one hand. To his right, Kinnison strode, each step placed with deliberate care. Instead of looking around, his eyes scanned the ground, avoiding every rock or dip, ensuring as smooth a ride as possible for Aeylin. For her part, despite the sweat which covered her brow and the grimace of pain which had become a permanent feature on her pretty face, the pregnant werewolf remained silent. The medicines Celeste has sent with them to ease her pain had been left in the castle in their haste to escape. Whenever Kinnison looked back to check on her, she managed to give him a faint smile, trying even now to spare him from her pain. Karn followed behind, guarding their rear. With every cluster of trees they passed, the dryad would pause long enough to place his palm against the tree's trunk, closing his eyes for a minute in silent communication before hurrying to catch up.

"The trees can all talk to each other, sending messages

carried on the wind with ruffles their leaves. I'm asking for their help to warn us of any danger," Karn said, in answer to Zara's baffled look.

The sun had reached its midday peak and heat beat down on the group, making them all sweat. They had been walking for hours, and Luca was about to call for a break when Symon suddenly froze. Karn, his eyes on the glade of trees ahead of them, almost walked into him. With a roll of his shoulders and a motion of his head, Symon signalled for the women to dismount. As soon as both hit the ground, Symon transformed, "There is someone up ahead. He's hiding up in the trees and doing a pretty poor job of it."

Lowering Nero to the ground, Luca released his grip on the stretcher. He scrunched his fingers which had become stiff, saying softly to Symon, "Friend or foe?"

"I doubt he's friendly. We're not even halfway to the border. Either way, better to not take any chances."

"Agreed. He's alone?" Symon nodded. With a hand signal, Luca motioned the group to form a huddle. "Nero, Beth, Marika, Karn, Emma, Zara and Aeylin stay here and stay hidden. The rest of us will find out if this watcher is any danger to us."

"I'm not leaving Aeylin," Kinnison countered, now in human form.

"We need you. You are the only one who can convince this guy that we are here with Tibarn's authority. Plus, he's less likely to shoot at us if it means risking hitting you. Myles," Luca turned to look at the boy, "If you're up for it, I would like you to walk with Kinnison. Having a servant along might make us less suspicious. But if you're too scared you can stay here."

"No, I'll come," Myles said, standing a little straighter.

"Good. If things turn ugly, then I want you to run as fast as you can to warn everyone."

"I can fight," Myles said indignantly.

"I'm sure you can," Luca said, managing to hide his smile, "But Marika will need your help protecting the others. I'm entrusting you to look after Beth and Aeylin." Myles nodded solemnly.

"Symon, Otto and I will walk with Kinnison. Let's try and give the impression that we are just out for a stroll. Kinnison is giving us an official tour of his father's lands. Let's try and be as non-threatening as we can." His words made Emma giggle, and she quickly put her hand over her mouth to stifle the sound.

"Sorry," she whispered. "But just how are you four meant to look non-threatening?"

"She has a point," admitted Karn. "Perhaps I should go, and Symon should stay. Even in this form, he looks intimidating." Symon was about to argue, but Luca cut him off.

"He's right. Stay here and look after the others. I'm sure that we can handle one watcher without you." Symon muttered something under his breath but stepped back to stand near Nero. "Let's go."

Kinnison strolled with Luca and Karn, one on each side, pointing out landmarks and rambling on about the borders of the pack's lands. The direction he led them in would pass the trees, hopefully giving the impression that they were unaware of being watched. The tension across the werewolf's shoulders betrayed how anxious he was leaving Aeylin behind. For someone who was seeing another side to life, Luca thought that he was holding it together pretty well. But the sooner they got Aeylin to safety, the better, preferably before Kinnison snapped.

Myles followed five paces behind his master as was expected of a servant, his eyes down. His hands were both clenched into fists at his side. Luca hoped his decision to bring the boy was the right one. If anything happened to him, he would never forgive himself. Otto, for his part, was the perfect actor. He'd wandered ten paces to the right, and the expression on his face could only be described with one word. Bored. Every few minutes he yawned so broadly that Luca had to fight the urge to yawn himself.

When they were in line with the trees, Karn said, perhaps a tad too loudly, "I'm going to go talk to those trees." He ambled off in their direction while the others stopped and waited. The plan was for Karn, the least threatening of them all after Myles, to approach first and suss out the situation. If the watcher appeared friendly, then he would signal for the others to approach. If he didn't, then they were only giving the enemy one potential hostage instead of five and Karn has assured them that the trees would defend him. At the slightest sign of danger, Myles would sprint back to where the others waited, and Otto, Kinnison and Luca would attack. Watching Karn disappear into the cluster of trees Luca felt a sudden shiver of foreboding run down his back. At his side, Kinnison tensed. Myles started bouncing on the balls of his feet, ready to run. Even Otto lost his vacant, bored look. Minutes, which felt like hours, passed and Luca was about to make the call when Karn came back into view. Luca released a breath, unaware until that moment that he had been holding it.

Karn held up one hand, palm open, the agreed signal that all was well, at least for the moment. Luca would have preferred if the stranger had come out with him but saw no sign of the watcher. Left with little choice, the party headed towards the trees.

"All is well?" Luca asked, voice low.

"Yes and no," admitted Karn, his face splitting into a wide grin. "But I've taken care of it." Karn led them further into the trees where Luca was a little stunned to discover a faun tied to a tree. Actually, on closer inspection, Luca thought that tied wasn't quite the right word. The faun was enfolded into the branches. One was wrapped around his waist, holding him tight against the trunk. Another was wrapped around the faun's throat, not quite tight enough to strangle but definitely enough to make movement uncomfortable. The faun was shouting what Luca could only guess to be profanities at them, his words muffled by the bushel of leaves stuffed into his mouth.

"He tried to jump from his perch and attack me. Would have worked too if the tree hadn't decided to interfere on my behalf," Karn chuckled.

"You are full of surprises," Luca said, clapping the dryad on the shoulder. So much for Karn being non-threatening, Luca couldn't have done it better himself. "Myles, go warn the others. Tell them to get ready to move." The boy sprinted off as Luca turned to Kinnison, "Do you recognise him?"

"No, but that doesn't mean a lot. My father has hundreds of tenants who work his lands."

"Karn, can you ask the tree to remove the leaves so we can question him?"

Karn placed his hand on the trunk, and at his request, the leaves started to extract themselves from the faun's mouth. As soon as his mouth was free, the faun began to rant.

"When Tibarn hears how you have treated me you are all dead. How dare you abuse me?"

Kinnison stepped forward. "Mind your tongue. These are my friends. How dare you insult them or me?"

"Oooh, I'm so scared," the faun spat at Kinnison. "The pup has grown claws. Don't fool yourself. Everyone knows that it's Tibarn who holds power, not you. You are nothing without your father. He sent word that if any of his tenants saw you travelling these lands without his wolves they would be richly rewarded for the information." Kinnison's face turned so red it almost matched his hair, and his body started to radiate heat. Raising his hand, the fingers sprouting claws, he was inches from slashing the faun to pieces when Luca grabbed hold of his arm, just managing with all his strength to pull the werewolf away.

"I don't think you will have a chance to tell anyone anything. Karn?" At Luca's words, Karn's hand returned to the trunk of the tree. On silent command, the leaves started to shove themselves back into the faun's mouth, despite the fact he tried his hardest to clamp his lips closed. Two of the leaves pushed so hard that they ripped his bottom lip and blood began to drip down his goatee.

Kinnison still looked ready to pounce so Luca maintained his grip on the werewolf's arm. In a calm voice, he said, "If your father has sent scouts to keep an eye out for us, then it is only a matter of time before they find us. Our time would be better spent getting the hell out of here instead of killing this worthless spy." When Kinnison still failed to react, Luca played his trump card. "We need to ensure Aeylin's safety." At the mention of his mate's name, Kinnison's body started to relax. With one last growl at the faun, he turned and sprinted through the trees. By the time he was out of their shadow, he was in wolf form, racing towards where his mate waited with the others.

"What should we do with him?" Karn asked.

"Leave him here. Tibarn's men will find him eventually. If they don't, then I guess he'll starve," Otto suggested.

"Will Tibarn's men hurt the tree for helping us?" Luca asked.

"The trees can look after themselves, but perhaps it would be better if he remained hidden for a few days. A few days without food won't kill him, and it might make him rethink where his loyalties lie," Karn answered with an evil chuckle. Luca was shocked by the suggestion. He hadn't known that the usually peace-loving dryad had such a dark side.

"Alright. Ask the trees to hold the spy for forty-eight hours, then release him. By then, we should be safely within the Guild walls, and he will be too weak to be any danger to anyone." At the declaration of his intended fate, the faun began to struggle violently against his bonds. But the harder he fought, the more the branches tightened their hold.

"You're only hurting yourself," Karn warned him, before turning his back and walking out of the cluster of trees. Otto and Luca exchanged a startled look.

"Remind me to never get on his bad side," Otto muttered. Luca nodded his head before following Karn out.

CHAPTER 31

Waiting sucked. Sometimes Zara felt like she spent her life waiting for Luca, but doing so while he was walking into potential danger was even worse. When Luca had told her to stay behind, she had wanted to scream at him and beg to be allowed to go with them. But she knew he would refuse. She wasn't a fighter, and her presence would only distract him. With so much at stake, they couldn't risk it. Marika and Symon patrolled the perimeter, making sure that nothing surprised the group while they waited. She had offered to help, but Symon had gently suggested that she check on Aeylin and Nero instead.

Aeylin rested against one of the trees, her eyes closed, her breathing calm. Beth sat next to her, softly stroking her brow. To distract herself Zara decided to check on Nero. Walking over to the wolf, she saw that his paw had started bleeding again, so she applied pressure to it. When she pulled her hand away, her fingers covered in blood, the bleeding had stopped.

"Try and keep it elevated," she said, moving to lie next to the wolf so that he could rest the injured paw in her lap. Wiping her hands through the grass, she managed to remove most of the blood, wiping the rest of it off on her jeans. Good thing the cupboard had chosen the colour black.

Emma, taking advantage of the quiet moment, came and sat next to Zara and, tearing more strips of yellow fabric from her dress, began to redress Nero's wounds. For a moment the two women sat in silence, listening for any sign of the others returning.

"So, what happened with you and Luca last night?" Emma asked, breaking the silence.

Nero's eyes, which had been closed, startled open.

"I don't think that now is the right time to discuss that," Zara said, eyes going from Nero to Emma.

"What time is better? Plus, so what if the wolf finds out. Won't he know any way through his bond with Luca?" Zara didn't think that was how the bond worked. "Come on," Emma prompted. "If I'm about to die trying to outrun a pack of werewolves at least let me die satisfied. Please," she begged, palms together in appeal to the gossip gods.

"Fine," Zara agreed with a laugh. She could never say no to Emma for long. She had to admit little gossip would pass the time. "What do you want to know?

"Everything," Emma said, moving and tucking her legs under her to make herself more comfortable.

"Well as you know, the smell of the meat was making me sick, so Luca took me outside for some fresh air and –" Emma cut her off.

"We don't have time for all that. Skip to the good bits."

"We danced under the moonlight, and then we went back to Luca's room and, well, it was amazing. He makes me feel beautiful and loved and like I'm the most precious thing in the world."

"Just like a fairy tale." Emma sighed happily.

"I guess you could say that," Zara laughed. "But waking up next to him just felt so right. Like it was where I'm meant to be."

Sitting up a little straighter, leaning forward, tone suddenly serious, Emma asked in a low voice, "Now tell me the truth. Does he look as hot without his clothes as I think he does?"

Zara was saved from answering by Myles who came rushing through the trees. He had sprinted so fast that for a minute he couldn't speak, struggling to get breath into his lungs. Marika and Symon returned as Myles finally managed to gasp out, "They're alright. Luca wants us to get ready to leave. They've captured a faun."

"A faun?" Symon asked, confused.

While Emma and Beth helped Aeylin to her feet, Myles filled them in on what had happened up until Luca sent him away. Symon had shifted, and Zara and Emma were clambering onto his back as Kinnison came bursting through the trees. Stopping just short of Aeylin, he started sniffing her all over, searching for injury. It reminded Zara so much of the way Bronson greeted her after she visited strange dogs that she almost laughed. But the next moment Luca, Karn and Otto came crashing into the clearing. Otto and Luca moved to the stretcher and, as one, lifted it up.

"Let's move. I'll fill you in as we go."

～

Knowing that spies could have sent word of their escape proved an excellent motivator for the group to increase their pace. Instead of walking, Otto and Luca began to jog with the stretcher. As they went, the two, with Karn's help, completed the telling of events that Myles had started. When they repeated the insults that the faun had thrown at Kinnison, Aeylin spat out, "That little piece of dragon dung," and ran her fingers through Kinnison's coat in comfort.

"So, Tibarn has spies out looking for us?" Emma confirmed.

"Seems that he was covering all angles. I doubt he actually credited us with being able to escape, but Tibarn didn't get to be Alpha by being a fool. The faster we get out of his territory, the better. Marika?" The centaur had been scouting out in front. At Luca's call, she circled and trotted back to the group. "I want you to gallop as fast as you can to the Guild. Falcon should have reached Skylar by now, and hopefully, there are Guardians on their way to us already. Find them, and update them on our position." Beth and Myles started to dismount, sure that the centaur would not want them slowing her down, nor the embarrassment of being seen with riders on her back. But Marika stopped them before they could complete the swing of their legs, "Stay with me, little ones. Your weight is not enough to slow me down, and I will not leave you. Hold on, tight as you can."

"But I thought you said it will hurt you?" Myles said eyes full of worry.

"I did, but I can stand the pain. It will hurt less than the fear of you two falling and being trampled under my hooves." With a gulp Myles grabbed tighter around her waist, making Marika wince slightly. Beth, seated behind him, scooted forward and wrapped both arms around him in a firm embrace. "Ready?" Marika asked, and when the two riders nodded, she flew into a gallop, leaving nothing but a cloud of dust behind.

Next, Luca turned to Symon and Kinnison.

"I know you're not going to like this, but both of you should also race on ahead. You'll make much better time without us. Aeylin needs to cross the border, or all this has been in vain. Emma and Zara aren't fighters, and they need to be kept safe." As Luca had expected, Symon shook his head violently at the idea of leaving a comrade behind. Zara and Emma both voiced their rejection loudly, but Luca stayed firm in his command. "If you go ahead then we won't have to worry about defending you and can make better time. They don't want us, so capturing us will mean nothing. Guardians make poor hostages. But if Tibarn catches two humans, it could lead to a war even greater than this one could be."

The bear growled loudly before giving the slightest nod of his head. He would follow Luca's command. Before the women had a chance to voice further frustration, he leapt forward, giving them no opportunity to dismount. Kinnison's dark eyes met Luca's for a long moment and then the prince, still in wolf form, did the unexpected. Reaching out one front paw he lowered his head and body into a bow. Then lifting his head, Aeylin clinging tightly to his back, he sprinted off after Symon.

"That's something you don't see every day," commented Otto, eyes wide. "The prince of a werewolf pack bowing to a bastard elf. No offence," He added with a quick smile.

"None taken. I'm still in shock myself. Karn, do you wish to go too?" With Luca's newfound appreciation of the dryad and why Skylar has chosen him for the mission, he kind of hoped he would choose to stay. Should it come to a fight, the Guardian would come in handy.

"No, I'm with you. Should Tibarn's wolves catch us, we can head for the trees. They will help us. Plus, I can swap out with you two. With three taking turns, we can share the load and go much faster." Luca nodded and gifted the dryad with a warm smile.

"The wise thing would be to hide me somewhere and leave me," Nero pointed out, but Luca ignored him. As far as he was concerned, that was not an option. Using his magic, Karn encouraged the stretcher to sprout longer handles, two feet in length instead of their original hand's breadth. Together, the three lifted the stretcher, Nero perched on top, so that the handles rested on Luca and Otto's shoulders. Once in place, Karn worked the handles so that they curved down the back of each, positioning the stretcher securely and comfortably. This new design gave them the ability to move much more freely, and Otto, who was in the lead, was able to face forwards. Luca was impressed by Karn's ingenuity. The dryad was a natural engineer.

At first, they made good time, covering miles at a steady

pace which swallowed the distance and yet could be maintained without too much strain. Or at least they should have been able to. However, after the first hour, Luca felt himself beginning to fade. Within two hours, his head had started to ache, and a sharp pain kept making itself known in his side. At first, willpower was enough to push past the pain, but they were still at least an hour's journey to the border when his knee spasmed and he stumbled. If Karn had not secured the stretcher so well, the tilt would have sent Nero flying. As it was, Nero almost slid off, but Karn managed to catch him and hold him in place.

"I'm sorry," Luca gasped, "I'm not sure what came over me. I need to stop. Catch my breath." With a signal to Otto, they lifted the stretcher off their shoulders and started to lower it to the ground. As they did so, Luca caught sight of Nero.

"Shit!" The ruff of Nero's coat was drenched in blood, and the wolf was barely conscious. The redesign of the stretcher had caused it to bounce and jar more than before, reopening his wounds, and the stubborn wolf has kept quiet. Blood had soaked the yellow bandage, dripping from his paw and throat wound so that the limbs of the stretcher were stained a dark red. Drops overflowed onto the ground below. Luca felt like a fool for not realising, and his anger rose. If this stupid act didn't kill Nero, he was going to. Stupid, stubborn wolf. No wonder that Luca was feeling poorly, Nero's life force was so drained he had started borrowing Luca's.

"We need to get help, and fast. Karn, can you take over this end from me?" Luca asked.

"Of course," Karn replied swapping places without hesitation.

"Thank you. You two need to go on ahead without me. If Nero doesn't get help soon, he will die, the stubborn fool. And I'll just slow you down." Otto and Karn exchanged a look before answering, almost in unison,

"No."

"But ..."

"No," repeated Otto, his voice firm. "You are in no fit state to command. We should cross the border soon. Without the weight of the stretcher, you should be able to make better time. We cross together."

"But ..."

"No buts, Luca," Karn added his own feelings to the debate. "You know as well as we that if you fall too far behind, it will affect Nero's ability to draw energy from the bond. If he dies, you will too, and I don't feel like being the one to tell Zara that we left you both to die."

"Emma might hit us with her candlestick," added Otto with a chuckle.

With a sigh, Luca gave in and gripped the edge of the stretcher for support. Together they began the slow journey towards the border.

CHAPTER 32

Zara, Emma and Symon crossed the invisible line which marked the border of Tibarn's territory with no sign of any of Lightfall's Guardians. The sun was bright, and Zara shaded her eyes, trying to catch sight of anything in the distance that might give her hope. But it was almost impossible to see and hold onto a galloping bear. Zara hadn't appreciated how much of an effort Symon had been making to keep the ride smooth for them until the necessity for speed had forced him to run at full pace. Every time one of his huge paws hit the ground, Zara felt a jolt run up her body, followed quickly by another as the other side hit, and another as each of his rear paws landed. It reminded her of the vibration platform her mother used to shake off extra weight. She just hoped that when they reached the Guild, her joints would still be connected.

Suddenly, Emma shouted, pointing to the sky in front of them, "Look, up there, is that Falcon?"

Zara squinted, searching the sky. The sun was so bright that at first, she could make nothing out. Then she saw it. The white bird soared overhead, flying in the direction they had been coming from. Zara and Emma shouted, waving their hands to try and catch her attention. But either she didn't see them or was choosing for some reason to ignore them. Either way, Zara felt relief wash over her. Falcon would find Luca, and he would know that help was coming.

Before long, the reason for Falcon ignoring them became evident. At first, Zara thought she imagined things when a blue hill came into view. As they got closer, however, it took on features, and she recognised Cansu, the blue water dragon that had worn herself out fighting the forest fire. Her scales were no longer a faded grey, but a vibrant azure blue which shimmered in the sunlight. Behind her, she heard Emma catch her breath, and then her friend started pounding Zara's back in her excitement. "Dragon!" Emma exclaimed, making Zara laugh. Her enthusiasm was contagious, and soon the two women were laughing and shouting together. Symon, catching their joy, started to bound. With each stride, more rescuers came into view. They saw Marika, panting hard, Beth and Myles still clinging to her back. Next to her stood Kinnison, no longer in wolf form, talking to an elf Zara didn't recognise, Aeylin cuddled close to his side. Their party had been met by a centaur, and four elves all mounted on horseback with two spare horses clipped to leads behind them. The last member of the rescue party Zara didn't recognise at first, obscured behind Kinnison's bulk. But as she stepped back, her red hair flowing in the breeze, Zara caught sight of Luca's sister.

"Brina," she called out. The fire witch turned, and, catching sight of Zara, broke into a run towards them, her red-painted mouth grinning widely. When Symon slowed enough so that she could dismount safely, Zara vaulted off his back and bolted to Brina. Brina's red hair mingled with Zara's black as the two friends embraced.

"I was at the Guild trying to find out what had happened when Falcon appeared. I demanded that Skylar let me accompany the others. You might need a healer and In could be spared," Brina explained. "Cansu offered to carry me, so Skylar could hardly refuse. Riding on a dragon was thrilling, but nothing compared the adventure you have had. I want to hear all about it."

"Of course. I'll tell you everything. But first, there is someone I want you to meet." Looking around, she spotted Emma standing awkwardly a few feet away and beckoned her closer. "Brina this is Emma, the amazing vet I was telling you about who works at The Haven with me. Emma this is Brina, Luca's sister." For a moment, the two redheads eyed each other speculatively. The two women were from two very different worlds and yet in some ways were so similar in their independence, sense of adventure and willingness to do anything to protect those they loved. Zara knew their meeting could go one of two ways. They would either love each other, or they'd discover that one realm wasn't big enough for both of them.

"Any friend of Zara's is a friend of mine," decided

Brina, and pulled a slightly startled Emma into a crushing embrace, kissing her loudly on both cheeks.

"It's a pleasure to meet you," Emma said warmly. Leaving the two to get better acquainted, Zara went to where Kinnison stood, still in conversation with the elf. The werewolf's brow was furrowed, and his shoulders were tight. Aeylin had a restraining hand on his arm. Not a good sign. Getting closer, Zara realised that the elf was trying to give Kinnison orders, something that the werewolf prince was not used to. Luca had earned his respect, so Kinnison listened to him. The tone the elf used, however, bordered on insulting. Stepping in before the two could come to blows, Zara asked, "What's going on here?"

The elf turned a frosty glare in her direction, and for a moment, Zara felt her own indignation start to rise. Then his gaze relaxed. She still didn't recognise him, but he must have been advised on her appearance for he greeted her politely.

"*Gode fen*, Mistress Zara. I am Jiel. Skylar sends instructions that you, Mistress Emma and Mistress Aeylin are to return to the Guild at once. The children will ride the spare horses and follow shortly after." When he said the word children, the elf had directed a dirty look in Kinnison's direction. Zara guessed that might be the reason behind his treatment of the werewolf, Helo had told her how much elves valued their children. "The rest of us are to continue on to meet Luca and the rest of your party."

"Aeylin stays with me," Kinnison growled.

"I'm afraid that is not an option. I am under strict

orders to ensure Aeylin is returned to the Guild. Her father is there, and I can assure you that she will be perfectly safe. No one will harm her while she is under our care," Jiel added the last with a smug look, unable to resist another dig at the werewolf. Kinnison's growl deepened, and Zara watched his lip curl but Jiel ignored it. Once again, though, it was Aeylin who got through to Kinnison. In a gentle voice, she said,

"Kinnison, I am exhausted. The sooner I can rest and see a healer, the better. Plus, you have a duty to Luca and the others. It would not be honourable to leave them in danger in your father's lands when your invitation is the reason they are there." To a werewolf, honour meant almost as much as family loyalty. Kinnison had already thrown one aside that day. Smearing his honour would break him.

"You are right, my love. I would be truly lost without you," Kinnison conceded, giving Aeylin a gentle kiss, first on her lips and then on her brow. Then he turned to Jiel with a cold stare, "But I will not leave until you are safely in the sky." The elf wisely chose to stay quiet. Lifting Aeylin into his arms Kinnison carried her towards the dragon.

His hands cupped, Symon boosted first Emma and then Zara onto Cansu's broad back. The dragon's scales were unexpectedly slippery, and Zara almost fell before she managed to grab hold of one of the spinal ridges. Waiting until both girls were in place Kinnison moved Aeylin so that she was positioned behind them, kissing the tips of her fingers before finally releasing her. If Cansu's flight turned out to be as bumpy as riding on

Symon's back, they would be lucky to make it to the Guild in one piece.

Zara had tried to convince Brina to come back with them, but the witch had refused. Brina would not return without her brother. A satchel was slung over Brina's shoulder containing lotions which she had brought to aid with healing. They wouldn't work as fast as Celeste's magic, but might mean the difference between life and death, buying Nero time to reach the fairy healer. Jiel had offered Brina the use of one of the spare horses. The other was already on its way back to the Guild, carrying Beth and Myles with Marika as an escort, the centaur refusing to lose sight of her young charges.

"Don't worry, we'll find him," Symon promised Zara.

"I know you will. I just wish I could go with you."

"Luca would want you out of harm's way. All will be well, you'll see." The smile Symon gave her fell short of his usual easy grin, not managing to entirely hide his concern for his friend. On impulse, Zara leaned down and kissed the bear shifter on the cheek, making him break into the genuine smile she was used to seeing on his handsome face.

"You come back safe, too," she ordered.

"Yes, ma'am." With a final smile and a slight bow in Aeylin and Emma's direction, Symon stepped back from the dragon.

"Hold on tight," Jiel instructed loudly as Cansu stood, propelled herself forward on legs as large as tree trunks, and with a sweeping whoosh of her wings, launched them into the air. The ground fell away below them as, with a dozen beats of her humongous wings, the dragon soared higher until the group were nothing more than tiny dots, miles below them. Zara and Emma screamed in delight. Riding a dragon was better than any rollercoaster. Behind them, in a voice barely loud enough to be heard above the wind, Aeylin said, "I think I'm going to be sick."

CHAPTER 33

Luca walked, one arm wrapped around Otto's shoulders, no longer able to support himself. His chest was a fiery ball of pain, and he gasped, trying to get enough air into his lungs. Every third step, he stumbled, and it was only Otto's strength that saved him each time. The group had been forced to reduce their pace to a slow crawl, as Luca's health had deteriorated with each mile. Three times, he had tried to convince the others to leave him behind. They had ignored him and instead did all they could to help him and Nero. Nero's condition frightened Luca. The wolf appeared to be hardly breathing. His eyes were closed, and their bond felt empty. Blood dripped in a constant stream, falling between the stretcher's branches to splash onto the road. It had been Otto who had made the call to move them onto the main road. The trail of blood would lead even an untrained baby werewolf directly to them. Ease of travel was more important than remaining hidden. Again, Luca had tried to debate against the choice, only to be ignored once again.

Licking his dry, cracked lips, Luca tried to focus all of his energy into moving forward. Putting one step in front of the other took more effort than he ever thought possible. Nevertheless, his thoughts kept returning to Zara and the others. If only he knew that she was safe and had reached help, he could relax. He should never have let her come with him to Tibarn's castle. He should have known that they were walking into a trap. He had thought that Kinnison's love for Aeylin would win over anything else, like his own love for Zara. But if this disastrous trip proved anything, it was that love didn't win all battles. And once they returned to the Guild, Skylar would send her home and he would never see her again. The thought was not helping him find the energy to continue.

Luca was trying to think of the right words to convince the others to leave him behind when he was startled out of his stupor by a loud cry as a dark shadow started circling them. His first thought was that it was carrion birds sensing that he was dying and coming to feast on his corpse. But looking up, he saw a large white bird circling over them before folding its wings into a dive and rapidly descending. Right before it smashed into the ground, the bird shimmered and transformed into Falcon. Her eyes went wide as she took in the sight, and Luca realised what a mess they all must look.

Taking up position next to Luca, Falcon moved one arm under Luca's other side, helping Otto to support his weight. With her help, they quickened their pace slightly, the bird shifter far stronger than her thin frame gave her credit for.

"Zara and Emma are safe," Falcon announced, starting with the news she knew would be most relevant to Luca. "So is Aeylin. Cansu has them and is taking them to Skylar."

"Cansu?" asked Karn in surprise.

"Yes. The dragon came with the elves and centaur that Skylar sent to find you. Jiel is leading them." Luca was glad. The elf was reliable and level headed, without the ego which often afflicted his race. "Brina is also with them." Usually, news of his sister meddling in Guardian affairs would concern Luca, but all he felt at that moment was relief. Brina would be able to help Nero. "But we need to hurry. There is a pack of wolves on your trail. They are still a fair distance away, but they are coming up fast. Good thing I found you when I did."

"It is indeed. How about we pick up the pace?" Otto asked. With silent agreement the party started to run, Luca no longer attempting to propel himself as he was lifted up, feet no longer reaching the ground.

By the time they reached the rescue party, Luca had lost consciousness, deadweight in Otto's arms. When Luca passed out, Falcon has taken the minotaur's position at the front of the stretcher, and Otto had lifted Luca to cradle him like a child. Had Luca been awake, he would have been embarrassed, but as both he and Nero were in no fit state to complain, or remember, the others decided for them. Watching them approach, a flicker of a smile crossed Jiel's lips, but it disappeared quickly as the elf greeted and got straight down to business. When Brina caught sight of her unconscious brother, she had almost fallen from her horse, she dismounted so fast. Pausing long enough only to grab to her satchel, she was pulling bottles and jars out as Jiel issued his orders.

"We cannot stop and tend their wounds or the werewolves will be upon us." Turning to the mounted elves, he said, "I need two of your horses. You will be swifter on foot than the others." Exchanging a quick look, two of the three elves dismounted. "Brina if we strap Nero in front of you on your horse do you think you can tend to him while we ride?" Brina hesitated, not wanting to leave Luca then nodded.

"You're right, of course. If someone can carefully strap Nero around his belly so that I have full access to his wounds, I should be able to help him."

"Done. Karn, can you take one of the horse and ride behind Luca? We can strap him to you so that he doesn't fall?"

"Yes, sir," the dryad quickly agreed.

"Good. That leaves the other horse for Otto. I recommend the stallion. It will be better able to support your weight." The wish to refuse flashed across Otto's face before he forced himself to nod agreement. It was rare for minotaurs to ride horses unless in dire situations. Their bulky weight, combined with their large horns and top-heaviness, meant riding could be difficult. He didn't have a wolf draining his life force, but Otto had to admit he was exhausted. The strains of a day which started with him being drugged and hadn't yet ended were wearing him down.

As fast as they could, the party mounted and prepared

to head back to the Guild. The dismounted elves helped tie Luca and Nero to their respective saddles before running out in front, ready to act as scouts. Kinnison and Symon took their positions at the rear, ready to guard their injured friends from potential attack. Sniffing the air, Symon stated, "I can smell the werewolves. They are less than a mile away."

"Thank you, Symon. Please keep us updated. Everyone, let's move out." As one the party picked up the pace and were soon racing back in the direction of the Lightfall Guild.

CHAPTER 34

Zara was surprised at how quickly Cansu covered the distance back to the Guild. To her, the ride felt like it had lasted minutes. Looking at the green pallor of Aeylin's skin, it had felt a lot longer for the pregnant werewolf. Poor Aeylin spent the entire journey trying her hardest not to spew the little food she had eaten that day down the dragon's gleaming blue scales. For Aeylin's sake alone, Zara was glad that the ride was short. For herself, she felt like she could have ridden on Cansu's back for hours. She had never felt so free.

Nearing the high walls of the Guild, Zara was struck by the difference from when they had left. Guardians, dressed in full armour, strolled the ramparts. The large gate was locked, and spikes had been set up around the base of the castle. Three archers aimed their arrows in the dragon's direction even when they were close enough to be recognised as friendly. The Guild was on high alert, and no one was taking any chances. Within the courtyard, more Guardians were distributing swords and crossbows, and the number of guards encircling the rift had tripled. As Cansu started to land, Skylar exited his office and met them in the courtyard as they touched down. The Commander was also dressed in battle armour. A polished steel breastplate covered his broad chest, and his horse body was protected by chainmail. Even his hooves had spikes attached to use as weapons should the need arise. In his hand, he held a wooden spear, its steel point razor-sharp and giving off a red glow.

Skylar stopped a few feet short of the dragon and waited for the women to dismount before speaking. The second Aeylin stumbled to the ground she held a hand over her mouth, eyes searching frantically. Guessing her needs, Skylar pointed towards the stables. Aeylin made it just in time, falling to her knees before emptying the contents of her stomach into an empty bucket.

"It seems that werewolves are not fans of flying?" Skylar asked, voice low.

"Poor Aeylin," Emma agreed. "She did not have a good time though that could be due to her pregnancy. But at least she's safe now, right?"

"That is yet to be determined. At the moment it is anyone's guess what Tibarn's next move will be."

"Surely he won't risk his position on the Council by attacking a Guardian Guild?" Zara asked, shocked.

Skylar gave her a long look. She couldn't tell if he was surprised at her understanding of Wundor politics, or thought her a fool for assuming Tibarn valued his position on the Council above the threat that Aeylin's child posed to his family. When he did speak, his answer surprised her with its openness.

"Tibarn can be persuasive. He has a long history of getting the Council to look the other way when he bends the rules. Will he attack us openly? My guess would be no. Would he bribe someone else to do it for him? Most certainly."

When Aeylin rejoined them, wiping her mouth on the back of her hand, he continued, "That is why I believe the three of you should wait in your world until this issue is resolved."

"And how long will that take?" Aeylin asked fearfully.

"I cannot say, but I don't believe things will take too long to come to a head, one way or another. Once it is safe, I will send Luca to collect you."

"Kinnison won't be happy," Aeylin warned.

"Kinnison will have no choice but to listen to logic, and will no doubt appreciate that you and his child are safe."

"Aeylin is carrying a wolf. I haven't assisted with a human birth, let alone one like this," Emma pointed out.

"I will ask Celeste to send some of her medicines with you. You will have to do the best you can. Hopefully, this will resolve itself favourably before the child comes. I have sent messengers to the other Guilds asking for their help, as I cannot risk conversing with them via a portal where there is a chance of being intercepted. When they arrive, we will have enough forces to push the odds in our favour."

A hundred questions flew around Zara's mind, but

before she could voice even one, Skylar said, "I must go. There is much work to be done. See Celeste, and then I bid you go." With a slight bow of his head, Skylar spun and trotted off in the direction of the mess hall.

The fairy was overjoyed to see them, greeting each with a hug and kiss. While Celeste scanned Aeylin to check on the health of the cub, she questioned Zara and Emma about the extent of Nero's injuries. A crease of worry appeared between her perfectly shaped brows when they mentioned the gash along his throat, and deepened when Zara said that Nero's paw had been gushing blood.

"But I managed to get it to stop by applying pressure," Zara tried to reassure Celeste.

"That worked?"

"Yes." Zara confirmed, "Why?"

"A wound that deep would usually take some sort of intervention to stop the flow. I wouldn't have thought that pressure alone would have worked."

"Zara has the magic touch," joked Emma. "She managed to get Aeylin's spasms under control too."

"Really?" The fairy looked Zara up and down, as if seeing her for the first time. She looked as if she was about to say something when Aeylin gave a sudden groan of pain. Instantly, everyone's attention was claimed by the image of the pup floating, suspended, above Aeylin. It was vibrating. "It would seem that your child takes after his father. I had hoped we would have more time, but he appears impatient to be born. Your labour had started."

"No, that can't be right," Aeylin cried. "He isn't due for

another couple of weeks. He can't come now. I'm not ready!"

"All mothers feel that way when their labour starts. I assure you that you will be fine," Celeste soothed, her voice barely betraying her own worry. No matter what Celeste said, everyone in the room knew that the timing of Aeylin's labour couldn't be worse. "The child is almost fully formed, so we don't have to concern ourselves with that. Plus, if you are anything like most first time mothers, this labour is likely to stretch out for hours if not days."

"If Aeylin comes to our world then with the time difference the fight could be over before the baby is even born," Zara offered.

"Time difference?" Emma asked, confused.

"Our time moves roughly five times slower than here in Wundor. It was why I was able to spend three days here last time, and you thought I'd only had a one-night stand."

"Yeah, sorry about that," Emma said looking awkward for all the teasing she and Josh had directed at Zara.

"It doesn't matter now," Zara said, accepting her friend's apology with a smile.

"I can give you something to help slow the contractions and something to ease the pain. The one advantage of him coming early is that his claws are one of the last things to develop, so there will be less risk of internal damage."

"I'm scared," Aeylin said in a small voice. Taking one of her hands, Emma reassured her.

"I'll look after you Aeylin, I promise. Nothing will happen to you or your pup."

"I'll help too. We won't leave you. We promise," Zara added, taking Aeylin's other hand.

Aeylin braved a smile.

"Thank–" she started before her words were cut off by a scream she struggled to muffle as another contraction coursed through her body. The image of the pup began to vibrate violently.

"Zara, stay with Aeylin. Emma come with me, and I'll show you how to apply the potions." Within minutes, Celeste and Emma were back. Emma carried a wicker basket stuffed with bottles, bandages, and an assortment of other medicines Zara didn't recognise. Helping Aeylin up off the bed, Zara and Emma each wrapped an arm around to help support her.

"Thank you, Celeste," Aeylin said.

Kissing her cheek, the fairy murmured quietly, "May the Goddess watch over you and your child." With a final hug for the woman, they turned and made their way out of the healers' quarters. They had to pause at the stairs leading down to the courtyard, and another contraction racked Aeylin's body.

"Hold on, Aeylin. Once we are through the rift, I can apply the potions to slow these down and ease your pain."

"Can't you give her something now?" Zara asked.

"No. Celeste was concerned about how they might affect her during the transit."

Zara shrugged, guessing that made sense. Being an only child, she knew less about pregnancy than Emma did. Once the last of the tremors passed, they continued down the stairs and into the courtyard. As they crossed out of the stairwell, the nearby Guardians stopped their work to watch them pass. Part of Zara expected to see hostility in their eyes at having dragged them into this fight. She wouldn't have blamed them. Instead, all she felt was support and friendship. As they passed, each paused to bow their heads and most offered quiet words of good luck.

Brax was waiting for them near the rift. When Aeylin's gaze met her father's, tears started to fall down her cheeks. Walking to meet them, head held high with pride in those he called brothers, Brax said in a voice loud enough for everyone in the courtyard to hear, "The Guardians are with you, daughter. You are my blood and as such, one of us, and we protect our own." Then, breaking his professional stance, he swept her up in his arms, hugging her as tightly as her swollen belly would allow. He whispered words in her ear, too quiet for anyone else to hear, but they had the effect of making Aeylin smile through her tears. After a long moment, he released her and turned to Zara and Emma. "For what you have done to protect my daughter, you have my gratitude and my protection. Consider yourselves family." At his announcement, all the Guardians in the courtyard started to cheer. Zara wasn't sure if she was more embarrassed by the sudden attention or proud, but either way, she was happy. These creatures from another world had become her friends, had welcomed her, had made her family. Catching Emma's eye, she wondered if her own smile looked as goofy as her friend's. She guessed it probably did.

Brax escorted them to the rift's edge. She felt Emma's hand find hers and give her a squeeze. As before, they would enter the rift together. With a smile, Zara said to Aeylin, "We'll wait for you on the other side," and without waiting for an answer, the two women stepped forward and disappeared, leaving the werewolves with a chance to say goodbye alone.

CHAPTER 35

O ver an hour after the three women had crossed through the rift, Marika, Beth and Myles came galloping through the Guild's gates. Pausing long enough for the two servants to dismount from their horse, Marika directed them to the healers' quarters before going off to find Skylar. She found him in the storeroom, directing provisions to be moved so they were spread throughout the Guild. If it came to a siege, he wanted to ensure that all the food stores could not be taken out with one well-aimed attack. Marika waited, trying not to stamp her hoof with impatience, while he finished communicating his plan to a nervous-looking pixie. As the pixie flew off to do his bidding, Marika said, "Commander."

Turning, a look of relief passed across Skylar's face at the sight of her.

"You're back."

"Yes, sir. Myles and Beth arrived with me. I've sent them to Celeste, I thought they would be safest with her."

"Good call. How far behind you are the others?"

"They shouldn't be more than an hour behind us, but I have bad news, I'm afraid."

The centaur shrugged his broad shoulders. The bad news was to be expected.

"Tell me."

"Nero is badly injured, and Luca is unconscious." Seeing his face fall, she quickly added, "But Brina is with them and doing what she can."

"I guess there is nothing we can do about that right now. Is that all?"

"No, sir. There is a pack of werewolves on their trail. Our team should outrun them, but it might not be by much."

"Tibarn's wolves?"

"I can't say, sir. Falcon spotted them when she was flying to Luca's group, and she didn't want to get too close and risk being recognised."

"Was she able to give you a count?"

"Fourteen, that she could see, although she did say that there could have been more hiding in the woods. She thought she spotted movement, but couldn't be sure."

"Well, at least that gives us something to work with," Skylar said, his nod making his dreadlocks bounce around his shoulders. "Thank you. Go tell Celeste about Luca, and then get some rest. You look exhausted."

"I am, sir, but I want to help."

"You have helped. I heard what you did, letting the young werewolves ride on your back." His comment made Marika bow her head, waiting for Skylar to scold her. Instead, his words were gentle, "There aren't many centaurs that would put the good of others above their own pride. I am proud to know that I have one such as you in my ranks."

Marika's head came up, eyes glistening.

"Thank you, sir."

"Now, rest. You've earned it, and it's an order."

"Yes, sir," Marika said with a shy smile.

Luca struggled to open his eyes. His lids felt so heavy, as if they were made of lead. He was tempted to give up, but a little voice in the back of his mind nagged at him, not letting him fall back into the peaceful darkness. It murmured that he forgot something, something important. He tried to remember, he honestly did, but the rocking motion of the horse lulled his mind. Then another thought began to tug at his memory, why was he riding a horse? Trying to move his arms, he was a little alarmed to find he couldn't. He tried again. Same result. Something was wrapped around him. His alarm peaking, he made a valiant effort once more to open his eyes. Tentatively, they opened. Blinding light assaulted them, and he fought the urge to close his eyes again. Instead, taking a deep breath, he started to blink his eyes rapidly, helping his pupils adjust to the light. As the sunlight slowly began to be bearable, he looked around and caught sight of Nero, strapped across the front of Brina's horse. The events of the day came crashing back. Zara, where was Zara? Luca started thrashing against his bindings as he struggled to look around him.

"Take it easy, Luca, you're upsetting the horse," Karn warned, slowing his horse, which was starting to fidget in reaction to Luca's struggles.

"Where's Zara?"

"Zara is safe. Cansu carried her, Emma and Aeylin to the Guild hours ago." Luca let out a deep breath.

"How's Nero?"

Brina, who had pulled her horse to stop beside Karn's, answered, "Not as well as you, but he'll be alright once Celeste gets a chance to heal him. It's good to see some colour coming back into your face. You scared me."

"I scared myself," Luca admitted. "Thanks for having my back."

"Always."

"You can fill Luca in on the rest while we ride. The pack is still on our heels, and I would like to have as much distance as possible between them and us before we reach the Guild," Jiel ordered, before pulling a dagger from his boot and passing it to Karn. "Cut Luca's restraints, assuming of course that he feels up to riding without them."

"I do. Thank you, Jiel, I owe you one."

"You owe me nothing, Luca. I know you would have done the same for me."

Watching him ride back to the front of the group, Luca couldn't help but smile as Karn said in a quiet voice, "You know for an elf, Jiel isn't half bad."

The gates were open when they came within sight of the

castle; one of the Guardians on lookout spied them in the distance and alerted those manning the gate. As Kinnison and Symon, the rear guards, stepped across the threshold, the gate was slammed shut behind them, and the heavy metal bars slid into place with a bang. Waiting until everyone was safe inside the guild walls, two witches started spelling the gate, and then, heading in different directions, they began creating a protection circle around the inside of the outer wall. They had taken, with Skylar's permission, all of the salt from the kitchens. As a result, the cook had threatened that should there be a siege and the food was bland, it would be no fault of his.

Skylar and Celeste met them in the courtyard. Not wishing to risk further injury, Celeste used her magic to lift Nero from Brina's horse, and hurried him up the stairs to the infirmary. Despite Luca's protests that he was fine, he was ordered to follow. Brina, having dismounted and handed the charge of her horse to a waiting pixie, wrapped one arm around Luca, promising Skylar that she would ensure his orders were followed. Once the injured were taken care of, Skylar turned his focus to the pending battle. But before he could start questioning Jiel for details, Kinnison, once again in human form, shoved past the elf, eyes wide and searching.

"Where is Aeylin?" Kinnison demanded, grabbing hold of Skylar's arm. His worry added to his strength and there was a scraping noise as the metal of the centaur's arm greaves dented under the pressure of his fingers. Abashed, Kinnison released Skylar's arm as if it had burnt him.

Skylar, with a slight frown on his face as he took in the four finger marks now gouged in his armour, said, "I sent her across the rift into the human realm with Emma and Zara. She will be safe there."

A range of emotions flashed across Kinnison's face. Anger, grief, and then finally acceptance, "What can I do to help?"

"I need to know how far away our likely attackers are."

"I estimate they will reach the castle within the next thirty minutes, at most."

"If you tell them to stand down, will they listen to you?" Kinnison shook his head.

"No. My father would not be foolish enough to send any of my own wolves against me. Whoever he sends will be loyal to him and him alone."

"What do you think your father plans to do? You know his mind better than I."

"He will do whatever he must to ensure that my son is never born." Kinnison sighed, finally admitting the truth to himself as well as Skylar. "I was a fool to think that my wishes and his own blood would make any difference to him. I led all of us straight into his trap."

Symon, who had been standing silently next to Kinnison while he conversed with Skylar, placed one large hand on the werewolf's shoulder.

"Do not blame yourself for your father's betrayal. Love blinds us all." For a moment, Symon thought that Kinnison was going to shrug his hand away, but instead, the werewolf prince simply nodded his head.

"I've sent for reinforcement from the other Guilds," Skylar informed them. "We just need to hold out until they arrive. We've warded the gates and the outer walls.

They should hold them off, but should they fail, we must ready for when the fighting starts."

Up in the healers' quarters, Luca was having a frustrating time. He wanted to be downstairs with the others, prepping to defend the Guild. He wanted to cross the rift and see with his own eyes that Zara was safe. But instead, he was stuck waiting on one of the beds until Celeste deemed him recovered enough to go back to his duties. He fidgeted, his left hand scrunching the bed sheet into a ball and twisting it over and over again. His right foot tapped an inconsistent beat onto the floor.

"Luca, if you don't stop that infernal tapping, I will knock you out, and you won't be any good to anyone for hours," Celeste threatened her voice stern. Luca's foot froze. "If you want to make yourself useful, sort that pile of bandages by size and distribute them between the beds. We may not have time to waste later when the patients come flooding in."

"Do you really think that the werewolves will breach the walls?" Brina asked. The witch had offered to help, and was busily crushing herbs and crystals to mix with creams and ointments, ready for the wounded. At first, Brina thought that Celeste hadn't heard her, as she took a long minute to answer. Her focus was all on Nero, who lay unconscious on her table. She had knocked him out to save him from the pain the healing would cause. His paw was a bloody mess, and despite their best efforts had become contaminated with splinters of stone and wood during his escape from the castle. If Celeste couldn't get every bit out before she used her magic, then the wound would never heal properly.

"In my years here as a healer, I have learnt to never underestimate an enemy," Celeste said, triumphantly pulling out a splinter and disposing of it in a tray. "Tibarn does not seem to me to be the type to give up easily, and he has powerful friends." Brina's eyes met Luca's, and they shared a worried look. If the usually optimistic fairy was predicting bloodshed, then they could only hope that reinforcements would arrive in time.

CHAPTER 36

Zara waited with Emma in the cluster of trees bordering the rift for Aeylin to join them. Night had fallen, and the stars shone like a blanket of wishes above them. The cool night breeze ruffled her hair and made the leaves chatter, reminding her of Karn. Breathing in deeply, Zara inhaled the scents of eucalyptus and felt her body relax. It was the smell of home. Despite the worry that she still felt for Luca and her friends, she couldn't ignore the fact that part of her was happy to be home.

"Maybe one of us should go and let Marx know we are here?" Emma asked.

"No point. Aeylin won't be long." As if summoned by Zara's words, Aeylin appeared, stumbling as she fell out of the rift. Shaking badly, her legs unable to hold her weight, Aeylin collapsed to the ground, just barely managing to put her hands out to stop herself from smashing her head open. Zara and Emma rushed to help her, but didn't reach her in time to prevent her belly hitting the ground hard. Aeylin let out a whimper of pain.

"Grab her under her other arm, Zara. We need to get her to the house now!" Together, they lifted Aeylin between them. The werewolf, on the verge of losing consciousness, was a deadweight in their arms and they struggled to move her.

"Marx!" screamed Zara, knowing that if the werewolf were anywhere on the property, he would hear them. A minute later, a dark brown wolf came running from the direction of the farmhouse. As he caught sight of them, he shimmered, taking man-form.

"What in all the worlds is going on?" Marx asked, sweeping Aeylin up into his arms.

"No time for that now. We need to get Aeylin inside."

"I'll tell you later," Zara promised before running ahead to the farmhouse, leaping the stairs in a single bound, and opening the door wide so that Marx could carry Aeylin through.

"Where should I put her?" he asked, looking to Emma for direction.

"The sofa will have to do. Do you have any blankets or bed sheets we could use to cover it? I have a feeling this is going to get messy." Marx gently lowered Aeylin and laid her on the sofa.

"I'll fetch the blankets."

Emma brushed her hand across Aeylin's forehead with one hand while taking her pulse with the other.

"Is she going to be okay?" Zara asked.

"She's really clammy, and her pulse is racing. I think travelling through the rift this late in her pregnancy may not have been the best idea. Can you pass me the vials that Celeste gave us?"

Zara opened the satchel and pulled out the two vials. Handing them to Emma, she helped her tilt up Aeylin's head so that she could swallow the contents. As Marx returned with the blankets, Aeylin's eyes fluttered open.

"The baby?" she asked in a shaky voice.

"He's alright, I think. I'm more worried about you. I'm going to examine you, okay?" Emma asked.

To give them some privacy, Zara and Marx stepped out onto the porch. Reclining into the porch swing, happy to rest her feet after a long day, Zara closed her eyes and just let the fresh air calm her nerves. Marx leaned against the wall, watching her, giving her time to relax, and a comfortable silence flowed between them. Zara was grateful that Marx was there and that, without the others, he seemed to have become the friend she remembered.

"So, for me, it's been about four and a half hours since you left. I'm guessing that it's seemed a lot longer for you?" Marx asked, unable to hide his interest for long.

Opening her eyes, Zara tried to think of how to simplify all that had happened between them crossing into Wundor and their desperate struggle to return. She could hardly believe that in this world, it was still the same night they left. It made her nervous for what was happening to Luca and the others while she sat safely here, gently rocking back and forward on the swing.

"It seems like forever since we crossed the rift," she admitted. "Kinnison invited us to his father's castle on the promise that Aeylin would be safe there. Turns out he was wrong."

Marx watched, brow furrowing and lips tightening, as she recalled everything that had befallen them. She thought he would be shocked when she mentioned Onyx's attempt on Aeylin's life, yet Marx stood stiffly, uttering no comment. "Now the Guild is trying to fend off Tibarn, who seems willing to do anything to remove the threat of Aeylin's child. Especially as he knows that it is a boy."

"The child is male?" Marx asked.

"Sorry, I must have forgotten to mention that. Celeste did a scan, and the pup is a boy. He will be Tibarn's heir after Kinnison."

"Not if–" Marx's statement was cut off when a scream of pain shattered the quiet night. Jumping off the swing so fast it was flung violently backwards and hit the wall, Zara rushed into the house. She gasped as she took in the sight of Aeylin, her legs spread wide apart while Emma crouched between them, madly mopping up the liquid with one of the blankets.

"Aeylin's water's broken, and her contractions have started. Celeste's remedies have had no effect, I don't know why."

"What can I do?" Zara asked, tensing as Aeylin let out a scream as another contraction wracked her body.

"I need towels and boiled water. God only knows what sort of germs are on this floor."

"I'll fetch the towels," Marx offered in a flat voice before heading out of the room.

"I'll get the water."

"I wish I had my gear," Emma said, voice agitated.

"I can call Josh. Ask him to bring it."

"Please."

Zara's phone was still on the kitchen counter where she had left it. She had taken two steps toward it when Marx commanded, "Stop right there, Zara." Something in the way he said the words, cold and stern, made her freeze and turn in his direction. What she saw made her blood run cold. Instead of towels in his hand, Marx was holding a gun, and the barrel was pointed right at her.

CHAPTER 37

S ymon was in the armoury with Kinnison, trying to find something which would fit the werewolf prince, when a shout came from the watchtower that figures were approaching. Dropping what they were doing, they both raced for the stairs, taking them two at a time as they ran up the three flights to the battlements. They looked over the stone walls in the direction every arrow pointed and saw the approaching dust cloud signalling that the pack of werewolves had arrived.

"Do you recognise them?" Symon asked.

Squinting, Kinnison tried to separate the individual wolves from the pack through the haze of dust.

"Some but not all. They are not all members of my father's pack. At least one is a lone wolf."

"Is that good news for us or bad?"

"We'll know in a minute," Kinnison said, his voice dark.

The pack halted ten feet from the gate. Symon could hear the bowstrings as they tightened around him. His eyes met Jiel's, who had taken charge of those on watch after returning and being debriefed. The elf gave him a slight nod. He would not give the order to fire, at least not until peace talks had been given a chance. As they watched the werewolves, the large black wolf at the front of the pack shimmered, and Onyx stood before them. He showed no signs of injury from his time stuffed into the cupboard. He had also changed out of his uniform.

"Give us the girl, and this can all end here," Onyx shouted up.

With a quick glance in Kinnison's direction, Jiel called out, "Aeylin is under the protection of the Guardians," in a clear, even voice, taking command of the negotiations. Symon thought it was a good thing that the elf was in charge, as Kinnison was vibrating with rage beside him. The werewolf prince's jaw was clenched so tightly that Symon feared he would shatter his own teeth. "Does Tibarn wish to declare war on us?"

"We are not here under Tibarn's orders. We are here because this is a werewolf matter and therefore comes under our jurisdiction. The birth of that child affects all werewolves." Onyx answered.

"Dragon shit," muttered Kinnison. Symon had to agree with him. Onyx was not known for his diplomacy, and his words sounded like nothing more than a script fed to him by his master. Despite that, Symon had to almost admire Tibarn's cleverness in the move. The Ruling Council would not interfere in a species' right to rule its own. By having the werewolves not wear his own pack's insignia, he also removed any accountability and any chance of losing his seat on the Council for misconduct. Clever indeed.

"If this is a werewolf matter, then I urge you to bring it before the Council. If they decree it we will, of course, step aside," Jiel countered, in a steady voice.

Kinnison started to growl, but Symon laid a reassuring hand of his arm. In a low voice, he advised, "Jiel is playing it smart. The Council could take days, if not weeks, to come to a decision. By then, your child will be born, and mother and pup can be moved to safety. He is trying to buy us time." Kinnison's growl stuttered to a stop, yet his body remained tight, ready to spring in defence of his mate. But instead of buying them time, calling Onyx's bluff seemed only to escalate the situation. The pack clearly had no intention of leaving without Aeylin.

"If you will not hand her over then you leave us with no choice but to take her by force," Onyx growled. "This is your last warning. Will you hand her over?"

"We will not."

"I was kind of hoping you would say that," Onyx said, a cruel smile flicking across his mouth.

"Light the barricade," Jiel commanded, and one of the elves let a fiery arrow fly. It hit the spikes that bordered the Guild, making them burst into bright purple flame. No werewolf would be able to climb the walls without being badly burnt. They would also struggle to escape the flame's grasp, as this brand of magical fire was designed to mould to them like wax. Symon expected Onyx to fall back, but instead the general only laughed. Looking to the sky, he opened his mouth and howled, the rest of the pack joining in.

"Do they expect a few howls to scare us?" Symon

scoffed. "They are fourteen, and there are nearly sixty of us within these walls. We need only wait them out."

"Those howls weren't to scare us. They were calling for reinforcements." Kinnison pointed to the edge of the woods. Symon watched as more wolves, ogres, dark elves, and fauns streamed from the trees. Each carried weapons, axes, swords, crossbows and in the case of one of the ogres, a club the size of a pony. Doing a quick headcount, Symon swore under his breath. Tibarn must have offered rich rewards indeed for so many to be willing to risk their lives on his behalf. Over a hundred creatures now surrounded the Guild.

"They won't make it past the barrier," Jiel said, yet the confidence had drained from his voice at the sight of so many opponents. "Only strong magic will breach our walls." Even as the elf spoke the words, Symon felt a cold shiver run down his spine as a large dark shadow crossed over him. Looking up, he felt dread wash over him, and for the first time in a long time, he felt genuine fear. For circling high in the sky, wingspan large enough to cover the Guild in his shadow, was the fire dragon, Aldebrand.

"Get back. Everyone down the stairs now!" commanded Jiel, pushing for those exposed to the dragon's fire to retreat behind the protection of the walls. He didn't have to issue the command twice as the Guardians turned as one and stampeded to the stairs, Symon and Kinnison following. Yet despite their training and fleetness of foot, they were too slow. Jiel, taking the rear to ensure all of his fellows made it, was not quite quick enough. Taking the first two steps down, Symon turned to look back over his shoulder for the elf. Their eyes met for a moment before Jiel suddenly burst into flames, taking the full force of Aldebrand's fire. The elf's scream of terror and pain were like nothing Symon had ever heard before. He tried to turn to go to him, even knowing as he did so that it was useless, but Kinnison grabbed his arm and, gripping him firm enough to bruise, half dragged, half carried him down the stairs.

Skylar was waiting for them in the courtyard. The look he gave Symon reflected his own pain, yet that shared look was all the time they could take to grieve for their friend. Later, if they both got out of this fight alive, they would grieve for Jiel and any others they would undoubtedly lose. That battle they had dreaded was coming to pass, and they had drawn the short straw.

"How long have we got until they breach the gate and your protection spells?" Skylar asked the witches.

"Not long. Perhaps fifteen minutes. Our magic is no match for dragon fire," the older of the two witches said, wrapping one arm around her younger sister, who was shaking badly. Skylar nodded.

"I'll take any time I can get. Both of you go to Celeste. She will need your help, and I don't want you getting yourself caught in the crossfire."

"Thank you, sir," the older witch said before guiding her sister towards the stairs which lead to the healers' quarters.

"Once the gate is broken, Aldebrand will be too large to fit through it. He will be forced to step back to let the others approach. It will cause them to funnel, and we can use that to our advantage. Archers, I want you ready to prevent them from rushing us all at once." The archers who had come down from the battlements took their positions, half on each side of the gate.

"What's to stop Aldebrand flying over the walls and burning us alive?" Karn asked. No one feared fire being used for a weapon as much as a dryad.

Skylar hesitated, eyes roaming the courtyard looking for a solution.

"Cansu says she will help, but she's not sure how long she'll be able to hold them off. We can manipulate her water to create a shield to hold Aldebrand at bay," one of the water nymphs offered. Skylar looked as if he was about to reject, knowing full well how rare blue dragons like Cansu were, and how they avoided war at all costs. But before he had a chance the nymph continued, "She wants to help us protect Aeylin's child."

"Tell her thank you, and that once again the Lightfall Guild is within her debt." The nymph bowed before sprinting off to help the dragon make preparations.

"Remember, our priority is to ensure that the rift is protected. It is our sworn duty to make sure no one species gains control over it. If the enemy crosses it, then they will take Aeylin, and all this will have been for nothing. They will win. We've trained for this, and I have faith in each and every one of you. Protect each other. Protect the rift," Skylar said, loud enough so that all in the courtyard could hear him.

As one, the Guardians raised their right fists and placed them over their hearts. "Lightfall!" they cried as one before moving to take defensive positions.

Symon looked to the gate. It had started to glow a warm red. It wouldn't be long before the dragon's fire melted it. He needed to get Luca; his friend was one of the Guild's best warriors. They needed him. Racing up the stairs, he pushed open the door of the healers' quarters to find Helo already there, having beaten him to it. Nero lay on one of the beds and, while still unconscious, his wounds appeared to have stopped bleeding. Symon assumed that Celeste must have given him something to force the healing process. Until he was fully recovered, it was better that the stubborn wolf remained where he was. But looking at Luca, Symon was relieved to see that his friend appeared fully recovered. Gone was his clammy skin, dried lips, and the dark circles under his eyes. Instead, he almost glowed with health and determination. Catching his eye, Symon gave him a determined grin.

Luca returned the grin. Leaning down, he kissed Brina's cheek and gave her a quick hug. Then turning back to his brothers in arms, Luca said, "Let's go show Tibarn why he shouldn't mess with Guardians."

CHAPTER 38

"What the hell, Marx? Where did you get a gun?!" Zara exclaimed.

"I need you to go and sit down next to Emma. I don't want to hurt you," Marx replied, voice and hand steady as he motioned the barrel in the direction of the sofa.

"Then, don't hurt me. Seriously Marx, what the hell is going on?" Zara was more angry than scared. After everything else that had happened, the idea of a werewolf holding a gun made her want to laugh out loud. It had to be some kind of prank.

"Last warning Zara. Go sit on the sofa!"

"I think you should listen to him," Emma said, voice quivering.

"It's okay, Emma, Marx isn't going to shoot me. It probably isn't loaded," Zara reassured her friend. Proving her wrong, Marx lifted the gun and pointed above his head. With a loud bang, he shot a bullet into the ceiling, causing bits of white plaster dust to fall like snow. The sound had Zara scuttling to the couch. Reaching Emma, she wrapped her arms around her, giving her a tight hug to make sure she was still in one piece. Suddenly, Aeylin screamed, and for a horrible moment, Zara thought that the werewolf had been shot. But looking at the struggling woman, she quickly realised it was another contraction trying to rip her body apart, instead of a bullet.

While Emma bravely turned her back to Marx and went back to helping Aeylin, Zara took a deep breath and tried to steady herself. She thought back on all the conversations she had with Marx over the weeks while she had waited for Luca. He had always been sympathetic and friendly to her plight with no indication of a hidden, vicious agenda. He'd told her about his family who he loved dearly. Perhaps she could use that to her advantage.

"Marx, what would your family think of what you are doing?" Zara asked in as calm a tone as she could manage.

"Why do you think I'm doing this?"

She hadn't been expecting that as his answer. Surely, Marx would want Aeylin's child to be born. It would mean power to the bitten werewolves, of which he was one.

"I don't understand."

"Tibarn has my daughter. If I don't kill the child, then he won't just kill my daughter, he will torture her until she begs for mercy, and then he won't stop until she is dead. You don't know what he is capable of," Marx said, voice cracking. "I don't want to harm any of you three. I won't unless you make me. You just have to give me the child once it is born."

"You can't have my child," screamed Aeylin as another

contraction took her. "He is the future for our people." The child, unaware of the horrible fate which awaited him, seemed determined to make his entrance into the world. Though Emma tried to hide what was happening, Zara caught a glimpse of tiny ears starting to be pushed out. The moment the pup let out his first cry, all would be lost.

"How do you know he has your daughter?" Zara asked, trying to distract Marx. As far as she knew, Marx had been in the human world the whole time.

"Because he sent a messenger. He had one of my daughter's ears in a box. It still wore the earring I gave her for her eleventh birthday."

"And the gun?"

"I have my sources. Luca isn't the only one investigating the defensive capabilities of the humans," Marx said, as if slurring Luca would balance out what he was about to do. The news came as a shock, but Zara pushed it aside to think on later.

"What if we help you get your daughter back? I'm sure Skylar will help. All the Guardians will."

"The Guardians are no match for Tibarn."

Aeylin screamed again. Meeting Emma's eyes, she saw they were glazed with terror. Carefully, keeping the movement out of Marx's line of sight, Emma held up two fingers. Zara wasn't sure if she meant two pushes or two minutes. Either way, they were screwed. Anxiously, Zara tried to think of something else to say to Marx but her mind was blank. She wished that Luca was there. Or that they had stayed in Wundor.

Suddenly Marx growled, drawing her attention back

to him. While the gun was still pointed in her direction, the werewolf's attention was focused out of the window. The brash side of Zara considered rushing him and going for the gun before her logical side took over, reminding her that she was no match for his reflexes or strength.

Looking out the window, she caught sight of the head-lights coming slowly down the drive. She recognised the car, Josh returning after family dinner. Together, they watched in silence as the car turned slowly and then came to a stop in the driveway. Turning off the engine, Josh took his time getting out, unable to sense the danger on the other side of the farmhouse door. Opening the rear door, he lifted a covered pie dish off the back seat and placed it carefully on the roof of the car. Then he walked to the back of the car and opened the boot.

"Make him go away," Marx said. "He doesn't need to be involved in this. If you value his life, make him leave," Marx warned. Zara simply nodded, unable to speak. Standing slowly, she moved cautiously to the door. Marx stepped up behind her so that he was only a few feet away. Opening the door, she stepped out onto the porch. The boot light was still on, and she could make out Josh's happy smile as he called out,

"I hope Wundorians like blueberry pie."

"I'm sure they do." She tried to think of an excuse for him to go, but the best she could come up with was, "But we don't have any cream. Would you mind going back and grabbing us some?"

"What's wrong?" Josh asked. The excuse was flimsy, and Zara should have known that she wouldn't be able to fool him. Josh called her an open book. Even if he was unable to read her face in the darkness of the porch, her tone had given her away. Now Josh would come up to the house, and then three people she loved, not to mention the baby, would all be at risk.

What the hell was she going to do? At that moment, Aeylin gave a scream of finality, and Zara turned to see a grey bundle of fluff and paws and ears come into the world. Marx, distracted by the pup's birth, took his eyes off Zara. Knowing she wouldn't get a better opportunity, Zara did the only thing she could think of. She screamed at the top of her lungs,

"Josh, RUN. Marx has a gun!" Then, spinning on her heel, she threw herself on the werewolf. If Marx hadn't been distracted, it probably would have been as useless as jumping against a brick wall. Instead, her momentum, combined with his angle to watch Aeylin, allowed Zara to push Marx to the ground. Time seemed to slow as they fell, Marx falling first, Zara collapsing on top of him, and as they hit the ground, the devastating bang as the gun went off.

CHAPTER 39

The Guild rang out with the sounds of battle, the screeching of metal as sword clashed against sword, the howls as werewolves leapt upon their opponents, the battle cries of the Guardians and the moans of the wounded. Mist drenched them all, so it felt as if they were fighting within a cloud, as Aldebrand's fire hit Cansu's water shield, turning it to vapour. Pixies darted around the fighters, dragging the wounded to safety and to the healers' quarters where Celeste worked with Brina to heal what wounds they could, or to bring some last comfort to those who couldn't be saved. Twenty minutes into the fight and already more than two dozen lay dead, most of those the attackers but not all. Otto, who had taken one of the ogres single-handedly, bringing him down by slashing through the tendons in his left leg, had been shot through the eye by a dark elf. Luca had tried to reach him, to save him, but the archer was too fast. Instead, he had time only to hold his friend in his arms as he died. Caught up in his grief, he didn't see the faun creeping up behind him with the knife. But luckily, as always, his friends had his back. Before Luca had time to turn, Helo was upon the faun, slashing his throat with his own sharp blade while Symon offered a hand to help Luca up.

"There will be time to mourn later," Helo told Luca, his own face grim.

"If there is a later," Symon added, his usual joviality gone.

Taking positions so that their backs were to each other, they took the opportunity to catch their breath. If it wasn't for Cansu, and the funnel at the gate, they would have been slaughtered. Despite them all being skilled warriors, there were just too many attackers. If help didn't come soon, Luca didn't think that they would last until nightfall. Looking around, he tried to gauge where best to attack next when his attention was caught by a deep growl. The sound had come from above. He scanned the upper walkways and saw Kinnison madly battling the werewolf general, Onyx.

The two wolves were moving so fast they became a whirl of grey and black. One moment Kinnison had Onyx by the throat, and the next the black wolf was on top of him. The two appeared to be evenly matched. When the general had first climbed through the broken gate, snapping the necks of not one but two archers with his powerful bare hands, Kinnison had snarled and claimed him. Before anyone could protest, he had leapt at Onyx. Seeing him coming, the general had shimmered, taking his wolf form to meet Kinnison's own. At first, Onyx had been hesitant with his attacks, holding something back, but now all bets were off. As Luca watched, Onyx took hold of Kinnison's ear and with a sharp thrust of his head ripped off the tip. Kinnison gave a howl of pain, fighting with all his might to get the black wolf off him before he lost more than just part of his ear.

"Kinnison needs our help," Luca urged his friends, pointing to where the wolves fought. As one, the three started to move towards the nearest stairwell. Each creature that attacked them or tried to block their path fell. At the base of the stairs, an ogre waited, grinning wildly. Reaching out, it attempted to bowl them over with its club, forcing them to take a quick step back.

"My quiver is empty," Helo said before Luca suggested he shoot the ogre.

"I could give him a bear hug?" suggested Symon, even though the ogre was almost double the size of his bear form. Luca looked around for another option, but could see nothing. He was about to suggest a rush attack when the ogre's eyes suddenly rolled back in its head and with an unsteady step, the colossal beast crashed to the floor. Three floors above, Myles rushing out of the infirmary to empty a chamber pot over the railing, had seen their plight. Hurriedly grabbing one of Brina's sleeping potions he had dropped it on the unsuspecting ogre. Luca gave the boy a wave, which he returned before disappearing back into the healers' quarters.

"Let's move," Luca ordered, and as one they headed for the stairs, climbing them slowly while Luca looked ahead and Symon covered their backs. Stopping before they reached the second-floor landing, Luca peered around the corner. The wolves were still fighting, droplets of blood and clumps of fur flying. Scanning the area behind them for danger, Luca could just make out a figure standing near the far stairwell. He couldn't tell if they were friend or foe, however, as they were hidden by the shadows. He reported their presence back to the others, wishing that Helo still had arrows in his quiver, for without them they had no option but to fight in close combat.

"Symon, can you help Kinnison?" Luca asked. In bear form, he would be the only one able to separate the two werewolves.

"Sure," Symon said, stripping off his weapons and passing them to Helo. While his armour would stay with him when he shifted form, the sword and knife would not. Leaving them in the stairwell for a potential enemy to find was not an option.

"I could throw the knife, frighten the stranger out of hiding," Helo suggested, twirling it across his palm to assess the balance.

"Not until we work out who they are or until we manage to get past the wolves. Otherwise, you risk hitting Kinnison or Symon," Luca said, earning him a look of disdain from Helo. "Sorry," Luca apologised. Helo was no fool, and he shouldn't have let stress make him treat him that way. "Ready?"

Helo and Symon both nodded. Moving out of the stairway, they split up. Symon shimmered, and in bear form, launched himself at the two combatants. Helo, agile as a cat, climbed up onto the banister, racing along the top to avoid the fight, while Luca clung to the building's wall. He moved as quickly as he could, keeping one eye on the fight and the other on the figure down the walkway. The figure hadn't moved, neither stepping forward to identify themselves or making a move to attack them. That changed, however, the second that Luca was past the skirmish, where Symon was pulling the wolves apart with his massive paws. Being distracted by the sight of Onyx making a slash for Symon's unprotected throat saved Luca's life. The arrow which came flying at his head missed him by a hair's breadth. If he hadn't turned his head to check on Symon's predicament, the arrow would have caught him straight in the eye.

Lowering himself into a crouch to become the smallest possible target, Luca sprinted towards the stairwell. Symon would have to dispose of Onyx without his help. Again, another arrow flew at him, and Luca rolled so that it scratched his arm instead of penetrating his chest. Despite the steel armour he wore, had the arrow hit him it would have pierced straight through, it flew with such force. He worried for Helo, who was exposed as he sprinted along the banister, but the elf seemed to be dodging the arrows. From the corner of his eye, Luca watched Helo use the pole of the railing to swing his whole body out over the courtyard to avoid being hit. For those few seconds, Helo hung suspended in the air. But someone in the courtyard below must have noticed for they took the opportunity to try and take Helo out by hurtling up a knife. By pure luck, the blade missed, almost catching Luca as it clattered to the ground in front of him. Helo wouldn't be able to risk that move again.

Putting on a burst of speed he didn't know he had to spare, Luca ran full-tilt towards their attacker. Passing the halfway mark, he managed to glimpse the archer. Dressed in black dragon scale armour, his legs and arms protected by black dragonhide greaves and boots, the dark elf looked lethal and caused Luca's blood to freeze. Only one elf wore such armour. Luca had never laid eyes on him, but the rumours of his misdeeds were enough to make anyone's blood run cold. Tacassa, a mercenary who killed on behalf of the highest bidder, had no moral code. He had killed hundreds of men, women and children, all for gold. If ever Luca needed proof that Tibarn was behind this attack, Tacassa's presence was it. Only someone well-funded and of high rank could afford his services. The odds of both he and Helo surviving against the dark elf were a hundred to one a best.

"Helo, help Symon," he called to his friend, wanting him safe, wanting at least one of them to have a chance. But either Helo didn't hear his shout, or he chose to ignore him because he kept running. They were closer now and looking up Luca could see that Tacassa's mouth was curved into a cruel smile. He was playing with them. Giving them false hope that they had a chance. The dark elf's gaze met Luca's, and with a wink, he notched not one, but two arrows to his bow and fired. Both hurtled towards Helo, still exposed on the banister. He would be able to avoid one if he risked swinging out over the court-yard, but he wouldn't be able to dodge two. Helo swung inwards avoiding the first but the second flew straight at his throat. Without thinking, Luca swerved to the side and leapt, reaching out a hand to block the arrow. Instead of hitting its intended target, the arrow pierced through the metal and leather of Luca's gloves, through the tender flesh of his hand and out the other side. Luca let out a scream of pain. Grabbing the end of the arrow with his uninjured hand, he tried to yank it out but he couldn't. The metal point of the arrow had split like a grappling hook. He screamed as the movement sent waves of pain shooting up his arm.

"Luca!" Helo shouted. Looking up, he saw that another arrow was less than five feet away and coming up fast. He had been so absorbed in pain, he hadn't noticed Tacassa take careful aim and shoot again. He knew that even if he moved, he wouldn't escape it in time. He tried to think where he could let the arrow hit with the least amount of damage. On instinct, he threw his body towards the wall. Hitting it with a hard thump, he waited for the pain of the new wound to catch him. Waited for the pain to shoot through his body. But it didn't come. Dazed from hitting the wall he looked around to find Nero, the arrow intended for him in the wolf's jaws as he sprinted towards Tacassa. The dark elf hadn't been expecting the wolf. As fast as he was at notching another arrow, Nero was faster. With a howl of fury, the black wolf leapt onto the elf, throwing him off balance and pushing him to the ground. Tacassa let out a scream of outrage which quickly turned to pain as Nero grabbed him by the throat. His dragon armour would defend him against magic and most weapons. It would not protect him against a broken neck. Within seconds the fight was over as Tacassa fell, limp, to the floor.

"Thank you," Luca said to Nero, passing all the relief and gratefulness he felt down their bond.

"Brina told me about the fight. Thought you might need my help. Turns out the witch was right," Nero replied, walking

over to Luca. *"Brace yourself,"* the wolf warned before taking the arrow head in his teeth and, with a quick jerk of his head, snapping it in two. Luca would have fallen had Helo not grabbed his shoulder for support. Before Luca had a chance to brace himself a second time, Helo grabbed hold of the shaft and yanked, pulling the arrow free. Luca's screamed in pain, so loud it made the windows rattle. Nero, feeling the pain through the bond, winced. *"You need to have Celeste take a look at that,"* he added, gesturing to Luca's hand which was now dripping blood onto the stone floor.

"I will," Luca gasped, "but we need to help Symon first."

"I don't think Symon needs our help," Helo said with a smirk. Luca turned just in time to see the enormous bear lift the black werewolf and toss him like a rock over the edge of the walkway. His landing was greeted by shouts. Rushing to the banister and looking over Luca saw three Guardians, Karn among them, making quick work of Onyx. He couldn't hold back a cheer, startling Karn slightly. Kinnison, the adrenaline rush of the fight leaving his body, collapsed as his hind legs gave out from under him. His left ear had been torn in half, he had a slash across his muzzle, one eye was swollen shut, and that was just the injuries to his head. His body was a mess of seeping wounds. A patch on Kinnison's flank the size of Luca's palm looked like it had been scalped. He was in such bad shape that he couldn't even shift form to speed his healing.

"Come on, let's get you to Celeste," Symon said, having changed back into his man form. Leaning over, he carefully picked Kinnison up in his arms. Kinnison let out a whimper of pain. "Sorry, I'm trying to be as gentle as I can, but there aren't many places that aren't damaged." Kinnison licked Symon's shoulder in a very un-werewolf-like gesture.

"You could do with getting that looked at too," Helo said inspecting Luca's hand. To his side, Nero gave Luca an 'I told you so' look. "Thanks for saving me, brother."

"Anytime."

The party had turned, heading for the stairwell, when they heard an almighty roar of a dragon's triumph, followed by screams of terror from the courtyard. Rushing to the banister, Kinnison still in Symon's arms, they looked down to see the yard in flames. One of the water nymphs had collapsed, her magic drained from maintaining the barrier, and as she had fallen so too had half the barrier. Seizing the opportunity, Aldebrand had descended, crushing over a dozen Guardians with his massive body. Now he roared, spewing hot flame from his maw, and the screams of the burnt rang through the air. Cansu, the barrier now useless, was attempting to block the blasts. But without the addition of the nymph's magic, her water was only able to quench half of the flames at best.

Luca gauged the distance from the banister to Alde-brand's back, thinking to thrust a sword through the back of the dragon's skull. But even if he took a run up, and jumped the banister at the optimum point, he would fall short. He was contemplating asking Symon to toss him when he spotted Skylar galloping towards the dragon from behind, his pointed spear in his hand. Luca could guess his plan. The confines of the courtyard's walls had forced the dragon to hold his wings in a suspended position, unable to fully close them. This meant that the unprotected skin under his wing was exposed. But as he watched Skylar's approach, the sound of galloping hooves alerted the dragon, and it turned its massive head in the direction of the centaur. Skylar was only a handful of feet away when the dragon opened his mouth and spewed fire at him. Luca saw his Commander's doom but was powerless to stop it. Skylar could only twist to the side so that instead of hitting him full in the chest, the boiling hot flame seared only his left side. Skylar screamed as his skin bubbled, yet the courageous centaur stayed his course, whether through willpower or momentum, and with a scream thrust the spear under the dragon's wing.

Luca's heart stopped, waiting for Aldebrand to fall but for a horrible second, which seemed to last an hour, nothing happened. The dragon continued to spew fire on the agonised centaur. Then, as if his heart took a minute to tell his brain that the impossible had happened, the fire stopped. With a stunned look, his large, cat-shaped eyes rolling back into his head, Aldebrand crumpled to the ground, trapping Skylar underneath him.

Ignoring his own pain, Luca sprinted down the stairs to Skylar's side, Helo and Nero behind him. With a growl of frustration, only Symon waited in place, Kinnison in too injured a state to be put down on the stone floor. Reaching him, Luca could see that Skylar was barely conscious, moaning in agony. His left side was a horror of burns and raw flesh. His hind legs had been crushed when the dragon fell. Looking around, Luca saw that four other

Guardians had also gathered around their injured Commander, and he took charge.

"You three, help Helo and I lift Aldebrand's body. When he is up, Falcon, you need to pull Skylar out. Be quick because this beast is too heavy for us to be able to hold up for long." Everyone moved to take their assigned positions, half of the Guardians on each side of the dragon's still body. The centaur was no longer moaning, the pain having stripped him of consciousness. Falcon hesitated for a moment, trying to decide on the best place to grab hold. With one hand she grabbed Skylar under his right armpit, where the flesh was still whole. The other hand hovered over the ragged left side, ready to grip the same spot when the time came, trying to save him the pain and damage of grabbing it too early.

"Ready?" Luca asked, looking at Falcon. She nodded, bending her knees.

"One, two, three," Luca commanded, and as one the Guardians lifted the massive dragon. Aldebrand weighed more than Luca could have guessed, but somehow they managed to leverage him up enough for Falcon to slide Skylar out. The movement woke the centaur, and he let out a scream as his injured body was dragged across the sand of the courtyard floor. The second he was free, the Guardians let the dragon fall.

"Let's get him to Celeste," Luca said, going to help Falcon lift Skylar's shoulders. But he never made it. Instead, before he had even taken two steps, he swayed. His face went pale, and his dark blue eyes rolled back into his head. Mere inches from the floor, Karn managed to catch him. In the anxiety of saving Skylar, Luca had pushed all the pain of his own wound aside. Gripping the dragon had applied pressure. But the second he let go his blood had begun to fall again in earnest, his body unable to lose any more.

"Quick, let's get them both to Celeste," Falcon said and, dodging the fighting which was still going on around them, the group carried both Skylar and Luca up towards the healers' quarters.

CHAPTER 40

Zara didn't have time to think about the bullet. All her thoughts and energy were focused on keeping Marx down, on stopping him from firing again. It was like trying to battle a boulder. The werewolf, even in two-legged form, was all muscle and strength. Trying to remember back to the self-defence lessons her father has forced her to take years ago, she decided to focus what little power she had on his tender spots. She thrust her knee up into his groin while also trying to crush his windpipe with her elbow. But Marx was too fast. In a blur, he grabbed her and spun them. Zara was slammed into the floor, the breath knocked out of her. He snarled and one hand wrapped around her throat, squeezing so hard that black spots appeared in her vision. His eyes were red with anger. Zara tried to kick out with her legs, to use her knees to gain leverage, but it was no use. Marx covered her body with his. She tried to gasp for breath, but nothing came. The black dots in her vision were expanding. She knew she was going to die.

"Take that you piece of dog shit!" Josh screamed and with as much force as he could muster, he smashed the tyre iron he had grabbed from the car down on Marx's head. Swinging it, he hit Marx again, and then again. He didn't stop until blood sprayed from the werewolf's head and he collapsed, dead, on top of Zara, his grip on her throat finally slackening. Zara struggled for breath, but Marx's full weight was lying on her chest, and she couldn't drag enough air into her lungs. She tried to push him off her, but her limbs were too weak from oxygen deprivation. Seeing her plight, Josh took a firm grip of Marx's hair and dragged the werewolf off. Zara took in three quick, deep breaths. The air felt so good, she took another three, almost hyperventilating as her body gorged on the air.

Reaching down a hand, Josh helped her up. "Take it easy," he said as she staggered and he wrapped an arm around her waist to steady her. Zara looked herself up and down, waiting for the burning pain to hit, surprised not to find herself covered in blood. But she could see no evidence of a bullet wound. By some miracle, Marx must have missed her.

"Zara ..." Emma's usually vibrant voice was quiet, and not full of relief like Zara expected. Looking towards her friend, she saw that Emma had collapsed at an awkward angle, like she had fallen, with her legs sprawled out in front of her. Her eyes were almost black, the pupils fully dilated with fear, and she was trembling violently. Her hands clasped her stomach, which blossomed with a blood-red flower, flowing across the tattered remains of her yellow dress and dripping down the side.

"I can't feel my legs."

Half stumbling, Zara ran to Emma.

"Oh no, Emma, no ..." she sobbed, tears running like a stream down her cheeks. Reaching her friend, she placed her own hands over Emma's, which felt cold and clammy despite the warm blood which washed over them. "Josh ..." Zara said planning to ask him to grab the medical kit he always had stashed in his car, but he was already gone, the tyre iron clanging to the floor as he sprinted to the car.

"What can I do?" Aeylin asked. Zara looked up, for a moment having entirely forgotten about the pregnant werewolf. But Aeylin was pregnant no more. In her arms, cradled against her chest, lay a silver ball of fluff, eyes closed. The pup was tiny, and Zara wondered how so much fuss could have been caused by such a little thing. Trying to calm her mind, to switch into work mode as Emma called it, Zara tried to think of what they could do to try and save Emma. Moving her wasn't a good idea, not until they knew what damage the bullet had caused. That left two options. The first was to call The Haven. They were closer, they weren't fighting a war, and they loved Emma. But they didn't have experience with bullet wounds or working on humans, and she would have to answer a thousand questions which Emma didn't have time for. She knew George would want to take Emma to a hospital, and he was right, except how do you explain to the doctors at Busselton General Hospital that Emma was shot by a werewolf. But the biggest argument against this option was that there was no guarantee that they could save Emma. Only magic could do that.

So that left option two. That someone had to cross the

rift, possibly deal with a war zone, and convince a fairy to come to the human realm to save Zara's friend. Assuming that Skylar would even grant Celeste permission. Plus, the only person, apart from Zara, who knew where the rift, was Aeylin, who had given birth less than ten minutes before. Could Zara really ask her to risk her own life, and her child's, to save Emma? Yet Zara couldn't face the idea of leaving Emma like this when she needed her.

"I'll go," Aeylin volunteered, guessing Zara's question before she could find the words to ask it. "She risked her life for my child and me. It's time for me to return the gesture." Not waiting for Zara to say anything, Aeylin swung her legs down off the sofa. But when she tried to stand her legs gave way, and she landed with a bounce. The pup in her arms stirred, letting out a little growl, and then went back to sleep. "You'll just need to give me a minute."

"I'll go with her," Josh offered. He had returned with the medical kit in time to overhear Aeylin's offer. "She can't go alone," he said, dropping the kit on the floor next to Zara and picking up the tyre iron. "There are pain meds and pressure bandages in the bag. We'll be back as soon as we can." Walking over to Aeylin, Josh offered his free hand, and she gratefully took it. Once she was standing, he wrapped his arm around her waist.

"Thank you both," Zara said. They simply nodded and headed for the door. Opening the bag, Zara breathed a small sigh of relief. Usually Josh would only carry the basics for first aid in his car but, instead, he'd packed the night visit bag, which had almost anything a vet could want when visiting patients away from the clinic. She found the morphine, syringes and needles in their locked case at the bottom of the bag. Fitting the needle to the syringe, Zara pushed the tip through the morphine bottle's seal. Carefully she pulled the plunger. She needed to give Emma enough to relieve the pain but not enough to knock her out. Losing consciousness now could be fatal. With a press, she sprayed drops of out the top of the needle, clearing it of air bubbles. Reaching in the bag, she found the length of rubber used to create a tourniquet and tied it around Emma's left arm, just above the elbow. Tapping the vein, it worried her how long it took to become rigid. Emma was losing too much blood.

"Stay with me, Emma," she said as she slid the tip on the needle into the vein and pushed the plunger. "It'll feel better in a minute. Just stay with me."

"Who would have thought, when I taught you how to do that, you'd be doing it to me?" Emma asked with a quiet chuckle.

"At least you know I had a good teacher," Zara said, attempting a smile. Reaching into the bag, she pulled out two large pressure bandages, some wipes, and a bottle of antiseptic. "I'm going to take a look, okay?"

Emma nodded.

Emma lifted her hands so that Zara could pull up her dress. The second she did so the blood started to flow freely, giving no sign of slowing. Gingerly, Zara pulled up Emma's dress and tried not to groan when she caught sight of the wound. The bullet had entered Emma's stomach two inches to the right of her belly button. It had left a trail of torn flesh behind, and Zara could see tiny bits of yellow fabric stuck in it. They would need to be removed or risk infection, yet Zara was hesitant to try and remove them now. Infection was the last of Emma's worries. If they didn't find a way to staunch it, Emma would bleed out long before a virus had a chance to take hold.

"How bad is it?" Emma asked.

"Not too bad."

"Liar."

"Well, nothing that Celeste won't be able to fix. We just need to hold on until she gets here."

While Emma bit her lip and tried not to scream, Zara wiped the wound and poured antiseptic over it. Once cleaned as best she could, she covered the wound with a bandage, the blood quickly soaking it through. Placing the other on top of it, she positioned Emma's hands over the wound.

"Do you think you can hold that there?" Zara asked. Emma nodded, no longer able to speak. Leaving her friend just long enough to fetch a glass of water from the kitchen, she held it to Emma's lips while she drank. Finding a hand towel in the medical kit, she dowsed it with water, folding it and placing it over Emma's hot forehead. Her friend was burning up, another bad sign. Sitting beside Emma, Zara placed her own hands over her friend's, and together they waited for help to come.

CHAPTER 41

"Are you ready?" Aeylin asked Josh, moving the pup into a firmer position against her chest. She hoped crossing the rift wouldn't do the child any harm. The idea of losing her grip on him as they travelled terrified her. Yet she knew she had little choice. She needed to return to find Kinnison, to show him their son, to show the other bitten werewolves what was possible. And she needed to find Celeste and save Emma. She could not let her incredible, brave new friend die.

"As ready as I'll ever be," Josh replied, gripping the tyre iron tighter. He tried to ignore the blood which still stained it, with his two friends and the thought that he, a healer who had sworn to protect life, had just killed someone. Sure, that person had been trying to kill Zara, but still. But now was not the time to dwell on guilt; there would hopefully be plenty of time for that later. Emma and Zara were relying on him. Taking a firmer grip on Aeylin's waist, moving slightly so that the pup was positioned between them, he let her lead him into the rift.

The rift threw them around as if they were feathers caught in a strong gust of wind, tossing them up, down, left, and right so that as they reached the exit, Josh could no longer tell up from down. Yet somehow through it all, he managed to keep hold of Aeylin and his makeshift weapon. As his feet hit the solid sand floor of the court-yard, Josh let go of both. Falling to his knees, he vomited his dinner onto the ground in front of him. Retch after retch, Josh continued until there was nothing left, reminding him of days when he'd come home after a big night out and spewed alcohol everywhere. When the last bits were gone, he wiped his mouth with the back of his hand, finally looking up to see the tip of a sword pointing at his throat.

"Identify yourself," a deep voice commanded.

"I'm Josh, I'm friends with Zara. We need Celeste," he spat out, trying to swallow another mouthful of bile which threatened to spill.

The elf who held the sword looked quizzical for a moment and then, looking behind Josh, spotted Aeylin. Taking in the pup held protectively in her arms, his eyes widened. He motioned for the Guardians to close ranks, tightening the circle.

"Symon!" he yelled, loud enough to be heard over the fighting which still raged around them. Within moments the large black bear was thrusting his way through the fighters to reach them. When he caught sight of who had come through the rift, he instantly shifted form.

"Where's Zara?" Symon demanded, a note of dread in his voice.

"With Emma. Marx shot her. We have to find Celeste."

At Aeylin's words, Symon looked like he had been struck by a hammer. But, thanks to his training, he recovered quickly.

"Come, I'll take you to Celeste," Symon said. "Can you walk?" he asked Aeylin.

"I think so," she said, though her voice didn't sound confident. With a look at Josh, who shrugged, Symon stepped forward and picked Aeylin up in his arms, careful not to jolt the pup.

"Hello, little guy. I know someone who will be very happy to meet you," he said, gazing down at the wolf pup. Looking to Josh, he asked, "I am assuming you are alright to walk?" Josh nodded. "Good, but stay behind me." Turning to the elf who had held a sword to Josh's throat, Symon asked, "Nitel, can you assign someone to guard us?"

"Of course," the elf nodded. But before Nitel could nominate anyone, a voice called out.

"I'll go," said Karn, and stepped forward. For a moment Nitel looked as if he was about to object, but Symon cut him off, smiling broadly at the dryad.

"Wicked."

Together the party made their careful way to the stairs. Symon did his best to shield his precious cargo from sight. If Tibarn's army found out that she had returned, they would move heaven and earth to destroy her. Josh walked next to Symon, the tyre iron held in a defensive position. When two werewolves tried to jump them a few feet away from the stairs, Josh smashed one between the eyes, knocking it out while Karn took care of the other.

"Nice weapon," Symon said. "Might have to get me one of those." Josh only smiled.

After two more short scuffles, one on the first set of stairs and the other shortly after they reached the third-floor landing, they reached the infirmary. Symon, arms full, kicked the door open with one large boot, revealing the chaos within. Every bed was filled with a patient, and more lay on the floor or sat against the walls. Brina, her red curls pulled into a messy bun on top of her head, moved from bed to bed looking frazzled. Sweat dripped from her forehead. She didn't even look up as they entered, her hands and mind occupied with trying to pick bits of rock out of a wound in a minotaur's leg. The two witch sisters were likewise occupied with patients of their own. Beth and Myles, for their part, ran from one bedside to another ferrying drinks of water and chamber pots. Symon looked around for Celeste and for a moment couldn't see her. Then he caught sight of the bottom of her turquoise wings just visible beneath a curtain in the far corner of the room.

Striding over, he paused outside the curtain's boundary, unsure if he should interrupt.

"Celeste," he called in a quiet voice and was startled when instead of the fairy, it was Luca who pushed back the curtain. Luca's eyes widened as he took in the sight of Aeylin in Symon's arms and Josh standing next to him, the tyre iron now slack in his hand as he gazed, mouth agape, around the room.

"What in the Goddess' name!" Luca exclaimed, stepping out from behind the curtain. But before it had a chance to fall back into place, Kinnison was pushing his way through. As the werewolf took in the sight of Aeylin, with the tiny grey wolf pup cradled in her arms, he fell to his knees, his body racked with sudden sobs. Aeylin tapped Symon's arm, and he gently put her down. Stepping in front of her mate, she held out their son. Lifting his head, his emerald green eyes sparkling with tears, Kinnison held out his large hands and gingerly, as though the babe was made of glass, took hold of him. As if sensing the importance of the moment the pup opened his eyes, green to match his father's, and stared up at the man who held him. Kinnison smiled brightly at his son, who yawned widely in response before closing his eyes again and snuggling against Kinnison's palm. Moving so that he was cradled into the crook of his arm, Kinnison stood. Wrapping his spare arm around Aeylin's waist, he kissed her on the forehead.

"I'm so proud of you," he said. "Are you alright?"

"I'm fine. But Emma is not."

"What's wrong with Emma?" Luca asked.

"She's been shot in the stomach, and she can't move her legs. It's why we came back. We need Celeste's help." Luca and Kinnison exchanged a frantic look.

"Celeste is with Skylar, she can't leave him."

"If she doesn't come, Emma will die," Josh butt in. "Isn't there anything you can do?"

"I don't know ..." Luca started trying to think of how to help the human woman who meant so much to Zara and had risked her life to help them, yet worried at the same time about his Commander, whose life was on the line. Suddenly, the curtain pulled back, and Celeste's head popped around the corner.

"You must be Josh," she said, directing her gaze to the lanky man. "Can you describe for me exactly what has happened?"

"Marx and Zara got in a fight, and Marx shot Emma in the stomach. He wasn't aiming for her, he intended to kill the baby, but it went off in the scuffle. Zara said we couldn't move her. We have pain meds and bandages, but they won't be enough," Josh said, trying to relay only facts but failing to keep the growing fear out of his voice.

"I can't leave Skylar right now, or he'll risk losing his right arm if not his life." At her words, Josh's face fell, and he went a deathly white. "But I will help. If I give you something to stabilise Emma so that she can be moved and show you how to use it, do you think you'll manage? I can't come to her, but perhaps you can bring her to me."

"I'll do whatever it takes," Josh said, a touch of colour returning to his face.

"Brina," Celeste called. The witch looked up from her administrations on the minotaur. "When you have finished with Tandor, can you please come to take over Skylar's care for me for five minutes?" Brina nodded, sparing time for a quick smile at Symon and Luca before turning back to her work.

"How's Zara?" Luca asked Josh quietly.

"Panicked, as you can imagine, but okay. I think hanging around with you has given Zara confidence, but maybe too much. She always was good at putting others before herself but shit, Luca, you should have seen the way she threw herself at Marx. It was scary."

"I'm sorry for exposing her, all of you, to this. It was

never meant to be this way. I'm coming back with you. You shouldn't have to handle this by yourselves."

"What about the fighting here?"

"They'll have to cope without me. I am not letting –" But Luca's words were interrupted by the sound of blaring trumpets coming from outside the walls of the Guild, loud enough to be heard above the fray. Relief rushed through Luca, and he smiled, grabbing a startled Josh into a tight hug, making him almost stumble. All around them in the room the patients, those who were conscious, let out whoops of joy. The minotaur that Brina was attending grabbed her and pulled her down for a kiss. Everyone was laughing, the gloom of the healers' quarters pushed aside for the moment.

"What's going on?" Josh asked.

"We're saved!" exclaimed Luca. "The Guardians from the other Guilds have answered Skylar's call. With them joining our ranks we'll outnumber our attackers three to one. The battle will be over. We will win."

CHAPTER 42

When Emma faded to the point where she could no longer support herself on the sofa, or keep her head up, Zara had moved to sit with her back against the wall, her friend cradled in front of her. She had to keep Emma in an upright position for as long as possible. It was the only way Zara could reach Emma's stomach wound and apply pressure, since Emma was no longer capable. Anytime she released the bandage, blood began to gush out at an alarming rate. But even more terrifying was the fact Emma had started to cough up blood.

The room was silent, the closed door and windows blocking out the sound of the birds outside. Zara wished she could hear them, wished Emma could, knowing it would give her comfort, but she was too scared to move. When she had lifted Emma to reposition her, she'd left a trail of blood behind. The bullet had gone straight through, and Emma was leaking blood from both sides. She could feel the warmth of it now, wet on her own stomach where Emma's body pressed against her own. The whole farmhouse smelt like copper, the tang of blood, the scent of Emma's mingling with Marx's, whose body still lay where it had fallen, a few feet from them. She wished there had been time to remove it before Josh and Aeylin had left. The sight of it creeped her out.

"Zara." Despite being inches away from her, Emma's voice was barely above a whisper. "Tell George and Karen that I love them and thank them for being my family." Zara shook her head.

"Don't say that. You can tell them yourself. As soon as Celeste comes and makes you all better." Emma was trying to say goodbye and Zara wasn't ready for it. Would never be ready for it.

"I'm not going to make it, Zara. I feel so cold and weak," Emma said, her voice breathy. She coughed, and Zara saw flecks of blood land on the front of Emma's shirt.

"Oh my God, Emma. You can't leave me. You need to hold on. This is all my fault."

"No, it's not." Another cough. "Don't blame yourself. We forced you to tell us." Another cough. "I don't regret it, none of it. I rode on a dragon, Zara, how many can say –" Another coughing fit stole the rest of the words from her.

"You need to hold on. Think of all the animals that need you. I need you!" Zara exclaimed.

"No, you don't. You have Luca, stay with him. Don't let him go," Emma said, a slight smile crossing her lips. Then, as Zara watched in horror, Emma's smile faded and her eyes closed, face going slack.

"Emma!" No answer. "Emma!" Zara tried again, this

time shaking her slightly. Again, no response. Letting go of the pressure bandage with one hand, she felt Emma's neck for a pulse, relieved to find it still beating even if it was slow and irregular. Next, she cupped her hand over Emma's mouth. She swore loudly, finding that her friend had stopped breathing. Sliding out from under her, Zara found the strength she didn't know she had to lift Emma's limp body and place it gently onto the floor. If she couldn't get Emma to start breathing within four minutes, she risked brain damage from oxygen deprivation. She wasn't sure if even Celeste's magic could cure that. Opening Emma's mouth, she checked to make sure that her airways weren't blocked but could find nothing. Her fingers did, however, come away red with blood, which worried her. Moving Emma's head so that it was tilted backwards, clamping her nose shut with the fingers of her left hand, Zara started to perform CPR, enclosing Emma's mouth with her own and administering two rescue breaths. Pulling back, she rechecked Emma, still no sign of breathing. Placing her hands in the middle of Emma's chest, she started compressing, more grateful than ever before that this had been part of her compulsory first aid training at The Haven.

It took Zara four repetitions before she felt Emma gasp and take a breath on her own. Monitoring it, an ear to Emma's mouth, she sighed as she felt the gentle movement of air as Emma exhaled.

"Emma, can you hear me?" she asked. No response. She tapped her friend's cheek and then squeezed her hand. Again, no answer. Moving Emma so that she rested on her side in the recovery position, Zara checked to make sure she was still breathing. Fear washed through her as for a millisecond she felt no stirring of air against the palm she held in front of Emma's mouth. Then Zara felt it, weak but still there. Sitting up, one hand pressed against the wound, Zara wracked her brain, trying to think of something she could do, something that she might have missed, anything which could save her friend. But nothing came. Stuck in the farmhouse with no one there to help, none of the necessary equipment, no fairy magic, there was not a single thing that she could do.

Where the hell was Josh with Celeste? It felt like he had been gone for hours. With the time difference in Wundor, he should have been back by now. With that thought, a new fear washed over her. What if Josh and Aeylin had been killed when they crossed the rift? What if, by sending them, she had signed their death warrants together with Emma's? Was it the wrong choice to not send Josh to The Haven for help? She had been so worried about getting Karen and George involved. Enough of her friends were already in danger.

Overwhelmed with panic, Zara started to hyperventilate, her own breath coming in quick gasps. Her whole world felt like it was collapsing around her. Looking down at Emma, so drawn and pale, she felt helpless. Terrified. Alone. Powerless.

Closing her eyes, Zara tried to clear her mind. Tried to think around her panic. Her fingers itched, but she ignored them. Pins and needles were nothing compared to what Emma was suffering. She concentrated on her breathing. In, holding for the count of six, then out. Repeat. Repeat.

Slowly her breathing steadied. But her mind continued to run wild, searching for a solution. She remembered the last time she had felt so helpless. Remembered what she had done to save Wysh, the unicorn foal, by bonding her own life force with the unicorn's. She wished she could do that now with Emma. She would happily lend all the energy she had within her to heal her friend.

Desperate enough to try anything, to just feel like she was doing something, she attempted to remember how it had felt when she had linked with the unicorn. Leaving one hand to keep the pressure on the wound, she moved the other so that it touched Emma's clammy forehead. She could almost imagine Celeste's voice in her head, telling her to open her mind, to sense some sort of connection between the patient and herself. She wasn't surprised when she felt nothing. There was no magic from Celeste to make the bond. But instead of giving up, she tried to imagine her energy, her own life force, flowing slowly into Emma. With every push of invisible energy, she also tried to send thoughts of love and of family. She infused the thoughts with memories of the times they had shared together. Of family dinners, girls' movie nights and long walks where they spoke of their dreams of the future. Of the confidences and laughs they had shared. She kept pushing, throwing all of her hope and love towards Emma, too scared to open her eyes and find that it had all been for nothing. Not ready to say goodbye to her best friend.

At first, she thought that the silvery, shimmering light which sparkled at the edge of her eyelids was purely her imagination. But slowly, a flicker at a time, it started becoming brighter. And it was throbbing. Throbbing in time with her own heartbeat. As this realisation hit her and excitement flooded her body, the throbbing also increased. Slowly, Zara opened her eyes. The exhilaration that rushed through her as took in the shimmery silver light which covered Emma's body was so intense that she almost broke the connection. The urge to pull off the bandage and see if the wound was healing was immense, and she fought to resist it. Not yet. Closing her eyes again, she thrust all of her energy into Emma, focusing it on her right hand which pressed onto the wound. She could feel her blood tingling in her hands where they touched Emma's skin, knowing this time that it wasn't pins and needles. Somehow, she had found a way to work the magic without Celeste.

"Zara?" Emma's voice broke through her concentration, the surprise making her let go. Opening her eyes, she looked down to find Emma staring at her, her eyes wide and her face flushed a slight pink. "What's happening?"

"Oh my God, you're awake!" Zara exclaimed, wrapping her arms around Emma, joy flooding her as she felt her friend's arms hugging her back. For a moment, they lay there, not speaking, enjoying the moment that had been so close to never happening again.

Letting go reluctantly, Zara said, "We need to check your wound." Emma turned so that she lay flat on her back and with gentle care, Zara peeled the soaked bandage off Emma's stomach. It was difficult, the dried blood sticking to the bare skin, and Zara was anxious that she might reopen the wound if she pulled it off too quickly. But her fears were for nothing. As the bandage released its hold and she pulled it free, she gasped.

"How bad is it?" Emma asked voice fearful.

"It's healed," Zara answered in awe.

"What do you mean?" Emma asked, trying to sit up and then lying back down quickly, as blood rushed to her head.

"There's no wound. There's blood, but it's all dried. There's no wound," Zara repeated. Reaching for the medical kit, she pulled out the bottle of saline solution and a couple of cotton pads. Drenching the pad in the liquid, she used it to wipe Emma's stomach. The blood came away easily, the cotton pad quickly turning red, and in its place was a fresh patch of pink skin where the bullet hole had been.

"How is that possible?" Emma asked.

"I don't know. It shouldn't have worked. Quick, turn over. I need to check the exit wound." Emma rolled over as instructed. Removing the bandage, Zara felt joyous relief. "It's healed." Unable to hold in the flood of emotions any longer, Zara began to laugh, setting her joy and her tears free.

CHAPTER 43

T hanks to the attackers bringing down the gates,
there was nothing to prevent the newly arrived
Guardians from entering. They made quick
work of the werewolves and others who tried to block
their entrance. The allies numbered over two-hundred,
and it wasn't possible for them to all fit within the walls.
Over fifty remained outside, rounding up those who tried
to escape.

The werewolves, those who had not been killed in the
battle, chose to continue to fight until none stood, not
allowing themselves to be captured. They knew that
returning to Tibarn as failures would be a death sentence.
But the elves, fauns and others who had made up their
force's numbers saw the writing on the wall and threw
down their weapons in surrender. There would be more
than enough to stand witness against Tibarn's denials.

Since Skylar was still fighting for his life in the infirmary, Luca had no choice but to assume command and
greet the leaders of the visiting Guilds. Symon and Helo

stood at his side while Nero paced at his feet, anxious as Luca to cross the bond and get to Zara and Emma.

"*Gode fen*, Guardians, you are a welcome sight. The Lightfall Guild thanks you for answering our call and coming to our aid," Luca said, greeting them formally.

Rillian, the second-in-command of the Farhaven Guild, nudged his black warhorse forward, halting him a few feet in front of Luca.

"You called, we answered, as is the Guardian way," the dark-skinned panther shifter replied, head slightly bowed. Then, breaking the air of formality, he grinned broadly, showing white teeth, "Plus we haven't had the chance for a good fight in ages. Wouldn't want you guys to have all the fun."

Looking around at the mess, the fallen Guardians, the scorched walls, Luca didn't think he would describe what had happened as fun, but he returned Rillian's smile none-theless.

"Skylar sends his apologies for not being able to greet you himself, but he is currently with our healer. He was badly burnt when he slew the fire dragon, Aldebrand."

Rillian whistled through his teeth.

"I wish I had been there to see that! Skylar will go down in legend. Songs will undoubtedly be sung about the battle." Then, his tone becoming more serious, he added, "But tell me, Luca. What of the werewolf pup? Does it live?"

Luca glanced around for Kinnison and found him looking down from the floor above, one arm wrapped protectively around Aeylin and the other his son. Father-hood must have brought out a wiser side of the werewolf, who would usually be the first to push his way into anything. Instead, he held his family back to see the outcome of the meeting. Wise indeed. Luca waved for them to join him, letting Kinnison know that it was safe. Rillian liked to joke, and cat shifters of any kind didn't often get along well with wolves, but the Guardian meant no harm.

As the three exited the stairwell, those still milling around the courtyard stood back to let them pass, bowing their heads slightly. Those who had not yet seen the child smiled, or let out whoops of joy. Stopping next to Luca, Kinnison took the pup from Aeylin's arms. Holding the tiny grey wolf up, he said, "I would like to present my son and heir, Kodan." Cheers broke out across the yard as the Lightfall Guardian's voices joined with those from their brother Guilds in chanting Kodan's name. The pup, as if sensing that the cheers were for him, let out a tiny growl, making those close enough to hear it laugh.

"The pup's life isn't out of the woods yet, but it is good to know that he has friends," Nero commented. *"Friends who would die to protect him. Friends like us."*

"Indeed," Luca said, looking down at the wolf, grateful to have friends like Nero, Symon, Helo and now Kinnison and Aeylin in his life.

As soon as the formalities were over and Helo had been dispatched to find food for the visitors, Luca bade farewell to Rillian and hurried off to see Josh. He found him waiting in the healers' quarters, a pack of supplies from Celeste slung over his shoulder, feet tapping a nervous rhythm on the stone floor.

"Ready?" Luca asked.

"I've been ready since we got here," Josh snapped, then looked guilty. "Sorry, I'm just anxious about Emma. I know that you are too."

Luca nodded. "Let's go." They were out of the healers' quarters and halfway to the stairwell when they heard a commotion from below. "What now?!" exclaimed Luca, hurrying to the banister. Looking down, he had to blink his eyes rapidly a few times, sure that they were playing tricks on him. For in the centre of the courtyard, woozy for having just come through the rift, stood a frazzled looking Zara with one arm wrapped tightly around Emma's waist.

"Emma! Zara!" yelled Josh, not doubting the vision for a second before sprinting off down the stairs. With his long legs, Josh was fast, but Luca was faster, skidding to a halt in the sand a few inches in front of the pair. He rapidly scanned Zara for any sign of injury and was relieved to find none. Blood covered her stomach and hands, but he didn't think any of it was hers.

"Are you alright?" he asked, reaching for her. Letting go of Emma, who was now being supported by Josh, Zara collapsed into Luca's arms. Wrapping her hands around his waist, she stood there silently for a moment, drawing strength from his closeness. Slowly, she shook her head.

"Zara, what's wrong? Is it Emma?" Luca looked at the woman. The front of what remained of her dress was soaked with blood, and she was pale, but she was standing with Josh's help. Perhaps they had overestimated how much damage the bullet had done.

"No. It's just ... I was so scared." The fear of the past hour broke out of Zara, and she started to sob. "She almost died, Luca. She stopped breathing. She lost consciousness. There was so much blood, and there was nothing I could do."

"But she's fine now, you must have done something?" Luca asked puzzled.

"It... was magic. I don't know how or why it came to me, but it did. It was like when I saved Wysh. It was a miracle." Her sobs had quieted now and, suddenly, aware of the crowd gathering around them, Zara wiped her eyes.

"Magic? You must be mistaken," Luca said, looking closely at Zara. He thought that the shock of what had happened must have screwed with her memory of the events.

"I'm not," Zara said, standing up straighter, voice firm. "One moment, Emma was bleeding out in my arms. The next she was covered with a silver, shimmery light and her wound healed. She can feel her legs again."

"But you're human?" Luca stuttered.

"I know." Zara shrugged, unable to explain what had happened any more than Luca. "But I'm telling the truth."

"I believe you," Luca said, or at least he believed she believed it was the truth. "Come see Celeste, maybe she can explain what happened."

The party made their way to the healers' quarters. As well as the warriors, the other Guilds had brought along two healers to help. Half of the beds were empty, their previous patients healed and sent to find food and rest elsewhere, so Josh helped Emma to one. The curtain around Skylar's bed was still closed, making Luca's brow furrow with worry. Sensing it, Zara asked,

"What's wrong?"

"It's Skylar. He was badly hurt during the battle."

"Maybe I can help?" Zara offered and before Luca could stop her, she had walked up and pulled back the curtain. Skylar's horse body was held in a floating sling which hovered three centimetres off the ground. His man half was strapped so that he hung, back straight, above it, suspended in place. His eyes were closed and his breathing shallow, his black dreadlocks hanging like a veil around his face. Zara gasped as she took in the raw, red burns which covered most of the left side of his shoulder and torso.

"Zara?" Celeste asked, looking up from where she sat in a chair next to the sling. The fairy looked worn out, her hair straggly, and her skin almost translucent. Even her turquoise wings seemed to droop.

"Celeste," Zara said, rushing over and giving the fairy a hug and a kiss on the cheek.

"I'm so sorry, Zara. I wanted to come, but I couldn't leave Skylar. How's Emma?" "Emma's fine, I healed her." Celeste's eyes widened.

"Did Josh make it through the rift in time?"

"No. I connected with Emma, I made the magic work like it did with Wysh, although I have no idea how."

"That's why we're here," Luca said, stepping through the curtains to stand behind Zara. "How is it possible that a human worked healing magic?" Celeste looked as baffled as Zara.

"I honestly don't know." Looking at Zara, she asked, "Do you think you could do it again?"

"I don't know. I'm not really sure how I did it the first time," Zara admitted.

"Well, I'm sure there is no harm in trying. See Skylar's hind leg? It was shattered when the dragon fell on him." She pointed to the leg which jutted out at an odd angle. Peering closer, Zara could see small fragments of bone poking through the chestnut coated skin. "I ran out of power before I got to that and the other healers are drained as well. I've managed to remove the sand, but I was waiting to recharge before attempting to heal the wound. How about you try?"

"What do I do?" Zara asked hesitantly, afraid of hurting Skylar more than he already was. Sensing her fear, Celeste put a steadying hand on her arm.

"Don't worry child, I won't let you hurt him. He is under a sleeping spell, so he won't feel anything. Just place your hands near the wound, where the flesh is whole. It gives the magic a guide of what you want, something for it to match. Then close your eyes and try and replicate what you did with Emma."

Looking at Skylar's body, it wasn't easy to find a place where the flesh and bone hadn't been damaged. Gingerly, Zara ran her fingers across his skin, barely touching it, just enough to be able to sort the ruined from the healthy. Her right hand found a spot by his fetlock, her left on the inside of his thigh. Closing her eyes, she tried to remember exactly what she had done with Emma. In her mind, she pictured her energy flowing from her own heart, down her arms, through her hands into Skylar.

With it, she sent the love and respect that the Guardians felt for him. She sent him her strength and the knowledge that the battle had been won. She sent her thanks for all he had risked for her and Luca.

Luca watched Zara, barely blinking, for a sign of the magic she had described. Seconds turned into minutes, and nothing happened. He looked at Celeste but the fairy simply held up one hand, urging him to be patient. So he watched and waited, hoping and fearing that the magic would come. Knowing that if it did, his world would change forever. Just when he was about to give up hope, he saw it. At first, it was just a faint glow. A dusting of light along the centaur's hind leg. Then, as he continued to watch, mouth agape, the light blossomed until it was almost blinding. Silver and shimmering, it looked like it was made out of starlight.

CHAPTER 44

Zara and Luca waited outside of Skylar's office, holding hands, watching the Guardians clean up the mess in the courtyard below. Symon, in bear form, was lifting rocks and rubble which had fallen from broken walls and pillars. Some of the walls were barely held together, there were so many holes caused by dragon fire and ogre's clubs. Helo lead a group of Guardians carrying the bodies of the fallen to large pyres outside the Guild, erected to burn them and send them on their way to their gods. Kinnison helped, getting his hands dirty beside those who had fought to defend his family. Aeylin looked on, sitting on a wooden bench against one wall, Kodan asleep against her shoulder, Emma and Josh chatting at her side.

"What do you think Skylar wants to talk to us about?" Zara asked Luca. The Commander had been in his office with the Guild representatives for nearly an hour, despite Celeste's protests that he should be resting.

"I think that Skylar is going to send you away," Luca

answered quietly, his brow creased with worry, his dark blue eyes clouded.

"What? Why?" Zara was startled. She thought she had won Skylar over, she felt that they had become friends.

"Because we just lost a third of our people fighting a battle we never should have been involved in and if you stay it could start another," Luca said as gently as he could. The idea of Zara leaving broke his heart, but if she were home in the human realm, if she cut off all connection with Wunor, she would be safe. In the Ruling Council's eyes, it was terrible enough that Zara was human. If they discovered that she had powers, he feared what they might do.

"But you did the right thing protecting Aeylin and Kodan. You know you did," Zara said, squeezing his arm.

"I know," Luca replied, shaking his head. "But the Ruling Council won't see it that way. They are already looking for any excuse to shut the Guardians down. Our interfering has just added fuel to the fire."

"Why would they wish to shut down the Guardians?"

"Power and control. Over the rift and the towns we are sworn to protect."

"Isn't there anything we can do?" Zara pleaded, biting her lip to try and stop the tears that threatened to fall. But when Luca shrugged, unable to find words to reassure her, she felt a tear slide down her cheek. Luca brushed the tear away with his thumb before reaching for her, pulling her close against him. Wrapping her arms around his waist, she returned his tight embrace. Neither said anything.

They were still like that five minutes later when the

door to Skylar's office opened. Rillian and the other delegates filed past them on their way to the stairs, the panther shifter gifting Luca a broad grin. But Luca failed to notice the smile, too caught up in the emotion of what was about to happen. Releasing from their embrace, Luca took Zara's hand and squeezed it, then unable to resist, leaned forward and kissed her gently on the mouth. Whatever was in store, they would face it together.

Walking into the office, they found Skylar leaning against the far wall, his face drawn and eyes weary. Dark circles ringed his eyes and wrinkles marked his face that hadn't been there before.

"Are you alright, Commander?" Luca asked, concerned.

"I'm fine. Just tired. I need to discuss something with the two of you, and then I will go rest," Skyler said, then added with an uneven smile which made him look more like his usual self, "otherwise Celeste will have me hobbled. Firstly, let me take this opportunity, Zara, to say thank you for healing my leg. Celeste tells me that if it wasn't for you, I would still be in that damn sling."

"You're more than welcome, Skylar. I'm just happy I could help." Zara said.

"Secondly, Celeste told me about how you healed Emma, which, in truth, has just led to a whole lot of questions that no-one seems able to answer."

"Sorry, sir," Zara said, looking sheepish.

"You have nothing to apologise for Zara. In fact, I should be the one apologising, I'm afraid. I have some news that I fear you are not going to be happy to hear." As Skylar's golden eyes bored into Zara, she bit her lip. She would not let herself cry in front of him. She would be brave, and she would go home with her head held high. The rush of magic she felt when healing would be forgotten. She would do what was best for the Guardians and for Wundor. She took a deep breath, steadying herself to hear Skylar utter the words for her to leave.

"The Guardian High Command have come to the conclusion that we cannot let you return to your world, or at least not yet. Not until we discover where the source of your power has come from and not until you can be taught to control it. If you were to use your power in the human realm, it could have devastating consequences," Skylar said in a heavy voice. For a beat, Zara felt her heart stop, and then with a rush, start beating wildly. She opened her mouth to ask a question, but all that came out was a gasp. She looked to Luca to find he appeared to be as shell-shocked as she did.

"It has been decided that you will go to the Farspire Guild. Their Commander is Yasri, a witch with great power of foresight, and we hope she can help you, and us, find some answers. Corsena, their healer, is second in skill only to Celeste. She will teach you to use your magic." It all seemed too good to be true. Zara felt joy rush through her. She was going to be able to stay in Wundor with Luca.

"Can I accompany her?" Luca asked, an edge to his voice.

"No, you cannot."

"But –"

"No, Luca, do not fight me on this. Zara needs to learn without you there as a distraction. And besides, someone needs to oversee the repairs here and the recruitment of new Guardians while I am recuperating."

"You're putting me in charge?"

"I am," Skylar said solemnly.

"After I went behind your back and helped Aeylin?"

"Yes," Skylar said, the side of his mouth flickering with a smile. "Sometimes you think with your heart instead of your head, Luca, but you were right to help Aeylin. I am hoping that taking command will help you learn to think with your head, also. Or at least have a healthy respect for the consequences of such decisions. Now, if you two don't mind, I need to rest. Rillian and his party are planning to leave tomorrow. I will ask Celeste to have a bag of supplies packed for you, Zara. I suggest you spend tonight saying your farewells."

It was late, the moon reaching its peak, and the mess hall was empty apart from the party of friends. The other Guardians, sensing their need for privacy, had quickly eaten their own meals or taken them to their rooms. Empty plates and tankards covered the table, but the kitchen pixies didn't disturb them to the clear the dishes. Everyone in the group was exhausted, and yet no one seemed ready to leave, knowing it would be their last night together for a long while.

Zara sat in Luca's lap, the distance of the seat next to him too far away to bear. His arms were wrapped around her. Every few minutes, he leaned in to kiss the back of her neck tenderly, breathing in her scent. Emma and Josh sat together on a bench seat, her head against his shoulder. Zara had tried to convince Emma to go to bed but had been bluntly denied, her excuse being she would have plenty of time to sleep when she was back at The Haven. Together they had come up with a feeble story to explain Zara's absence, that she had to fly to Sydney urgently as her father was in poor health. If that didn't work, then they would tell a simplified version of the truth, that she had run away with Luca. Zara hated lying to Karen and George but knew there was no other choice. Brina lay, barely able to keep her eyes open, on another bench, her head in Symon's lap and her feet in Helo's. Nero contentedly crunched a dragon bone under the table. Kinnison and Aeylin had said their farewells a few hours earlier, going to bed in Brax's room with Kodan. Until it became safe for them to come out into the open, the Guardians had come up with a plan to move them from one Guild to another. Brax, a very proud grandpa, would act as one of their personal guards. Zara looked forward to seeing them in Farspire.

She still wasn't sure how she felt about travelling across Wundor to the far north region. One minute she couldn't seem to sit still with excitement, the next she was trying to breathe away her fear. Since coming to this magical world, she had visited a tiny fraction of it. What she had seen had been breathtaking, awe inspiring and beautiful. But she couldn't forget that she had been in life-threatening danger multiple times. But most of all, she felt sad. Sad to be leaving Luca and her friends, both the humans and those she had made here. She felt like she was being forced to give up a part of herself, and without them wasn't sure who she would be.

Sitting up, her red hair a ruffled mess, Brina announced, "I'm sorry, but I need to get some sleep. But before I do, I want to make a toast." Picking up one of the half-full tankards, she raised it above her head. "To friends and family. May we never forget each other, may we always be there for each other, and may we meet again. Goddess make it be." The others grabbed up their own drinks and as one clinked them against Brina's. Zara didn't know if it was the words, or if Brina had woven a spell into her toast, but as she swallowed the ale, she felt contentment wash over her. No matter what adventures awaited her, no matter what trials lay around the next corner, she loved this group of people with every beat of her heart. And one day she would be with them all once again.

ABOUT THE AUTHOR

By day Miranda battles numbers and spreadsheets. At night she adventures into fantasy worlds of her own imagination using her powers as a wordsmith to bring her characters to life. She lives in Western Australia with her husband Andrew and her dog Kira.

To find out more about her books and her adventures go to www.mirandaharvey.com.au